FINDING EVER AFTER SERIES | BOOK ONE

THE GILDED MIRROR

K E BARDEN

Cover Design by Miblart

Chapter Artwork by EthericTales

Map designed by AdrianoBezerra

Typography and Formatting by Turtle Publishing

Paperback ISBN 978-1-7635308-0-5

eBook ISBN 978-1-7635308-1-2

Distributed by K E Barden and Lightningsource Global

To Mum and Dad,
It all started with a fairy tale.

N
NW
NE
W
E
SW
SE
S
Beast Cove
CRULLFELD
Lake Moss
ASHENFELL
The Luna Lighthouse
The Tower and the Maze
Candot
Grim
Xersailles
ARDENBEAX
Annce
Mountains Le Bleu
The Lantern Lighthouse
Lake La Belle
White Bridge
The Channel
Waters Keep
The Black Cove
THE ISLAND OF MYORCAI
THE EVER AFTE

THE REALM

G Isles
The Realm of Dragons and Giants
The Northern Lighthouse
The Coral Coast
AURELIA
KING'S KEEP
Butterpond
Blarney Forest
Hasleholme
MAELSTROM
The Briar Rose
The Marshes
MINES OF PARADOR
Ellendale
CARNELL
THE MOUNTAINS OF EYRIE
SHADOW FOREST
PEAKS OF CARFELL
Eastborne
Arrow's Den
The Crystal Lake
Ivywood
Bell's Peak
THE DARK FOREST
THE SILVER CITY
PERRIDORM
Roserock
Dove Port
Witches Hut
The Skinny Piglet
BELLATORRE
The Elysian Fields
LLDRYN
Wolf's Den
The Queen's Mines
TEAL COVE
NYSA
ATLAS
THE ISLE OF NYSA
Lighthouse Luvon

Once, long ago, there lived a little girl and her merchant father.

The father lived for his daughter's laughter and doted on her. The little girl wore a crown of lilacs, and had the most beautiful voice. Her father would clap as if he stood in the grandest theatre with the finest company. They would dance until sundown and laugh until blue.

He would tell her stories by firelight, ones filled with dragons and swords and heroes.

Although they were poor – the house but a ramshackle cottage in a glen – the little girl never wanted for anything.

For he was her king, and she his princess.

Myrenna had a *wrinkle*.

It was an awful little thing, staining her skin with a small crease by the side of her amethyst eyes. Her manicured nails stroked over it, a hiss escaping her lips at the audacity of its arrival.

Never mind that she already looked tired, her sharp cheekbones lined with a fine dark powder to hide the exhaustion. Not to mention the sheer amount of cover she had smothered on her face to hide the discolouration.

Her hair pulled as she turned her face in the mirror. It'd been secured by diamond-encrusted pins, placed artfully in a way she could never have achieved without her handmaidens. Though it was so tight she couldn't be sure whether her headache had stemmed from that or the fact she was travelling by road.

The black carriage jolted, the twilight of the full moon flickering through the curtains. Myrenna threw down her mirror, annoyance stirring in her chest as she peered out the window.

Being fashionably late was a queen's prerogative, but being late to the point where she would miss dinner was not an option. She needed this alliance despite hating herself for it. She had too many cultivated plans for a singular girl to ruin them all.

A girl who had somehow escaped from the castle.

Princess Snowfall.

Heir to the crown of Bellatorre, and a royal pain in Myrenna's arse.

Myrenna's amethyst eyes flashed in the window's reflection, the name stirring a rage so cold she wouldn't be surprised if she turned to ice.

The driver knocked on the roof, the trotting hooves of the horses slowing to a stop.

What in the realm is the problem now?

Myrenna had probably been patient once, back when she'd been mortal. Maybe she'd even been kind. But she was no longer that girl. No longer naïve.

She was a queen, a powerful one. With that responsibility came the harsh reality of the realm. How long had it been since she'd been mortal anyway? She couldn't remember.

Sometimes it didn't matter. Sometimes, dreams of her past revisited her anyway, as vivid as if it had been only yesterday. As vivid as the wrinkle by her right eye.

Cruel faces still flashed behind her eyes in the late hours of the night, regardless how much time had passed. Each silent scream as she killed and killed and killed.

Her driver's footsteps crunched against the road as she pulled herself together, hiding her shaking hands in her skirts.

The driver rapped on her door twice.

'What is it?' she hissed.

'Road's blocked, Your Majesty.'

She rubbed her temples. This was the price she paid for making an entrance, and always cursed herself for it. Why take a carriage when you could fly?

But tonight wasn't about her subjects or making a powerful entrance; it was about politics. And the carriage was her white flag.

You wish to strike fear, her gilded mirror had said, *then build an army which you can steer.*

Despite her misgivings about the mirror, it had been pivotal in her climb to power. A gift, in a strange, twisted turn of fate. And though she'd wanted to argue, it was right that she needed an army.

Hers was busy on the edge of Perridorm, the two young royals putting up a better fight than expected. Not to mention the mines she'd commanded over the country. With a rebellion brewing, she was short of resources, but luckily for her, Carnell was short on brains.

Myrenna blamed her dishevelled appearance on stress. Stress, and the fear of the unknown now that she didn't have the princess. She needed more power, more time. More control.

And she needed to get rid of that *damn* wrinkle.

'Your Majesty?' a raspy voice echoed. 'You may want to see this.'

The crisp night air hit the queen as she opened the door and found her Tinker waiting. His eyes peered at her in that calculating way of his as she descended the small steps, her dress pooling around her ankles.

A girl was standing by the road alone. She looked to be fourteen or fifteen. Myrenna watched with mild curiosity as the Tinker dragged the girl forward, her thin shivering form coated in dirt.

Myrenna tilted her head. 'What do we have here?'

'Please,' the girl begged. 'We did not know.'

'Did not know *what?*' the queen cooed, reaching out to wrap one of the girl's pale locks around her finger. Myrenna thought her beautiful, in a frail innocent kind of way. She reminded the queen of a bird about to take flight.

Myrenna couldn't help but smile.

What a virtuous evening, indeed.

The girl blinked at Myrenna's touch, looking hesitant and too afraid to move. 'We did not know it would break,' the girl sniffled. 'It was not meant to break. *Please* help him.'

The queen turned towards her Tinker, who pointed his spindly finger to the broken cart strewn across the road. A man lay unmoving on the ground, his face oddly pale and blank.

Myrenna knew death when she saw it. Had caused it more times than she could count.

'A minor inconvenience,' Myrenna mused, turning back to the girl. 'Sorted with a small payment.'

The Tinker nodded before disappearing, leaving Myrenna and the girl alone.

'Payment?' The girl trembled. 'Can you save him?'

'Of course, my little bird,' Myrenna replied. 'It's just a token. Nothing you'll miss.'

The girl swallowed.

Myrenna trailed her hand across the girl's collarbones, her diamond rings stark against the plain, worn dress.

Myrenna may not have started as queen, but by the cauldron she looked the part.

She laid her palm on the girl's chest, her cold eyes watching as it rose and fell in shallow breaths. She could feel the trill of the girl's heart, alive and whole and *young*.

'Just a small token,' the queen repeated.

'Y-Yes.'

It was all the confirmation she needed. Within a breath, the queen's hand clawed, the sharpened talons piercing flesh as the girl screamed. She tried to pull away, but Myrenna was too fast, one hand latching onto the back of the girl's neck to bring her close.

From here, Myrenna could smell her fear, the sweet stench of it bringing a familiar rush she craved. Though her body trembled from excitement, Myrenna's voice was as soft as a caress as she whispered in the girl's ear. 'Your heart will do just fine.'

The girl gasped as Myrenna tore flesh from bone, her body falling with a quiet thump onto the dirt. And in Myrenna's palm lay the girl's fresh, beating heart. It felt like velvet, the hum of life reverberating as if it still remained inside the girl's chest. In one long stroke, Myrenna's tongue danced along the flesh and she shivered. There was nothing in this realm she savoured more than a maiden's heart. Nothing else that satiated the constant hunger for *more*.

Except, perhaps, for the destruction of three witches.

Ignoring the invasive thought, Myrenna bit into the heart's flesh, and a groan involuntary escaped her lips.

It tasted like youth and power and revenge. Reminded her that she was a queen.

She was beautiful. Regal. Powerful.

But she was also so, much, more.

She ignored the gnawing voice inside her that always screamed. The whispers telling her it was *wrong*. She ignored the hole inside her own heart as it shrivelled after each passing year. And chose to revel in this one victory, instead.

Blood still coated the queen's mouth as she whipped her wrist forward, the broken cart flying apart and opening the road for the carriage.

Already, she could feel the wrinkle smoothing, the shadows under her eyes disappearing. Power crackled under her skin.

Her Tinker bowed. 'Ready when you are, my queen.'

She gave him a dark red smile before stepping back into the carriage. The heart had given her more than just a youthful face or an undercurrent of power. It had soothed her fear, her lingering doubt vanishing as fast as the girl's life had.

She licked her fingers, sucking off every last drop, as the carriage jostled.

Myrenna would make a grand entrance in Maelstrom, as she'd always done. If everything went to plan, the King and his sons would be eating from her palms.

And she didn't need a heart for that.

I

The Skinny Piglet

Eveline sat in the corner of the Skinny Piglet and picked at her nails, ignoring the sprawled-out fairy on the table by her elbow. The fairy's wings spread out behind her in a sheen of pink, her blue hair a tangled mess. Bored, she blew away strands from her face in a game of tag.

The inside of the Skinny Piglet wasn't large by any means, but it was warm. Springtime usually meant pleasant days but cool nights, which became even cooler this close to the mountains.

The fireplace blazed, the wooden rafters tucking in the heat against the bitter wind outside. There was no rhyme or reason to the layout, each wooden setting just as decrepit as the next. But it was central, a hub for those travelling along the border of the forest.

The thin golden knife in Eveline's hand shone as she peeled some of the dirt out from under her thumbnail. 'I've decided, Porchid. That when we grow rich and old, we'll never have to deal with a tavern again.' The fairy grumbled an agreeance when the bell from the door tinkled. Porchid's ear twitched and Eveline sighed. 'Not them.'

Porchid huffed, kicking out her small legs in irritation.

This was the way jobs went sometimes. Waiting and pacing and breathing. Whilst Eveline hated waiting, she needed the income.

And she needed it desperately.

Eveline had kept her hood low since arriving, thankful for its cover as the smell of salt and seaweed filtered through the tavern. Among the sea nymphs dancing by the window, there was one with wine-red hair. The blue scaled skin and full lips were familiar.

'By the cauldron,' Eveline muttered. 'Just once, I'd like to remain anonymous.'

Pulling her hood lower, Eveline tucked herself deeper into the corner, but she was too late. Already the creature had noticed her presence, the curve of her pale lips quirking as she stood.

Eveline didn't take her eyes away from the creature, tracking each graceful step that left pools of liquid in their wake. It stirred an old hate within her.

Eveline didn't like sea nymphs much. In fact, she'd avoided them successfully over the years. They were known to be cruel and selfish. Even a little mad.

Unfortunately for Eveline, this nymph was an old acquaintance. She took a deep breath to calm herself, stabbing her knife into the table. Porchid crossed her tiny legs, her face proud and determined.

'Go away, Cyrene,' Eveline drawled. 'I'm busy.'

'So busy that your drink's gone warm?' the sea nymph mused, dragging her long finger down the edge of the table.

Eveline leaned back. 'I didn't ask for your opinion.'

'You are terrible at greeting your friends,' Cyrene said as she slid into the seat facing her.

Eveline grumbled, failing to hide her distaste.

Cyrene lifted the cup in front of Eveline and sniffed before running her finger over the rim, the drink's surface chilling. Cyrene raised her brow, waiting for gratitude with a snarky smile.

Smug show off.

Eveline pulled the hood of her cloak down, hair curling on her brow, and looked into Cyrene's dark eyes. 'Can't you find anybody else to annoy?'

'Why?' Cyrene asked. 'When I have the grand Seeker at my disposal?'

Eveline hadn't missed the use of her job title, Seeker. She was known for her peculiar gift across the land. She'd wanted people to know so the jobs came to her instead of the other way around. It hadn't made her rich by any means, but she led a comfortable life.

Porchid shuffled closer to Eveline's elbow, the light of her skin changing from orange to green. Porchid was unique in that way, her emotions flickering over her skin like the moods of the wind.

Cyrene clicked her tongue. 'Sour as ever, it seems. And here I was coming over to help you.'

Eveline narrowed her eyes. 'I highly doubt that.'

Sea nymphs never just came over to help. They prided themselves on their bargaining skills and the deep treasure they hoarded beneath the sea.

Eveline picked up her knife again, stroking the golden blade with her fingers. She was here for a job, not for social engagement. Eveline would be damned if Cyrene was going to ruin hours of utter boredom by distracting her for five minutes.

The tavern's music clashed together in a mismatched array of sounds. Eveline cringed as the violinist squealed off key.

'What is it you want, Cyrene?' Eveline asked. 'It's certainly not for another job.'

Cyrene hissed, flashing those sharp teeth of hers. Eveline shivered at the thought of what those teeth would do. Sea nymph's teeth were designed to pierce through the hard-protective layers of shellfish for food.

But it could just as easily be a throat.

'You don't speak of that,' she warned, pulling back her rage. But Eveline could see it lingering behind her eyes, the threat still there. 'I've heard rumours. Dark whispers of prophecies and old magic that have even reached us in Nysa.'

Nysa was the coast on which the sea nymphs lived. It bordered that of Teal Cove where mermaids dwelled. The relationship between the two kingdoms was tenuous at best, but they seemed to remain civil despite the two species' history.

A history that remained long, bloody, and vicious.

'And?' Eveline queried.

'Something wicked brews,' Cyrene replied, lowering her voice. She grabbed Eveline's wrist and pulled her closer. 'Even my queen keeps deep within our caverns.'

Eveline shot her a warning glare before prying her arm free. Calmly, she shuffled her drink over, narrowly missing the nymph's arm. Eveline noted the dark circles under Cyrene's eyes, her hair duller than it had been in years past. 'Something evil is coming, Seeker,' Cyrene continued, 'and I fear we may all be doomed unless we can find a solution.'

Porchid's light went dim at the words, her aura shadowed. Now Cyrene was really pissing Eveline off. 'Do you realise how insane you sound? I find lost things, Cyrene, not solutions to dark prophesies and magic.'

'I'm not insane.'

This time, Eveline leaned in, her braid pinching on her collar. 'And what does the Sea Nymph Queen care about some whispers of dark times?'

Cyrene hissed. 'This is not some joke to take lightly. We are not safe, and neither are you. We do not care for your kind, but we do care about this land and what that entails for us.'

Eveline held the nymph's stare. She could see the fear behind her eyes, yet she couldn't understand it. Why in all the kingdoms should she care about some dark rumours that may or may not come to pass?

'I'm unsure, Cyrene, why you believe this information is relevant to me, or why I would bargain with you for it.'

'This is no bargain,' she replied, stiffly. 'It's a warning. One I would wish for my *dear friend* to heed.'

'That's the second time you've referred to us as friends.'

Cyrene scoffed. 'What else would I call you?'

'You literally tried to kill me the last time we spoke.'

Cyrene waved her hand. 'That was years ago.'

'Still happened,' Eveline mumbled.

Cyrene stood up. 'My kind may bargain, and we may take, but we are not evil. We do not wish for darkness to take reign, and we do not wish for death.'

With that, she walked away, gliding into a seat beside her kin.

Eveline looked to Porchid. 'That was strange.'

Porchid only twinkled in concern.

She didn't have time to ponder Cyrene's words as the door rang. A troll stumbled in, followed by a human male in brown leathers.

Smirking, Eveline winked at the small fairy. 'It's time.'

Eveline wasn't familiar with trolls – not on a personal level, anyway. She'd seen them around and read about them in books, but mostly they were tales from the north. Trolls were known to be harsh, unforgiving. Their beliefs centred around a vicious magic where bloodshed came easily. In every story, they bore weapons and grimaces, ready to strike at an enemies weakness.

The troll's skin was the usual shade of mucus green, his ear glittering with piercings of gold. But it was the way he smiled at something his companion said and the ease in which he walked that puzzled Eveline.

The troll's companion was no different, his echoing smile matching a chiselled jaw with dimples. He was young, stocky in build, with an axe strapped to his side. As he shook off his jacket, the sleeve of his shirt lifted, revealing corded muscle.

Porchid twinkled in glee at Eveline's side, her eyes roaming over him like one of her favourite berries. When she dramatically swooned, Eveline groaned.

'You just can't help yourself, can you?'

Porchid blushed a deep pink. The fairy had always liked pretty things. It was a trait Eveline had desperately tried to wring out of the little creature. Eveline might have chastised the fairy, but even she couldn't deny he was gorgeous – in an unrefined sort of way.

He moved with grace despite his hulking form. And though his brown hair stuck out, the disarray was a little charming.

She was curious. How had a young man come to be in the company of a troll with a stolen object in hand? He looked too young to be in this sort of business. It was all a little odd. But Eveline's gift had not been wrong so far, and despite her grumblings with it, she still trusted it.

Most beautiful creatures could puncture your soul with poison. She'd known that firsthand.

Eveline twisted her knife, the familiar grip soothing her nerves.

Her best weapon over the years had been her size. When you were short and small, most people treated you more like a child than a warrior. Her father had always told her brute strength was a fool's belief. Strength wasn't found in the high, solid walls of kingdoms, or the sharp, deep cliff face of the mountains.

Because even the smallest of cracks could tear them down.

She smiled at the memory. She was the crack. Her skills were honed with vicious training years before she'd begun this life. Her knives may have been slight, but when aimed with her skill, they were flying death.

Porchid tilted her head to peek around Eveline's elbow and watched the two strangers enter through a hallway behind the bar.

Eveline took a sip from her drink, Porchid shivering with anticipation as she looked to Eveline for direction.

The Seeker didn't have a plan exactly, but luck was on her side.

She waited a heartbeat before she stirred, and like a shadow, crept out of her corner.

Eveline's hand hovered over her blade as she peered around the corridor. Paint peeled from the walls, and while she'd thought the reek had been bad in the main room, it was nothing compared to that of the back hall.

'Are you sure about this?' the young man asked the troll, keeping his voice low.

'He said it's the real thing. Hard to obtain, and expensive,' the troll replied, his accent rough.

The man's hand moved to his axe, holding onto it with white knuckles. He looked like a huntsman.

Eveline stuck to the shadows as the barkeep fiddled with his keys.

'You better be right,' the huntsman replied, 'or she'll have our heads before we ever get close to Snow.'

Snow?

Were they talking about the Princess? Eveline didn't have time to think about it as light peeled into the hallway. She remained silent as she grasped her twin golden knives, their familiar weight and shape a comfort. She was careful, but when the huntsman looked back, she held her breath.

She was a ghost. A shadow. A crack.

Her gift had led her to the Skinny Piglet and the troll. After some bribing in the surrounding towns, she'd also found out more than she needed. Old gossips they were. The barkeep – Marcellus – was a known smuggler, the Skinny Piglet a trove for his illegal goods.

She moved cautiously down the small stairway, hoping to avoid any old steps with a creak. Voices echoed ahead, the muffled sounds travelling across the stale air.

If Porchid did her job, they would be in and out of this cauldron of a place without a hiccup. She didn't want to be here longer than she had to.

The layout was not ideal. She strained her ears at the muffled voices as she reached the doorway. A nail protruding from the wall snagged on her leathers and she pulled free, glaring at the tear in her clothes. Another stitch she'd need to do despite being horrible at it.

Her eyes darted to the dusty window, hoping to spot the familiar pink wings of Porchid, but the fairy was nowhere to be seen. The voices echoed across the timber floors, and she dropped to a crouch, pulling free a small mirror. With some manoeuvring, she managed to get a clear outline of the room. The huntsman stood off to the side, watching as the barkeep and the troll assessed a large crate.

'This is it, then?' the huntsman asked.

Marcellus grunted, rolling some barrels to the side. 'In pristine condition, no less.'

'We'll need something to open it,' said the troll.

'You can't just open it?' asked Marcellus.

'I'm a troll. Not a crowbar.'

The huntsman chuckled as the barkeep grumbled, 'I'll get one from the office.'

'A troll or a crowbar?' the huntsman asked.

'Don't touch anything, ye hear?' Marcellus shot back.

Eveline froze, pulling herself further into the shadows. The barkeep's heavy-set steps passed her and disappeared down the hall. She released the breath she'd been holding.

'I don't like this,' said the huntsman, moving closer to the crate. 'I don't trust him.'

'Really?' The troll laughed. 'I hadn't noticed from your casual sarcasm.'

The huntsman grunted.

The troll pulled at the crate's edge, testing it. 'He's the only lead we have.'

Eveline hissed as another nail dug into her shoulder. She ducked as the huntsman's eyes looked towards the door.

'I'm not even sure we can use it without its owner,' the troll continued.

'True,' said the huntsman, 'but we have to try. She has nobody else but us to look for her. Nobody else knows.'

'Nobody but the Queen.'

The huntsman grimaced. 'Don't remind me.'

Eveline shivered at the casual reference to the evil queen, as if she were just a standard maiden they knew. Eveline had never met her, of course, but she'd travelled to enough towns to know the stories.

The Queen had come to power after marrying the King of Bellatorre, where he'd conveniently died. Soon after, everyone – other than humans – had fewer rights, and those who opposed her were sent to her mysterious mines. More than that, she had *magic*. Not the pitiful kind that witches held, or the small gifts some fairies could bestow, but truly powerful, horrible magic.

Eveline grimaced at the thought when her head was yanked back. Too late, the stench of ale hit her nose, sharp pain making her hiss. The cold edge of a knife pierced the skin at her throat.

Hot, wet breath touched her ear. 'This is a staff only area, lovey. We don't like unwelcome visitors.'

She swore.

The barkeep pushed her forward roughly, leading her into the room with the troll and huntsman. 'Look what I found lurking in the shadows,' he said.

The troll's eyes widened, probably noting how short she was in comparison. She'd heard all the jokes before and had never found them funny.

She tried not to swallow, narrowly avoiding the blade's bite as she peered at the strangers, before assessing the room.

'This is an interesting turn of events,' the huntsman said.

The troll moved forward in long, slow strides and sniffed her. He was smaller than most trolls, but still stood several pixies taller than the rest of the humans here. 'She smells … pretty.'

She'd almost have taken it as a compliment if he hadn't cringed as he said the words.

Eveline snarled, and the huntsman snorted.

'She smells like a spy to me,' Marcellus said from behind her.

It surprised Eveline he could smell at all, considering his own odour dominated all other senses. His body was too close, and she shuffled under his weight. She never liked people in her personal space.

Nobody except Porchid, at least.

'She looks too young to be a spy,' the huntsman replied.

Eveline didn't like the way he was looking at her, like she was some curiosity he couldn't figure out. His gaze was piercing, his shoulders strong. From the way he stood, she figured he must have been a soldier at one point, his stillness only obtained from years of training. Which made this situation all the more confusing. Why was a huntsman involved in a theft? What was the link?

Eveline's eyes darted to the circular window on the back wall. She swore she'd seen Porchid's pale light.

The chamber was dimly lit, the glow of the burnt candles spread about the room. Most of it was filled with barrels, large and small. Full of brew, no doubt. Bags of flour lined the top shelf, creating a mismatched pattern of brands above the barrels and rope.

'Young or not, she's a snoop. I've killed for less,' Marcellus stated.

A staircase sat off the centre, probably leading to the bartender's personal quarters, or an office if he even bothered with the paperwork required for running a business.

'Are you a spy?' the huntsman asked, still staring at her in that unnerving way. His eyes were golden-brown, reminding her of honey. It was intimate and uncomfortable.

Eveline held her head high, her throat grazing the knife's edge. 'I'd be a terrible spy if I was getting caught this quickly, don't you think?'

The huntsman's lip quirked.

'Marcellus,' the troll said, 'Release her, for cauldron's sake. She can't go anywhere. Not with three against one.'

'This isn't your establishment,' Marcellus hissed, holding his knife towards the huntsman.

Eveline saw her opportunity. Barely a second after the knife left her throat, she moved. With a stomp on the barkeep's foot, his scream shattering the silence, Eveline dived. She'd barely rolled to a stand when the huntsman raised his hands. 'What is it you're looking for?'

'Revenge,' she said with a smile.

'Hansel,' the troll warned. 'This is taking too long. Forget the girl.'

The huntsman turned to his friend, some internal battle taking place.

Eveline eyed the flour bags above. Her current situation wasn't ideal, but it also wasn't impossible. Three opponents, she could handle. Four or more would be cutting it close.

She followed the crate, feeling the huntsman's piercing gaze. Did he know something was about to happen? Her skin tingled, her gift recognising the thing within the crate as she eased closer to it.

'What will we do with her if we can't kill her?' Marcellus growled.

The huntsman tilted his head, watching, waiting, though she wasn't sure for what. 'Perhaps,' he said, 'she could help us.'

'Help us?' the troll replied, annoyance clear in his voice.

'Why are you here?' the huntsman asked her.

'Why are *you* here?' Eveline retorted.

Despite knowing what was inside of that crate, she didn't know the why. Even eavesdropping, she'd only managed to link them to the Bellatorrian royals somehow, but it didn't explain why they needed the crate, or the object within.

The huntsman smirked. 'You've got an attitude for someone who's outnumbered.'

'You're not the first person to tell me that,' she replied.

Her eyes caught the small light flashing from the window.

Good little fairy.

'I don't doubt that,' the huntsman said with a laugh. 'If the first impression is anything to go by.'

'A troll, a huntsman, and a barkeep, all hiding in the shadows with a mysterious object,' she said. 'Sounds like the start of a bad joke, but also interesting enough to follow.'

The troll crossed his arms. 'Except, in this instance, there's no punchline.'

She raised her brow, surprised at the troll's use of a joke.

'I told you we were conspicuous,' the huntsman said. 'If you had just stayed behind like I suggested—'

'As if I'm going to let you do this alone,' the troll interrupted. 'I took an oath.'

The huntsman rubbed his temples. 'Yes, Malak, we know you took an oath. You seem to enjoy reminding us at every opportunity.'

Porchid peeked over a barrel near the back, giving Eveline the thumbs up.

Eveline slid her twin blade into the palm of her hand and closed her eyes.

The huntsman would be first.

Right on cue, a barrel rolled across the top of the others, falling with a loud crash to the floor. Marcellus yelled from behind her as the others looked up.

Porchid, zipping through the rafters, pushed a large bag of flour and let it fall in a burst of white flakes and dust. The little fairy moved along one by one, kicking each bag with a strength Eveline didn't know she possessed. Flour fell like snow around them, coating the ground in white layers. There was something about it that soothed Eveline. Something that let her focus and slow.

Her left foot swung out first, hitting the huntsman with a satisfying grunt before she twirled towards the barkeep.

A thrust into his neck and he choked. A smack with her right fist and his knife clattered to the ground. He hissed as she sunk her blade into his arm.

Eveline was already moving before he hit the ground, his shirt stained in crimson. She held her cloak over her nose as she bolted across the room and darted along the barrels lining the walls.

She was a storm. An arrow. Wind.

She dived for the troll. His eyes were wide as she flew above him and dropped onto his back. She hit his head with the hilt of her knife, and he growled. When she went to hit him again, he tried to rip her away. Eve braced as he narrowly missed her long braid. She climbed his back and dug both feet into his shoulders, years of practice with her old mentors keeping her balanced.

Porchid dived above Eveline, pulling at the rope of the barrels and flying it around the rafters. The troll stumbled back, and she wobbled, his hands barely missing her. Eveline grabbed his black hair and yanked, his howl echoing through the room.

Porchid dropped the rope. Without hesitation, Eveline reached for it and slid it around the troll's neck. He lunged left, throwing her into the barrels. Pain shot up her left side as she groaned.

Brew poured onto the floor. The flour became thick and gluggy. Eveline could feel it in the troll's steps, the way he wheezed as he looked towards his companion, his hands tugging on the rope. Her thighs burned and her head was woozy as the troll thrashed.

With another tug, Eveline cut off the troll's air supply. She ignored the burn of the rope on her palms. Ignored the thrashing body of the troll beneath her. She only watched in fascination as his eyes rolled to the back of his head. Then he fell. Eveline dived off, narrowly missing the sharp blade of the huntsman's axe as it sliced through the rope choking his friend.

Eveline rolled along the ground and came up in front of Marcellus. His eyes opened in terror. She spun so fast her knives were a blur, and she smacked him twice with their hilts. He dropped like a limp fish.

Two down. One to go.

Breath heaving, she turned to face the huntsman.

He held his axe in his hand, his eyes darkening. 'Who are you?'

They circled each other, both ready to do their worst. His axe was the size of her torso, her knives a needle point. No matter.

She exhaled and smiled. 'Right now, I'm your biggest problem.'

His brows furrowed, and she couldn't help but notice his strong chin.

'You almost killed my friend,' he said.

Eveline smirked. 'Trolls don't have friends.'

'I forget how small-minded people are in this realm.'

His axe shone against the candlelight. Flour coated their skin. The floor was sticky, but she'd dealt with worse. Her steps were light, sure. So different from the tense stance of the huntsman. 'Who are you?' he repeated.

'I have many names,' she said, 'but Seeker is one you may recognise.'

Acknowledgement dawned on his face. 'Seeker?' He paused. 'You came?' She frowned, her confusion deepening as he said, 'I wondered if the deception spells would work on you. It seems not.'

Porchid floated above, her light dimming at the sight below her.

Eveline straightened her shoulders, the turn of events tonight grinding across her bones. Cyrene had been one oddity, but this was another. She twitched, her fingers splaying across the handles of her blades.

'Enough,' she said, and launched herself towards him.

Her knives met his axe in a clang, metal sparking off metal.

Eveline threw her full force into the huntsman, but he was too strong. Overwhelming. He pushed her back and swung his axe. She ducked. He swung again, the sharp edge of his blade meeting another barrel. Eveline scrambled across the floor, the flour and brew leaving a viscous layer on her clothes.

She swore.

The huntsman came back at her, raising his axe, and landed his blow with a loud snap next to her head.

She gasped.

'I don't want to hurt you,' he said.

'That's not overly convincing when you're swinging an axe at me,' she retorted.

'You came at me with your knives!'

'Well, you came at me twice,' she shouted. 'I only did it once.'

She scuttled back, her hilt digging into her palm as she broke free.

'That's your logic?'

Panting, she turned to meet the huntsman. His face was pink, his clothes and body drowned in dust and flour and brew. But this time, he didn't attack.

He raised his arms slowly and eyed her carefully. 'Ceasefire?'

'Not until I get what I came for.' She dived at him again, knives poised. He might be strong, but she was nimble. Eveline used every bit of energy she had to dodge and cut and parry. When he raised his arms to strike, she used her short height as an advantage.

And sliced at his legs.

With a shout, the axe dropped under him. He hit the ground with a heavy thud and groaned. Without a second thought, she twisted her blades and jabbed the hilt into the side of his head, letting him fall unconscious.

Panting, Eveline looked over at Porchid, who glowed gold in smug pride.

'This had better be the real deal,' she said to the fairy.

Eveline picked up the crowbar and tugged at the crate's edge. It took a few tries, but eventually the crate's wall fell and filled the air with more dust.

Eveline turned to Porchid. 'You took your time today.'

The fairy scowled and punched her sharply in the shoulder. Her light faded from red to blue.

The dust cleared, making way for the glare of the candle to light the crate's inside.

Eveline's brows squeezed together in confusion, but her gift flared in response, declaring its authenticity.

The object was small.

Porchid small.

The carvings upon its surface were immaculate, heavy detail showing swirls and suns with sand and sleep.

Eveline picked it up and smirked at her newfound prize.

Rumpelstiltskin's dream-weaving spindle.

II

The Dream Weaver

Rumpelstiltskin was not disappointed when Eveline handed over the spindle.

His golden-and-black teeth shone in the afternoon light of the following day as his spindly fingers delicately took hold of his treasured possession. Even though he stood a mere three feet tall, Rumple had a big reputation. He'd taken maidens throughout the ages, and when the stories had woven tales of gold, he'd not corrected them. For it was not gold that Rumple dealt in, but dreams.

Rumple caressed the spindle's wooden surface, the hairs on her arms raising at how intimate it seemed.

The only thing Eveline truly knew about the spindle was that it granted Rumple the ability to weave dreams. It was a dangerous magic, and it'd made him powerful, though slightly unhinged. She envisioned him diving into people's dreams like a pool of velvet and submerging himself in the wishes of others. Was it those dreams, those deepest parts of people, that gave him his long lifespan?

Porchid huffed at Eveline's shoulder in impatience, giving her the nudge she needed to expel the creepy thoughts. 'Well?' she asked.

He looked at her with narrowed eyes, his irises clouded but lucid. 'You have proved useful.'

'Great,' she drawled.

The dry pine needles on the forest floor cracked as she shuffled, eager for what they'd agreed upon. She hadn't bargained for gold or glory or a prince. She'd bargained for a dream.

Rumour had it that Rumple still held the dreams and secrets of those long lost. Those who couldn't be found even with her gift. The ones beyond the void who would never return, even with magic bound so tightly to this land.

Rumple lifted the wooden spindle, cleared his throat, and took a breath. Green smoke poured from his lips as he blew on the spindle. One moment the smoke was curling, and the next it swallowed Eveline whole.

She choked on the harsh scent of blood and grass, the world seemingly turning inside out. Porchid tensed on her shoulder, grasping on for dear life as they were suffocated. The ache behind Eveline's eyes built until she was panting over her knees, staring down at verdant grass.

Eveline reached for Porchid, only to find herself alone. The only sound came from the trill of a bird, the world eerily quiet despite her thrumming heart.

Blinking, Eveline took in the scene before her. She'd been transported into a glen, the rolling hills and treeline distinct despite this being a dream.

A familiar cottage sat at its centre, falling apart at the seams. To the left was the stream where her mother had bathed her on hot summer days, and to the right was the forest, where her old swing set remained. The last time she'd seen the swing it had fallen to decay, lying morosely on the ground, untouched and heavily broken. Here, she found it intact. Eveline moved towards the trees, and her hands shook as she held the rope.

Laughter echoed, breaking the silence. Eveline whirled to find a girl dressed in blue, hurdling towards the swing. A crown of lilac adorned her head and her curls fell in neat brown coils around her face.

Eveline hid out of instinct behind the trunk of the tree.

A man with brown, rugged hair wandered behind the young girl, laughing, his face lit with joy. He wasn't nobility. That much was clear from his tired, worn clothes and the dirt under his fingernails.

An ache that had long been suppressed awoke with a jarring stab in Eveline's heart. He looked older than she remembered. More weathered and aged. The crinkles beside his eyes showed a life full of laughter, but his skin was wan, the worry lines evident.

She'd remembered his smile clearly. His calloused hands knotting flower stems into crowns. The way his eyes shone a bright blue when he laughed.

He was familiar yet wholly different.

The sky rumbled up ahead, lighting the earth in flashes of purple and green. It crackled, moving at odd angles and too fast for any ordinary storm.

Eveline had tried to remember this moment for years, tried to focus on which direction it had come from, how it'd happened.

'No,' the man croaked, before rushing to the girl. With swift surety and a surprising amount of strength, he enveloped the girl in his arms and whispered in her ear.

Eveline's eyes pricked. She remembered the whispered warning of that day. The way his voice would calm her with stories. Most evenings she learnt how to cook whilst watching his weathered hands. Took comfort in the way his breath always smelt of mint from the leaves he chewed. But it was this moment, this memory that she'd seen a thousand times in a thousand dreams. She knew how it ended, and yet she was always powerless to stop it.

Droplets of rain began to fall. The clouds were thick and heavy, bulging at its belly like a mother's womb. Lightning shot down, striking the forest beyond. It filled the air with a sulphuric, acrid smell.

Panic alighted his face as the man pulled the girl close.

She lifted her lashes, looking curiously towards the forest where the shadows stretched deep. The man pulled her towards the small hollow of a tree. Their secret spot, he had called it, as he had named so many others of their shared places.

'Just as we practised,' he said.

The little girl nodded. No tears threatened to spill as her small, determined body weaved its way down into the burrow. The man collected branches from nearby, pulled them together to create a makeshift doorway, and buried the entrance.

When the shadowy figures emerged under the rolling thunder, he stood tall.

Rain fell in sheets, darkness creeping in. The air was static, its thunderous sky a warning. A warning that had forever echoed from Eveline's father, the man meeting his doom.

For someone who could supposedly find anything, Eveline had spent the better part of eight years searching far and wide for her missing father. Everything. *Everything* she'd done led up to this moment inside this dream.

The last time she'd seen those clear blue eyes had been as he mouthed, 'I love you,' whilst she scrambled down into the hollow of the tree.

She remembered shaking from the cold. Wondering when he would return.

The dream Rumple had given led her to the history she didn't know. When she'd found her way out of the burrow and back to the glen, it'd been only ashes. She didn't know what had happened outside, or how he'd disappeared.

Watching it unfold now made her heart ache.

Rain pelted down as the man raised his chin. Three figures emerged from the tree line, wrapped in shadow.

Even as an observer, Eveline felt their power, their pull. They were creatures of myths and legends. Stories that should have been nightmares.

Lightning split the sky and set the cottage alight. The flames ate at the wood, illuminating her father's stern brow, the heavy set of his footsteps.

Despite knowing the devastation to come, it hurt as if it was the first time. As if the remnants of her broken home left shards inside her broken heart.

Eveline dropped to her knees, a scream clawing up her throat as a shadow draped over the glen.

When Eveline blinked, they were gone.

Everything was gone.

Her home. Her family. Her hope.

All because of the sisters Grimm.

Eveline awoke to Porchid kicking her face. She groaned at the daylight, her body heavy and aching. She checked her sides and found her knives intact, but her coin purse gone. Swearing under her breath, she looked to Porchid, who was swathed in red.

'Great,' Eveline croaked. 'Just what I need. A pissed-off fairy.'

Porchid swatted her and she ducked, then stood on wobbly feet. She dusted off her pants.

Despite the dream, the most Eveline managed to gauge was that her father had been taken by the sisters Grimm. If anybody had told her that the three most powerful witches of all time had taken her father before she'd seen it, she would've laughed. They were the mothers of the realm, the all-powerful beings that created every creature in it.

But they were also terrifying. At least, if you went off the stories told by children. Three witches, three mirrors, and a cauldron with magic so potent you'd die on the spot.

Supposedly they liked to eat children who behaved badly or ignored their parents.

And yet, it wasn't a child they had taken all those years ago, but her father.

Eveline stewed in silence as she followed Porchid, thankful to get away from Marcellus as they made their way back to the road. It forked off in multiple routes: one to Wolf's Den, one to Roserock, and the others to the coast. With no money, she needed to find work.

She pondered for a moment and turned to Porchid, a crack in her voice escaping. 'The sisters Grimm took him.'

Porchid's light dimmed to an evening blue, her colour for sorrow. Reaching out her small hands, she flew to Eveline's side and touched her cheek. It was enough for Eveline's eyes to prick, and she swallowed, biting down the grief.

But she wasn't alone. She'd been with Porchid a long time, the fairy becoming an accidental companion when she'd found her injured. They didn't speak the same language, but it didn't matter. They communicated in other ways.

Eveline took a deep breath and put on a brave face. She didn't want to stew in her heartache, or pity. The reason she asked for a dream was because she wanted the truth, wanted answers. But most of all, she wanted revenge.

Except, revenge cost money.

If she was to seek out the witches, then her next job lay on one of the paths ahead. Wolf's Den was too close to the borders of Perridorm, where the Evil Queen waged war, and the coast was not a place to be if you were an earth walker. Teal Cove and the Isle of Nysa were full of mermaids and sea nymphs.

The option to turn back towards the Skinny Piglet was a fool's errand, considering she'd left Marcellus alive. Porchid left her shoulder and sat on the sign, seemingly already knowing their destination. She shrugged her small shoulders.

The only choice, really.

'Roserock it is,' Eveline said with a sigh.

III

The Promise of Revenge

Roserock was a village between the Shadow Forest and the Crystal Lake. Despite its size, it acted as a hub for those travelling from the west and south to the Silver City.

Mostly made up of humans, it was one of the smaller towns who had rebelled when the Queen started hunting the species in the realm – fairies, trolls, nymphs, elves and more had been hidden within the houses, protected by those willing to risk themselves against the queen's wrath.

Which meant, it had also been hit the worst when she'd taken her revenge.

Whilst it thrived now, a decade ago it had almost been ash.

Eveline had never been comfortable in any large town. She was used to being alone, working the odd job to feed her and Porchid's bellies before moving again. She didn't like to stay in one place, nor did she like the roving eyes of strangers looking her over. Judging, observing.

She moved with practiced ease through the streets, Porchid clinging to her collar as they passed stalls coated in flowers. During spring, Roserock prepared for the festival of flowers. Petals of blue, green, pink, and yellow blended into each other like a painter's dream and Eveline couldn't help inhaling the floral air. She remembered the crowns of lilacs her father used to make. The way he had called her his princess. Warm afternoons by the stream as she laid her withered and dying crown into the water, watching it float away. Her father's hand had sat on her shoulder as she cried for its short life. He'd made her a fresh one, but the overwhelming sense of how finite time was loomed over her.

'It is not the length of our lives that matters, Eve,' he'd said, 'but how much we fill it with during our short time. The new crown does not replace the last, but it brings something new.'

She'd still cried, still mourned the wilted lilacs as they floated downstream. But those words had made her appreciate all her flower crowns. Neither ever replaced the other, but each remained unique. A gift. One had been made by the tree in the glen, another made in the bustle of a city, the last by a stall filled with boxes of her father's goods.

The shout from a passing cart pulled her back to reality. The town was packed with tourists travelling from all over, stopping in to see the festival in full swing. Claustrophobia began to wrap its tendrils around her, and she dragged her feet, unenthused by the hustle and bustle surrounding them. Vendors shouted through crowds, their stalls made of coloured silk.

Porchid flew between the laid-out crafts, glowing pink with excitement. Eveline took note of the visitors coming in this time of year, looking for a job. She'd either do several little ones or find a big pay day through one of the richer families. Hopefully, if she booked a couple of nights in an inn, her reputation would be enough.

She started by helping a mother who'd lost her child – free of charge – and then moved up to a merchant who had lost his wagon wheel. Slowly she made her way around with Porchid's help and earned a few coins. Enough for a hot meal and a night or two in the local inn.

After a bath, she made her way to the tavern downstairs.

Eveline spent most of her time travelling and dropping into taverns. It's where loose lips came after a few pints of brew, and secrets ran as currency. She picked out a corner, much like she had in the Skinny Piglet, and ordered some food.

Eveline watched the crowd, lost in her own thoughts when a silver skinned arm delivered her meal. Eveline stiffened when she gazed up, noting the braided pale hair and dark eyes.

She was a changeling.

Porchid twinkled a reprimand, enough for Eveline to mumble a thanks. When she'd gone, Eveline turned to Porchid. 'Sorry.'

Porchid pouted, and bit into a berry, sweet red juice dripping down her chin.

Eveline took a spoonful of stew. 'I know. Just because she was swapped at birth doesn't mean she's any different from you or I.'

The changeling turned as if she heard, and Eveline's ears went hot – she hoped they weren't visibly red. It was hard to let go of stigma. Especially when most of Eveline's time was spent in Bellatorre, a country bent on separating creatures.

Changelings were fairies that'd been swapped with a human child in the crib. When most were discovered, they were killed or sold into slavery. It was an unpleasant, harsh reality. Eveline watched the changeling work her way through the tables and pondered whether or not she'd had to claw her way to freedom, or whether she'd been lucky like so few had been.

Eveline was just about to ask Porchid about their meal when a palace messenger came in. He panted as he whispered to the barmaid, leaving as abruptly as he'd arrived.

When the changeling finally came to collect their plates, Eveline lay her hand upon her silvery skin.

The changeling startled, pulling away.

'Sorry.' Eveline smiled. 'My friend here just wanted to know your name.'

The changeling eyed the small fairy.

'Piccadilly,' she replied, with a thick accent. It came off sharp, so unlike the demure persona she'd displayed when serving them dinner.

'What word do you have from the Queen?' Eveline asked.

Piccadilly reached out to collect the plates on the table. 'It's the Princess. She has been poisoned. Possibly dead.'

The words were clipped, tinged with something Eveline couldn't place. Piccadilly kept her head low, carefully avoiding Eveline's gaze.

It was strange. For months, she'd not heard a whisper of Princess Snow and yet in the last few days she'd been brought up twice. Digging out whatever coin she had left, Eveline placed it in the changeling's palm.

'Just poisoned?' Eveline asked.

The changeling eyed the patrons before facing Eveline. Her eyes were dark, but something behind them seemed bright, like a fierce star in the night sky.

Piccadilly sighed. 'Rumour is she's poisoned, but I'd say she's run for it.'

'Is that likely, given the Queen's reputation?' Eveline asked carefully.

Piccadilly snorted. 'No, I suppose not.'

Thanking her, Eveline ordered another round of brew.

Eveline had known from years past that Roserock had been secretly building a rebellion. Sure, it was small, mostly made up of farmers, millers, and bakers, but since Myrenna had been in power, the realm had fallen into decay. The people were slowly starving with the higher taxes and shrivelling crops. And with the laws against humans and the other species, things were tense. The people of Bellatorre hoped Princess Snow could bring back prosperity when she came of age. A time not too far away.

It was said her skin was white as snow with lips as red as a rose. Her beauty was highly regarded, and it was no secret the Evil Queen had her locked away in the castle.

But to kill her?

Snow had been under the Queen's thumb for years. Was she the one who'd poisoned her? If so, why wait until she was eighteen? Why not kill her off when she was a child?

Porchid poked her finger in Eveline's brew and licked it, wrinkling her face in disgust. Eveline laughed but was cut off when her skin tingled.

She eyed the room, noting a stranger swathed in a dark green cape. They weren't subtle with their gaze.

The stranger downed their drink and took careful steps towards Eveline's table. She repositioned herself, ensuring her knives were nearby as she leaned back in her seat.

The stranger sat and laid down a large bag of coin.

Straight to the point, then.

'No polite hellos?' Eveline asked casually over the rim of her cup.

The stranger grumbled, hood still covering their face.

The stranger spoke, his voice deep. 'I just need your business, not small pleasantries.'

Eveline leaned forward. She knew that voice, and the axe he wielded.

'Do you think this is a joke?' she hissed. 'I was kind before, but I could easily just cut your throat here. In fact, now I'm regretting not doing so.'

That was a lie. Eveline didn't kill if she didn't have to.

Her father had always said that when you killed, a little piece of your soul was left with the victim. After a time, you had no soul left.

The stranger pulled back his hood, his face grave. His jaw showed stubble, but his hair remained a mess. She sucked in a breath when the same golden-brown eyes from the Skinny Piglet met hers.

The huntsman.

'I need your help,' he said.

Eveline sneered. 'No troll to help you this time?'

'No.' He paused. 'He has a hard time blending in, and I knew this discussion might have been a bit… heated.'

Heated? This guy didn't know when to quit.

'He's confused as to how you put him under so quick.'

'I have no doubt he's always confused,' Eveline replied drily.

It was another lie. Whoever this troll was, he was by far the most educated one she'd ever come across. Considering she only had stories to go by, it wasn't much, but from the trolls' reputation, they were barbaric, brutal, and quick to anger. The troll might've been sceptical, but he'd communicated fine, and had even shown a sense of humour.

The huntsman leaned forward. 'I'm here to make a deal.'

Eveline watched him with narrowed eyes, not trusting a word from his mouth. His gaze was steady, honest even, and it unsettled something within her. She sighed. 'You have five minutes, or I'm walking out.'

'Maybe somewhere more private?' he said, looking around the tavern.

'So you can slice my neck with that axe?'

'So wandering ears don't overhear us.'

Sighing again, she waved down the changeling. Eveline told Piccadilly to bring the brew to her rooms, and made the huntsman follow her up the stairs.

Whatever this was. It had better be worth her time.

Eveline's room was small, but it had a mattress and hot water, which was all she needed for the moment. The huntsman sat by the table next to the window and removed his cloak, revealing broad shoulders.

'Make yourself comfortable,' she drawled.

Ignoring her, he placed his axe on the table and raised his hands in defeat. 'I'm not here to swindle or thieve or deceive you.'

Placing her hands on her hips, she took him in. His hair was thick, still sitting unkempt and unbrushed. His fingers were callused, and even though she didn't trust him, his eyes were earnest. She couldn't believe she was doing this.

'Forgive me if I'm wrong,' she said, turning about the room, 'but the last time I saw you, you had stolen an object from someone, and I had a knife held to my throat for trying to return it to its owner.'

He cringed. 'I can see how it looks, but please hear me out.'

Eveline took a seat on the edge of the bed and held her hands to her knives. 'Then talk.'

He ruffled his hair and fidgeted on the stool. 'I'm looking for someone, and I thought I could find her by using Rumpelstiltskin's spindle.'

His hulking form was comically too big for the small stool and Eveline wondered if it would break. She secretly hoped it would.

'I need you to hear me out before you say no,' he continued.

Eveline raised her brow. Whatever this was, it made her wary. But she sat still, the movement trained into her from childhood. She remained silent, waiting.

'Okay,' he breathed out. 'This is going to sound bad. But Queen Myrenna hired me to find Princess Snow.'

At that, Eveline snorted.

Queen Myrenna. The same queen they also called the Evil Queen – a well-known joke to the peasants and prisoners.

'She has tasked me to find her, and when I do—'

He paused, contemplating how much he should share. 'I have a skill with the axe you see, and I'm to seek her out and … cut out her heart.'

Eveline raised both eyebrows. *Cut out her heart?* The Queen needed to find her own heart before she started devouring others'. It was grotesque.

He stared at her, waiting, but Eveline didn't move. She was placing the pieces together but still finding no answers. The fact that he was owning up to wanting to cut out the heart of a person was disgusting, let alone the fact it was a princess. A well-loved princess, to be precise, with a rebellion at her call.

Maybe he didn't know about the messenger.

Eveline picked at her nails. 'Well, that shouldn't be hard, considering she's already dead – or haven't you heard the news?'

He wasn't shocked like she'd suspected. 'That's part of the reason why my mission is so dire.'

Eveline only blinked.

'I'm not explaining this very well,' he replied.

'You think?' she retorted.

'What I mean is, yes, I'm trying to find the Princess, but not to kill her. I want to save her.'

Now, that was not an outcome Eveline had expected. Going against a direct order of the Queen was suicide. Either he was brave, or a complete moron. She believed he might be the latter.

'She's dead, not missing,' Eveline pointed out.

'That's what Myrenna wants everyone to believe. Snow has been poisoned, yes, but she isn't dead. If we can—'

'Let me guess,' Eveline interrupted. 'You want me to find Princess Snow?'

He nodded. 'I've been searching for weeks, and she hasn't turned up. I'm afraid the rumours are true, but I must find her to be sure. She was alive the last time I saw her.'

'The last time you saw her?' Eveline asked, confused.

Nobody had seen the princess in years. She didn't make public appearances. Didn't go outside. She was a living, breathing mystery, with little-to-nobody knowing what she truly looked like.

'Malak and I worked at the castle.' He swallowed, his eyes pleading with her as she crossed her arms.

'So, you think the news from the Queen is a lie?'

'I think the Queen has other plans at play,' he replied.

The Queen was not a person to trifle with. She was cruel and cunning. Either she killed you or placed you into a life of torture in those horrid mines of hers.

He pulled out the heavy coin purse again. 'I was given fifty gold medallions. Upon my return, if I'm successful, she has promised fifty more.' He held her gaze. 'If you help me find her, then the whole sum of money is yours.'

Eveline couldn't help but be taken aback. One hundred gold medallions were a king's ransom. It would set her up for years in the finest establishments and go a long way in procuring the means to help her find and destroy the sisters Grimm.

It was too good to be true, and far too easy. Eveline stiffened, tilting her head at the man before her. 'If you plan to save Snow, then how do you plan to return her to the Queen and collect these so-called medallions?'

'Fifty medallions, then,' he amended.

Fifty medallions was still better than no medallions. She licked her lips. 'What is it the Evil Queen wants with Snow's heart, exactly? Why now?'

He shook his head. 'She eats hearts. Specifically, hearts from maidens with youth and beauty. I believe the Queen's mirror has advised Snow is of age.' he said, 'Meaning her heart is ripe for the picking.'

'She means to eat the Princess's heart?' Eveline asked in disgust. Maiden's hearts she understood, but her own stepdaughter was another thing entirely.

The huntsman nodded gravely. 'We believe the Princess's heart is the heart – the most powerful of all. But we don't understand why.' He stood, running his hands through his hair. His large shadow crept across the floor, and Eveline's fingers twitched at the hilts of her blades.

Even dishevelled, he was beautiful.

Her eyes flicked to the stain on her leathers from dinner, and a flush crept up her neck at the thought of how long it'd been there. Chastising herself, she crossed her arms. He was a man, not a prince, and if she was smart, she wouldn't take his deal regardless of the exorbitant reward.

'Will you help?' he asked.

She frowned, torn at the prospect of such a large sum and the surety of death that was the Evil Queen. 'I don't know,' she breathed.

'That's not a no, though,' he said.

'It's not a yes.'

'But it's something. If you say yes, please meet me on the main road out of town at dawn. I'll be heading through the Shadow Forest towards the Mines of Parador. It's rumoured to be where Snow was last seen.' He paused, as if unsure how to continue. 'Even if we met on bad terms, I hope we can at least strike a deal.'

He collected his axe as she stared at him in silence. When he reached the door, he hesitated. 'I hope to see you soon. Just, please don't choke my friend this time. He's sensitive.'

Eveline snorted.

When his footsteps faded below, Porchid whistled.

Eveline grimaced. 'You like him, don't you?'

Porchid's colour went fuchsia as she dramatically swooned. Eveline rolled her eyes and dropped on her bed. Handsome or not, his deal involved going up against the Evil Queen.

That meant danger and death.

But also, her mind whispered, it meant a chance at vengeance.

Roserock was famous for the tunnel of kissing trees entwined along its entrance road. The branches weaved in an intricate tangle, so close to one another you could never tell where one began and the other ended.

The locals believed the trees were long lost lovers, a warning to those who made bargains with magic not heeding the price. If the tale was to be believed, there'd been a couple who could not conceive. Upon this news, they approached a witch, who promised them a horde of children. The witch's only price was the payment of their first child.

The couple had agreed, but upon the child's collection the couple refused, fearing they may never conceive another. Not trusting the witch, the couple went to flee only to be met with the witch at the entrance to town.

The witch had cursed them on the spot for their lies, turning them into the trees which now stood side by side leading the way into Roserock.

Eveline frowned, hating that most of the tales held some sort of truth. The fact she could be sitting in something that used to be a person soured her stomach. She crunched into the apple she held, swinging her legs as she watched the sun rise over the trees.

She hadn't slept much. She'd tossed and turned all night over whether to take up the huntsman's deal.

Her dreams were filled with memories – a red tent with the grey-blue eyes of her old tutor, the warm hug from a lost friend, a storm that raged in a small glen.

She'd woken in a sweat, turning to the clock as it conveniently chimed dawn. She'd taken it as a sign. Perhaps this was the path she was meant to follow. The one carved out for her long before she lost her father.

She heard the two of them before she saw them, their voices echoing over the road. Eveline leaned down from her perch, eyeing the troll as he strolled through the gates with the huntsman. Despite the huntsman's height, he only reached the troll's shoulders, meaning Eveline would only reach his nipple – if she was lucky.

The two of them seemed to be companions, though she was still sceptical. It wasn't normal for a troll to befriend someone who wasn't another troll. And in Bellatorre, it wasn't normal for a human to befriend anything other than human. Sure, she had befriended Porchid, but she wasn't from Bellatorre. Not originally.

Eveline stabbed one of her knives through the apple core and waited, noting how the huntsman continually looked behind him.

As they came closer, she timed the pace of their steps, and took aim. Her wrist flicked, the knife flying free. Eveline grinned smugly as the blade landed in front of their moving feet. One inch closer and she would have sliced their toes. They halted as she gracefully dropped from her perch in the tree.

'Stealth is going to be an issue, with how large he is,' she said by way of greeting, pointing her second blade towards the troll.

The troll frowned as he picked her up her knife. 'Why is she here?'

Eveline raised her brow at the huntsman. 'You didn't tell your companion about your late-night visit?'

The troll stared daggers.

The huntsman turned to his companion. 'I knew you wouldn't agree.'

'Of course I wouldn't agree,' he said. 'We know nothing about her. She could turn us in.'

The huntsman flinched.

'I don't work for the Queen,' Eveline said, trying to assuage his reservations. 'I work for me.'

'That's the problem,' the troll retorted.

Eveline plucked her knife from his hand and placed it back into the holster at her hip.

'I assume you've agreed to help us, then?' the huntsman asked.

The troll's mouth dropped, his head twisting between the two of them as if they'd suddenly changed into sea monsters. 'Did I speak another language? Or are you choosing to ignore me?'

Eveline shrugged. 'The pros outweigh the cons.'

'That's still not a yes,' the huntsman said.

'It's as close as you're going to get.'

The troll scoffed. 'I can't believe this.'

The huntsman gave Eveline a small smile as the troll spat out curses. 'That's good to hear, Seeker.'

'She's the seeker?!'

'Slow on the uptake there, Mr Troll,' Eveline said, extending her hand. The huntsman clasped it, his rough, calloused fingers gripping hers firmly. She bent in a mocking bow. 'The Seeker, at your service.'

The huntsman smiled, which lit up his entire face. Eveline's breath hitched at the sight. 'This is Malak,' he said. 'My companion and a good friend.'

Eveline couldn't understand the concept. They were an odd pair, but she guessed they had been that way long before she'd first seen them step into the Skinny Piglet. She shrugged and swung her pack over her shoulder.

'This is Porchid,' she said pointing to the fairy on her shoulder. 'She likes pretty things, long walks on the beach, and hates water.'

The fairy shone proudly, and Eveline smirked. 'Well, let's go, then. If the Princess is indeed poisoned, she'll need assistance. One hundred gold medallions better be worth the death wish.'

'Fifty,' the huntsman reminded her.

'As you say,' Eveline replied, walking off ahead of them.

The huntsman and Malak hurried after her to catch up. The first stop would be the Mines of Parador and the dwarves that dwelled in them. Maybe she could pick up one of their famous gems whilst she was there. It was never a bad idea to have a couple of magical objects in your possession should trouble find you. Especially when you've just picked one cauldron of a fight.

IV

The Mines of Parador

The Mines of Parador were a hidden labyrinth deep within the Mountains of Eyrie.

It'd once been a great kingdom, the dwarves mining deep into its thick rock to search for diamonds and gems. The diamonds were worth a heavy price, but it was the gems which held true value. Each gem contained a gift depending on the type you managed to pull from the rock.

But the dwarves had become greedy, digging so deep they'd brought about their own ruin. If Eveline recalled correctly, her father had mentioned something about unlocking monsters, or a madness of some sort. Her brain went foggy at the memory.

Now, if you were looking for a dwarf, you'd find them in the Peaks of Carfell, bordering the edge of the mountains between two kingdoms. As for Parador …

It was haunted.

Eveline puffed as the land steepened, her muscles aching after walking for so long. Spring hadn't yet arrived in the mountains. As they reached the base, the cool air bit their skin. The ground was withered, the frosty grass cracking underfoot until it turned to rock.

By the time nightfall came, the wind had a chill, carrying the promise of snow. Eveline pulled out extra clothing from her satchel, wrapping it around her leathers. 'We'll stop here tonight,' she said. 'You'd be suicidal to attempt the climb after dark, and here we have fairly good cover from the trees, with a vantage point.'

The huntsman agreed and left to collect some wood for the fire. Eveline had barely begun to unravel her bedroll when hot breath raked her neck. She turned to find Malak's giant green nose inches from her eyeline.

'I don't trust you.'

Eveline motioned her hand in front of her nostrils to wave away the stench of its breath. With a sneer, she stepped around him and began to build a pit for the fire. 'Yes, troll, and I find you ever so trustworthy, considering you were harbouring a stolen object the last time I saw you.'

He huffed in response and walked away to grab his bedding. 'My name's Malak. Not Mr Troll, or Troll, or whatever you wish to call me. It's Malak.' He paused. 'And we were going to give it back.'

Eveline watched him as he neatly laid out his and the huntsman's rolls in perfect symmetry. With the fire going, they'd have optimal heat.

'I could just call you sook and be done with it,' she huffed.

'I could call you many things, too.'

She ignored him, looking down the crest of the hill to where the huntsman had gone. The area seemed clear of hunters, with no evidence of other camps. That was a good sign; the last thing she needed was raiders trying to rob them.

Twilight fell, giving them enough daylight to ensure the perimeter was secure. A crackle echoed as the huntsman lit a fire. He settled himself down with ease and motioned to the pheasants he'd caught. 'Hungry?'

'You were gone for two minutes,' Eveline said. 'How did you hunt them so *fast?*'

He shrugged in response, prepping the carcass. 'I'm a huntsman.'

She scoffed. Like it was perfectly acceptable to catch dinner within minutes instead of hours.

Porchid flittered nearby, inspecting Malak as he rolled over. He didn't swat at her, which was positive, but still, Eveline was cautious.

The huntsman noticed her gaze. 'He won't harm her. He's not built that way.'

'And how is he built?' Eveline asked, careful to lower her voice.

'He's not like other trolls. He's smaller. Kinder.'

'You called him sensitive,' she said. 'At the tavern.'

He nodded, a hint of a smile appearing. 'I did. You can't tell him I said that, though. He'll be rather offended.'

She grabbed one of the pheasants he'd caught and began to pluck. 'Why? Will the troll eat you?'

The huntsman chuckled. 'No. But his tears are far worse than his teeth.' Her lip quirked. 'I know you think it's strange,' the huntsman said after a moment, his eyes focusing on Malak and Porchid. 'I'm friends with a troll. But how is it any different from you and Porchid?'

The fairy floated carefully around the troll, her colour changing as she sniffed his clothing. Malak remained patient as Porchid rested her small hands on his cheek, poking him.

Malak rumbled a laugh.

Something about the interaction made Eveline shuffle. It wasn't that she was abhorred by other creatures, it was that she wasn't used to seeing a troll engage with others outside of his kind.

The huntsman watched her expectantly, his curious gaze just as piercing as it'd been in the Skinny Piglet. If she considered it like a human and a fairy, not a troll and a human, then she supposed it was the same. Though she was loathe to admit it.

'It's not any different,' she conceded.

The huntsman smiled. 'No, it's not.'

Eveline stood amongst flashes of green and the rolling hills of the mountains. A glass casket frosted in ice. She whirled to

meet deep amethyst eyes and a black gown whipping against the wind.

Smoke covered the land, turning the world to ash. A scream tore from her throat as a great beast dove from the blanket of trees and swallowed an eagle whole.

Eveline awoke in a pool of her own sweat.

The flashes in her dream had been quick, concise. She rubbed at her temples before noticing the troll's snores. Malak laid sprawled out by the dying fire, Porchid in a ball nearby.

She held her hand against her chest as her heart slowed, the breaths turning from shallow to full. She didn't know what the dream was, only that it'd haunted her since her father's death.

Eveline's skin prickled. Raising her eyes, she found the huntsman staring.

She tried to focus on the thrum of her heart. This was how her gift worked, never in succinct patterns or possibilities. Sometimes it was a tug of her heart, or a stirring in her gut, or a tingle. Tonight, it had been a dream.

'Nightmares?' he asked.

Eveline ignored his question. 'How did you know to start looking for the Princess near the mines?'

If he was taken aback by the question, he didn't let on. 'I heard several raiders bragging about it in Roserock. They found a cart, robbed it blind but mentioned leaving the body of a girl behind.'

Eveline frowned. 'How do you know it's Snow?'

He shrugged. 'Call it a gut feeling.'

The conversation was over after that. The huntsman looked away from her and rolled over.

Eveline did the same, facing away from him before those golden-brown eyes of his saw more than she wanted.

Eveline's dreams bit at her like shards of glass. A few nights of lacklustre sleep had settled deep within her bones. The huntsman and Malak moved in strides ahead of her, the trees thinning out as they got closer to the mountain. Her feet dragged, the early mornings not uncommon for her, but still a burden. Malak ignored her if he could, focusing on the fairy instead.

Eveline pretended the betrayal didn't hurt.

Sometimes the huntsman would walk with her, sometimes they'd even speak. But it was when she couldn't sleep that he invaded her space the most. One morning, she'd awoken covered in sweat and left the camp to train in a clearing. Despite her best efforts, the huntsman had found her.

'You're training,' he'd said.

She hadn't bothered to give him a response. It wasn't a question anyway.

Eveline lifted her blade and aimed for a white poplar tree. The blade flew from her fingers with ease and landed with a plonk in the bark.

The huntsman grinned. 'Impressive.'

Eveline held back her eye roll and headed towards the tree, but he cut in front of her and grabbed the knife. Eveline growled. Nobody else had held those blades since—

She didn't want to think about it.

'Give it back,' she ordered.

'You know,' the huntsman said, 'you haven't asked for my name once.'

Eveline watched him twirl the blade in his hand, his palms too large to handle it properly. It brought a sick feeling to her stomach. 'You never offered it.'

He pointed the blade at her like a finger, the move casual. 'I'd hope to offer mine when you told me yours.'

'Seeker is fine.'

He looked at her pointedly. 'I'll hand this back if you tell me?'

Eveline narrowed her eyes and he laughed. 'Okay, I'll hand it back *then* you give me your name.'

When Eveline went to grab the blade, he dodged, but she moved faster. Before he could blink, she elbowed his ribs and swung her foot into the back of his knee. He dropped, and Eveline swiped the blade off him before he could react.

'I suppose I deserved that,' he said.

Eveline peered down at him, baffled by his smile. She'd just put him on his knees!

'I'm Hansel.'

'Eveline,' she replied with a grunt.

'So, can I join?' he asked. 'It's always better to train with someone else.'

She'd had no logical reason to turn him down, except for her own selfish pride. Eveline nodded. Mild curiosity plucked at her with how he wielded his axe. With a skill like that, he must've been trained.

Reluctantly, Eveline had begun to enjoy their morning sessions, the movement of another body taking her training to higher levels. He was graceful despite his height, his moves sleek and sure. Sometimes she won, but only through sheer force of will and an ability to surprise him.

The training from their latest morning had been the hardest yet. Hansel had been waiting for her before dawn, his eyes sparkling in challenge. She'd met it with an excitement of her own, pushing herself further than before. Whoever had trained him had done it well.

Her muscles ached from the climb they'd started at dawn, and she knew fresh bruises were blooming all over from their sparring as well. She was getting stronger, but still felt tiny between her two massive companions.

Hansel slowed as the wind chilled, meeting her stride. He held out a handful of nuts, that easy smile of his on his lips. 'Thought you'd be hungry.'

She nodded in thanks, watching the landscape turn more barren ahead.

'You're quiet again today,' he commented. 'Where do you go?'

She eyed him warily, frowning in confusion. 'I'm right here.'

He laughed. 'I mean in here'—he tapped his skull—'where do you go inside there? You always look so focused.'

She'd never been asked that before. Never even been aware it was a habit of hers. Heat flushed her cheeks as she looked at him. But there was no judgement there. Only curiosity.

'I don't know,' she replied, 'perhaps into a dream.'

'Where you stab people with those little knives of yours?' She choked out a laugh, and he smiled. 'I now count five.'

'Five what?' she asked.

'Five smiles.'

Her breath hitched, and she whirled on him. 'I smile.'

'No,' he replied, 'you smirk. There's a difference.'

Her eyes met Porchid's, who giggled from Malak's shoulder. Eveline frowned. Did she smile so little? Was she so miserable? She blinked, trying to squash down the urge to flee.

'You have a beautiful smile,' he said casually. 'I'm just trying to see it more often.'

Before she could utter a retort, Malak called from ahead. 'You might want to see this.'

Glad to get out of the conversation, Eveline pushed forward, only to halt where Malak stood.

Before her was blackened soil, so dark it was as if it were coated in shadow. She leaned down and touched it, the soil crumbled like ash. The roots of the trees were decayed, the landscape dead, almost as if a fire had been set but contained.

'What is this?' Hansel asked.

Malak picked up a stick that dissolved at his touch. 'Dark magic, by the looks of it.'

Porchid flew to the ground, her bright colours stark against the dead landscape. She touched the root of a tree and looked back at Eveline before shaking her head.

'It's as if the life has been sucked out of everything.' Eveline said, making Porchid shudder.

'Is this common?' Hansel asked. 'Surely if something was moving through the forest and killing everything it would be posted around every major town.'

Eveline scooped up the fairy and turned to them. 'I don't think it's widely known yet. But I know the Queen of Nysa is worried about it.'

'You knew about this?' Malak asked.

'Not exactly,' Eveline replied, 'I just ran into an old friend. She mentioned something about evil things happening, but I took it as speculation.'

'Let's hope it's only one area and can't spread,' Hansel said.

They stood in silence, seemingly all unsure on how to proceed. The silence was broken by a caw, followed by a chorus in response. A murder of crows flew over them, their cries piercing.

'We should move,' Malak interjected. 'The mountains are close, and this place gives me a bad feeling.'

Eveline could tell he was on edge. She nodded. She wiped her hands on her pants, thinking back to Cyrene's words in the tavern. Cyrene was known to exaggerate, to flash tales and twist them to her own purpose. But something about this lifeless forest told Eveline that the sea nymph may have been telling the truth.

Which unsettled her more than she cared to admit.

The group trekked through the snow-capped mountains, making their way up towards the pale blue sky. It wasn't as harsh as it would've been during the midwinter, but it still stung Eveline's cheeks.

She pulled a cloth around her mouth to stop the chafe as best she could. She hadn't spoken much – the wind made it hard – and she would disappear into her head, where prophecies and rumours and questions blurred together.

Cyrene's prediction about the darkness coming didn't sit well with her, and her dreams had echoed in response.

Hansel called out as they came to a narrow path. 'Running away again?'

His mouth was covered in his own cloth, but she could see the slight crinkle of his eyes. He was always bloody smiling.

'Just tired,' she yelled back over the wind. It wasn't a lie, not exactly. The harsh change in weather had turned bitter, and their food stores dwindled. With her reoccurring dreams, Eveline was unsteady, her waking hours too long and too few at the same time.

Hansel surprised her when he said, 'I don't sleep well, either.'

Porchid shivered in her pocket. The wind had been too strong for her small wings to fly, so she'd remained hidden, Eveline packing an extra set of cloth to keep her warm.

Despite being hidden, you couldn't miss that Porchid was there. If for a second she thought they'd forgotten her, Eveline received a little flare of red or a pinch as a reminder. Honestly, if Eveline had known fairies were this fussy, she'd have never taken one as a companion.

Hansel took her hand, helping her over a particularly rocky path. 'I have nightmares, too.'

The wind picked up, ushering them back into silence.

By the second day, the path veered downwards, Eveline's legs thankful for the reprieve. When dusk hit, they made their way down a winding path, narrow enough that the sheer drop was only a pixie's length on her left. Malak barely even fit. His shoulders brushed snow off the rocky face, his brows squashed in concentration as the mountain groaned every so often.

Eveline picked at her dreams, letting the tug of her gift pull them onwards. Analysing the flashes, one of which had shown a worn path accessed only by this side of the mountain. She'd found the marking that told her they were heading in the right direction. She looked behind her, watching the troll indelicately stomp through the snow. He wasn't graceful, but he was steadfast. At least he was large enough to block the wind.

Her teeth chattered and her eyes stung. Eveline missed the warmth of the sun. She missed the warmth of anything, really. She'd even take a matchstick at this rate if it gave off something other than ice.

She knew they were close, but she couldn't help the slice of frustration that cut through her as her eyes watered from the wind. They should've reached their destination by now. Surely, they hadn't passed it. She paused to eye the path, checking she hadn't missed anything, and Porchid pinched her from inside the pocket. Eveline hissed, swatting at her jacket. The fairy emitted a blazing red against the snow.

Porchid hit Eveline again and pointed to the cold rock surface beside them. Almost invisible at first, but hard to miss once seen, was a small fissure. Eveline looked at the huntsman. 'Don't touch the wall,' she yelled over the wind.

'What?' Malak asked, his heavy steps moving towards them. It was like slow motion, the stomp of his heel and the graze of his shoulder eliciting a chain reaction she couldn't stop even if she tried. Her hand reached out, her eyes wide, but before she could call out a warning, the troll slipped.

That's when she heard it. A groan and a creak of the mountain.

The fissure split, the rock shuddering as the crack speared up the rock like a web. Then snapped.

Eveline threw herself towards the ledge up ahead, a scream escaping her lips.

Malak fell.

Porchid thrashed inside Eveline's pocket. The ledge she'd managed to dive onto was narrow, her body aching as she clung onto the huntsman. His gloved hand was clasped around hers, and she began to feel its slip.

Hansel must have seen the fissure at the same time she had, diving only moments behind her. But where Eveline had made it, he had not.

He swung over a break in the path, the fog below hiding the drop. Eveline eyed the chasm but failed to see Malak in its depths.

Pulling at the vestiges of her energy, she wrenched Hansel up bit by bit, his large frame a struggle. Her hair lashed her face, the wind violent and relentless as she heaved. 'I need you to help me, you oaf of a man. I can't do this myself.'

She didn't know if he could hear her but understanding seemed to flash in his eyes. When he was closer to the edge, he managed to find a foothold and used his legs to propel himself up. When his arms reached the edge, he scrambled over, and they collapsed.

Eveline rolled over and pulled out Porchid, whose light was blood-red with anger.

'Sorry,' Eveline mouthed knowing it was pointless until Porchid calmed down.

The fairy was hard to predict. One moment she would collect flowers and cry over a lost babe, and the next she wanted to poison someone.

Hansel's eyes raked over Eveline. 'Are you hurt?'

Eveline's cheeks flushed at the concern. She shook her head and he sighed with what sounded like relief.

Hansel peered over the ledge and shouted Malak's name. The only response was an echo of his voice and the sharp wind. He removed his pack, took out some rope, and motioned for Eveline to anchor it. His mouth was slightly blue. The snow had bitten into his cheeks, turning them pink along the stubble that had begun to grow into a beard.

Eveline tied a strong knot around a rock near the far wall of the cliff. The huntsman tested its strength, nodded to her, and made his way off the ledge. Her heart quickened, but she held firm as his shape disappeared into the snowy winds below.

Porchid's light went white. If Eveline wasn't so panicked, she might have scolded the fairy for her impulsive moods.

Minutes ticked by, and when the huntsman returned, he motioned for her to follow. The decision should have been simple. With nowhere to go forward, she didn't really have a choice but to follow. Still, it didn't stop the swell of sheer panic that tore under her skin. Regardless of whether Eveline could see the ground or not, heights were something she avoided. A tree where she could only break a bone was fine. But when the ground was invisible, death certain, she hesitated. Especially when it came to free-falling down a rope.

A memory flashed of a girl descending from a high tower. Her crown of lilacs wilting from her skull like dead confetti.

Her mouth went dry as the wind howled.

She swore under her breath as she grabbed the rope, and wished to the fairy godmother that she'd make it down without falling to her doom.

Eveline descended into the bleak abyss. Her feet slid as she tried to grip onto the frozen surface, her hands burning against the rope. Her limbs shook and her heart was hammering. A tower of pink flashed in her mind.

It's not the same, she told herself, willing her body to hold its grip. *It's not the same.*

She urged her body down inch by inch, arms groaning in protest. She blinked as a memory crept over her. The rope turned into golden hair and weaved lilies, the wall now a light pink brick.

It's not the same.

Snow and spring swathed across her vision, flickering in and out as reality and memory fought against each other in a battle of wills.

The memory won.

The wind whipped at her hair. The flash of a vine crawling up its surface. A knife glinted from a window high above. A princess with shadows under her skin was screaming with betrayal.

Rapunzel.

That long ago night, Rapunzel had murmured no names, her deep breath the only indication of her dreamless sleep. Eveline remembered pulling the rope from her secret place after weeks of tantrums and apologies and indecision.

She'd looped it over the hook at the side of the window and looked to the only friend she'd made since climbing into that burrow beneath the tree.

Her descent had been treacherous. A cackle and a crow as a figure above her peered from the window. Eveline's body locked up, just as it had then.

Nonononono—

She was in the mountains in snow, not in the springtime maze of a stone tower.

Her heart thundered, her breath seizing as Rapunzel lifted the knife and cut.

Eveline had fallen then, a silent scream escaping her lips.

Porchid pinched her skin, and she blinked. Her breath was hard and heavy. The wind stung her eyes as she swayed. Her fingers were white from straining them so hard when she heard the far away voice of the huntsman below.

Her father had always said that courage came from within. Fear could not control you. Only you could control you.

The words were weak, but enough for Eveline to start moving again. She took a deep breath, then another, lowering herself down the mountain through sheer will alone. Porchid twinkled something, her voice a solace as Eveline descended into the mist.

Eveline's breath hitched as green arms wrapped around her waist and gently placed her on solid ground. Her heart hammered in her chest and her muscles retracted as she collapsed. Her breath came in short, hot bursts as she gasped, clutching at the solid ground. Hands came into view and lifted her up – Hansel, grabbing her by the shoulders.

She couldn't hear him, could barely see him. It was only his smell that pierced through the haze of her fear. Pine and wood.

His demeanour was calm, his eyes like the shade of buttered pastry. He coaxed her back with each word, his voice as warm as melted chocolate.

When Eveline came back to herself, his hands gripped her tightly, his face inches away. She licked her lips at the proximity, noticing for the first time a freckle in his eye.

He pulled back before she was ready to let go, the cold piercing the space between them. He swallowed, seemingly as uncomfortable as she was. The only being who had been that close to her over the years had been Porchid.

Porchid—!

She panicked but found the fairy peeking from her pocket at Hansel like a love-sick idiot. She sensed it then. The stirring in her gut. The familiar tingle of its power.

'It's here,' Eveline whispered, a frown pulling her brow. She remained shaken, but she refused to let it show. Her tongue was like sandpaper and her lips were cracked from the cold. She held her arms to her chest and noticed Malak coming into view through the mist.

'I found something.'

Just as Eveline had predicted, mere metres away stood the opening to the Mines of Parador.

The cave wasn't warm, but the relief was palpable in the group when the harsh wind wasn't stabbing their skin. The caves themselves were a labyrinth built under every rock and crevice in the Mountains of Eyrie. Hundreds of years old, each generation of dwarves had carved their mark upon these passageways and done it with perfection.

The walls were carved with intricate depictions of wars and myths and history. Eveline ran her fingers over them as they descended into the dark. Hansel handed her a lantern, and Porchid sat upon his shoulder, her impish smile enveloping her whole face.

Little flirt.

Malak took the front; Hansel took the rear. All of them had their weapons out, ready for anything that might crawl from the dark places. They followed Eveline's gift through paths covered in dust; paths it seemed that hadn't been touched in many, many years.

'Before we get any deeper, I think we should make camp,' Hansel said. 'We don't know how long we'll be inside, and it's a labyrinth down there.'

They all agreed, finding a small alcove in the wall. The wind howled through the tunnel, its echo a high-pitched wail as Porchid's light changed from blue, to yellow, then white.

'Watch for her,' Eveline said to Hansel. 'She's afraid of confined spaces. And the dark.'

'And water,' he replied. 'Unless your introduction was a lie.'

Eveline's mouth quirked. 'And water.'

She unravelled her bed roll and sat, meeting Malak's eyes across the cave. His gaze flickered between Hansel and her, suspicion behind his eyes.

With the shake of her head, she rolled over.

Stupid troll.

The next morning, they veered through the tunnels arriving at a grand opening. The arch was made of carved marble, though it was chipped and aged. The stairs ahead fell into blackness.

Hansel leaned forward and raised his lantern. 'It just keeps getting deeper.'

'Are you sure this is the right way?' Malak asked Eveline. 'I don't particularly want to die down here.'

Her gift flared in response, urging her forward. 'It's the right way,' she said, sounding braver than she felt.

Hansel touched her elbow lightly and nodded at her in encouragement. She tried to focus on the fifty medallions, and whether this was worth it.

Taking the stairs slowly, she led them into the underground depths. Eventually, the group approached a throne room covered in gold. The ceiling was so high it was impossible to predict where it ended and where it began. Eveline gazed at the craftsmanship, a pit forming in her stomach at the thought of how much work it would've taken to create.

Malak forged ahead, his irritation all the more palpable the deeper they went.

Hansel paused beside her. 'Beautiful, right? The story behind it is dark, though.'

Eveline raised her brow, and the huntsman leaned in. 'Legend says the hall belonged to a great dwarf king who deemed the tunnels unworthy. Wanting to leave behind his legacy, he implored the fairies to help him build this grand palace beneath the rock. He believed the dwarves, even with their craftsmanship, couldn't achieve such magnificence.'

The floor displayed figures on great cliffs and mountains. A king ruling his throne and a pile of treasure so large even the Evil Queen would weep with greed.

Hansel continued. 'Though the dwarves hated fairies, and for a time, they worked together to achieve the impossible.'

Eveline's eyes lit up. She never could ignore a good story – it was one of the gifts her father had left her, though she was terrible at telling them herself.

Porchid seemed equally enamoured, her glow bright as she pointed to the throne.

'They say the dwarves' and fairies' animosity grew, and bit by bit the resentment festered. When the king had turned his attention elsewhere, their hatred for one another turned vicious, and they fought. Bloodshed ensued, and when the king's own son perished in the fight, he lost control, murdering the survivors as punishment.'

Eveline looked back at him and blinked. 'That's dreary.'

A wailing sound echoed through the great hall and Hansel shrugged. 'Supposedly there're wraiths, too.'

Eveline waited a fraction, about to ask more questions when he smiled. This wasn't the smile from when he calmed her earlier, or the one he used in the mountains as encouragement. No, this smile was entirely made of amusement, and she called it straight away.

'Fairy shit,' she said, crossing her arms. Malak's chuckle came from the other side of the room. He'd made it up, and what'd been worse was that she almost fell for it. A deep groaning came from below, and the ringing of a bell.

He stopped laughing and motioned for her to move. 'The story might be made up, but the wraiths aren't.'

Eveline went cold. 'We need to go that way,' she said pointing past the pillar by the throne. But even as she followed the others into another tunnel, the coldness didn't leave her. All myths were spurred by truth, after all.

Illuminated by her lantern, the floor was stained, dark patches covering the faces of the heroes. Some were worn with age, but others wore the stain of death. Bloodshed had undeniably happened here, regardless of Hansel's tall tale.

She hurried her footsteps, desperate to get as far away from this place as possible.

V
The Gems and their Keepers

The smooth surface of the tunnels became more rugged the deeper they travelled. Sharp edges jutted out, grabbing at Hansel's sleeves as the passages narrowed. The temperature continued to drop, and with it, the group's spirits.

Here was where the term 'mines' became more accurate.

The ceiling lowered drastically, its sharp edges looming over the four of them. Malak had to slouch to squeeze through, and Hansel grimaced at the proximity. Sometimes, he hated how tall he was.

Eveline led the group with her gift. Whether it was by instinct or some intrinsic magic within her, Hansel didn't know. He was still trying to puzzle her out.

She seemed withdrawn most of the time, losing herself in thought, frowning on occasion. She was quick with her blades and quicker with her temper. Hansel watched Porchid glow nearby, her twinkle having a calming effect on the Seeker.

When she'd unexpectedly dropped in on the deal with Marcellus, he'd been pleasantly surprised. He'd been ordered by the Queen to hunt the Princess, but with little information or a magical gift of his own, it was like fate had stepped in. He'd heard tales of the Seeker – a woman who was gifted at finding lost things – but he'd envisioned an older woman, one aged with travel and hardened by time. Instead, he'd found Eveline.

Eveline halted at a crossroads, the paths dividing into five directions. The roof extended higher than before, giving Hansel and Malak a reprieve. Porchid flew, her glow turning gold as she flitted towards the cave.

A cave, no less, sprouting clusters of gems.

Hansel held back his gasp. He'd never seen anything like it.

Sure, he'd dabbled with the rich, had guarded royalty, but even those treasures paled in comparison. It was as if the glittering horde had been collected and then forgotten. It was a dragon's dream.

Porchid flitted between gems, squealing in obvious delight. Hansel waited by the doorway, watching as

Eveline selected a green peridot from the floor. She froze at whatever she felt, no doubt a surge of power of some kind.

'Careful,' Malak warned from the other side of the cavern. 'Parador's gems are dangerous.'

Eveline managed a glare that could wound. Hansel glanced around the room, taking it all in before his feet found their way to her side. He stared down at the peridot she held, a warning trickling at the back of his neck. 'All he means is that dwarves' gems hold special properties.'

He didn't usually beg forgiveness for his friend's misdemeanours, but Malak and Eveline had started off on the wrong foot. Malak wasn't always this grumpy, but he was close to Snow, just as Hansel was, and his worry displayed as irritation.

Hansel met her eyes. 'In the wrong hands, they can be dangerous. They aren't something to take lightly.'

Eveline paused a moment before she placed the gem back on the pile.

He surveyed the room with caution, his gaze halting on a dark-blue gem near the back. It glowed brighter than the rest, a whisper echoing over his skin as if to say, 'Choose me'.

His steps were cautious, but when he picked it up, he assessed its smooth surface with curiosity. The inside held a vein of silver, sparkling in the low light. It whispered again.

Seeker.

He turned towards Eveline, who ran her finger along a trunk of gems, the familiar frown peppered between her brows.

Hansel didn't know why he did it, but he suddenly found himself in front of her, closer than he'd anticipated, the words spilling from his mouth before he could stop them. 'Open your hand.'

Eveline froze. She was always so steady, so sure. In training she was like a bird, light and fast and free, her twin blades a blur in combat. She'd challenged him, reminded him that he still had a lot to learn. But she was still a curiosity.

She bit her bottom lip, caution warring behind her eyes, but obliged. His touch was careful as he placed the deep blue stone into her palm.

'What does it do?' she asked.

Every gem was known for its individual properties. Each could destroy or create, depending on the type. The magic they held was unlimited, and it surprised him this many had survived untouched.

'I'm not sure,' he replied, 'but I feel good about this one. You should have it.'

Her thumb grazed over it.

'It's beautiful,' he said. 'Like you.'

He didn't know where the words came from. Why they'd chosen this moment to stir. He cringed as Malak snorted, the troll listening in despite how silent he'd been.

Hansel tried to reel it back. 'You don't have to take it if you don't want.'

Eveline held the stone close to her chest, protective. It stirred something like pride in his chest, as if he'd done something *right*. Almost as if it belonged to nobody but her.

Without another word, Eveline pocketed the stone.

'They are the dwarves' gems.' Malak said warily. 'You should ask them first.'

'There's nobody to ask left,' she replied.

Malak's frown deepened.

Eveline picked a tunnel, her steps never faltering as she led them on. As Hansel went to follow, Malak stopped him. 'I hope you know what you're doing.'

Hansel hoped he did too.

Hansel had been watching Eveline for days.

At first it was from caution, the Seeker known to accept coin from anywhere. Though, he could never guess her motives.

He appeared casual, but inside he was wary. He'd tried many times to coax Eveline out of that little box she'd locked herself in. She didn't smile much, so the times he had seen a smile, they were brilliant.

After the first few days, he'd deemed her trustworthy enough. He'd already revealed he'd planned treason against the Queen, and told her that Snow was his priority. The money had seemed to be enough incentive to keep his secrets. More than that, she'd saved his life.

Even if she stayed silent and had her own secrets; who was he to ask them of her? He had his own secrets. After all, not many had a clean slate in this realm.

She clenched her fists as she focused, her hair falling loose from her braid. Her eyes questioned everything. Hansel had the urge to reach out and tuck the loose strand behind her ear. They'd been so close in the snow that he'd been able to smell her, something like lilac and grass. It'd been strangely intoxicating.

The dark tunnel grew damp as they descended deeper under the mountains, the tracks rusty and broken.

He watched Eveline lightly trace the lump of the gem in her pocket, her strong, steady shoulders feeling whatever it was when she followed the call of her gift. Did she feel attached to it? Was it the stone she was attached to, or the fact he had been the one to give it to her?

They were useless thoughts, ones he shouldn't be having when so much hindered on his actions. He tried to focus on his steps, on the cursed princess, on the promises he'd made to others he wasn't sure he could keep.

But then there it was. The whiff of lilac and grass. And he was wholly entranced again.

Malak shook his head with a snort of exasperation, as if reading Hansel's thoughts. They'd been friends for years, spending time together in the castle, and though Hansel was practiced at hiding his emotions, he was an open book to Malak, just as the troll was to him. Malak's face told him he thought him an idiot. In this moment, Hansel had to agree.

Once the Princess was found, Eveline would disappear anyway, on another adventure, finding another treasure, and her fairy would follow suit.

He didn't know why, but deep down in the pit of his soul he cared, even though he knew he shouldn't.

VI

The Thieves and their Ghosts

Porchid didn't like small spaces. Or enclosed spaces. Or dark spaces.

Above all, she disliked these mines.

She flew behind Eveline and kept close, her gaze flicking to the handsome boy behind them. Oh, how she loved to look at him. Even if Porchid disliked these mines, and was bored out of her wits, it at least had one pretty view.

'Stop it,' Eveline hissed, her voice quiet.

Porchid pouted before she perched on Eveline's shoulder. Despite the Seeker's grimace, Porchid hasn't missed the twitch of her lips or the way her gaze had skirted over the huntsman.

The fairy twinkled. *Don't lie and tell me you don't like him too.*

Eveline raised her brow. Despite the language barrier, they'd been companions for long enough that most of their moods weren't a secret. Even with the scowl etched into Eveline's features, the Seeker could be quite soft when she wanted to be. Porchid had seen it in the way she spoke gently to children, or ensured she found some token for a peasant free of charge.

Eveline had been the only one to help when Porchid had lain dying by a creek, her wings half cut off. The ache of the saw-shaped knife still lingered sometimes despite the number of years it'd been.

Porchid supposed Eveline hadn't always been this way, but she liked the sour expressions, the clipped tone. The way Eveline wielded her blades as well as her tongue.

Eveline was abrupt, but she was also loyal. Down to a fault sometimes.

Porchid counted the steady rhythm of Eveline's footsteps, the loud breaths of the troll, and the steady thrum of their hearts.

Eveline was her anchor, her home.

Sinking into Eveline's shoulder, Porchid hummed a tune.

Only to be cut off when the haunting call of a thousand voices pierced the tunnel's silence.

Goosebumps spread over Eveline's skin as the call of the dead echoed through the tunnels. Her breath turned frosty, Porchid's wings iced over. The voices rose and fell like that of a terrifying lullaby.

'Wraiths,' Hansel whispered.

'You said they were make-believe,' Eveline hissed, not hiding the venom in her voice.

He didn't even have the decency to look sheepish. 'The story was made up, but I warned you wraiths were real.'

Malak prayed. 'By the Godmother …'

Eveline turned away, squashing the rage coursing through her veins. She hated being led astray, and his careless attitude rubbed her the wrong way. She was about to snap again when the wraith's song came in a chorus.

> *Thieves, thieves, come out and pay,*
> *Take what's ours and become our prey.*
> *Thieves, thieves, come out and dance.*
> *Return what's ours and take the chance.*

Eveline's skin crawled. Ice crept along the walls, chilling her to her bones. The tunnel creaked. 'We need to *run*.'

The others didn't hesitate. Eveline took the lead, hoping the Fairy Godmother and her gift led them swiftly through the right tunnels. Dozens of forks and breaks, the ice on their heels, and the tunnels a maze.

> *Thieves, thieves, we smell your dread,*
> *We taste your guilt, you'll soon be dead.*
> *Thieves, thieves, we'll chill your bones,*

And crack them clean and leave them stones.

Eveline was closed-in, claustrophobic. The tunnels never faded, never ended, each resembling the last. She wondered what it would be like to be trapped here, in a labyrinth of rock. Cold, isolated.

Alone.

She didn't have time to ponder as the tunnels became colder, her breath coming out in cold bursts. Porchid clung to her, her light a blinding white beacon in the enveloping gloom.

Thieves, thieves, you cannot flee,

For we can smell what you cannot see,

Thieves, thieves, run through the dark,

Where you are blind, we seek our mark.

She heard it then, the sound of running water.

Hansel yelled from behind, his voice far away as her ears pricked, honing onto the possibility of freedom. A crack ricocheted through the tunnel and the ice spread like a disease, its great white arms reaching for them.

She knew the others were close behind, but was it enough? Was her gift enough to get them out of this?

Knives were not useful when it came to ghosts, nor was combat. Only the hearth of a fire had the strength to deflect pure frost. Her body was slowing down, her heart rate slackening as the chill turned her lips blue. The voices grew louder. The chimes of a bell waiting to kill.

Thieves, thieves, come out and bleed,

The dead rule here to hear you plead,

Thieves, thieves, the end is nigh,

Return what's ours or choose to die.

A breeze coated her skin as she surged towards the light at the end of the tunnel. Straining, her legs pushed her forward until she broke free of the oppressing rock – and halted at a ledge. The crash of a waterfall muted her senses. Water dampened her clothes, soaking into her skin.

She whirled to see her companions close behind, followed by hundreds of dead pale faces.

Wraiths.

Eveline assessed the ledge, the drop at least a thousand pixies deep.

'By the Godmother,' she swore.

Cold bit into Eveline's skin, desperation rearing its ugly head when she spied a reprieve. There to their right was a bridge of wood. An arch of black crystal and purple hues stood in front like a doorway.

Hansel pulled free his axe, his eyes wide, as the wraiths stepped close. 'So, we have a bridge that looks as if it's about to rot away, or a hoard of angry ghosts.'

'I know where I'd rather take my chances,' Eveline said, bolting for the grand archway of the bridge. The arch glowed as she crossed, flaring a bright white.

Eveline didn't know why, but magic coated her, silencing the world for a split second before the bridge wobbled underfoot.

The wraiths roared with fury, chains and screams and decayed faces charging like a nest of wasps. Eveline screamed as Malak raised his club, the spiked wood cutting through a head of mist. The wraith laughed, lunging towards him, and he yelled.

Hansel was almost at the archway, Porchid providing light as he swung his axe, only for the wraith's form to dissolve and regenerate.

'Run!' she screamed.

Porchid crossed through the arch first. Malak urged Hansel through before him, ice frosting his skin.

And just as Hansel made it onto the bridge, the ghosts screamed. Malak stumbled back as a girl in chains bit him. Blood leaked from his arm, a roar escaping his lips.

White light bloomed, the wraith's gaping mouths screeching incoherent words. The chasm carried it, echoing it like an orchestra.

Eveline blocked her ears as Malak backed through the arch, club raised in front of him.

'They aren't following,' Hansel called. 'The arch is keeping them back.'

Eveline snapped her gaze to the arch, noticing its shade properly for the first time.

Black tourmaline.

It was a protection against evil.

The bridge groaned as Malak stepped onto the decaying wood. The snap of a rope rebounded, and the bridge shook.

Eveline didn't wait.

She ran.

Unbelievably, they'd managed to cross the bridge before it'd broken. The wood spiralled into the depths of the water as Malak reached the other side. They could still hear the wraith's screams, the echo of it haunting and loud.

Despite their escape, the tunnels twisted, and so did Eveline's gut.

The encounter with the wraiths had unsettled her. None of them spoke as they walked, the darkness closing in once again. She was exhausted, not just in her bones but her soul. The only thing left alive within her was her gift, that pounding presence of the Princess nearby.

When her energy finally waned, she slowed, the silence eerie and yet comforting after the chanting wraiths.

Hansel spoke first. 'We need to rest.'

'We're so close,' Eveline argued.

The tug in her gut had grown, the tunnels becoming narrower with each turn.

'Malak needs his arm checked,' Hansel said.

But Eveline didn't listen, she pushed forward, rounding a corner. Then stopped short. The walls widened out, but where she'd expected another tunnel, or a door or anything besides rock, she found a dead end.

Her mouth went dry.

What in the cauldron?

Eveline's gift still tugged as if the Princess herself were encased within the depths of the stone. This couldn't be right. Her gift had never failed her before, not when it came to finding things for others. 'I must have missed something,' she whispered, 'misread the signals, or the tugging. Maybe we've taken a wrong turn?'

Her eyes pricked as Porchid's small hands touched her face. 'I don't understand,' she said more to herself than the others. 'What did I miss?'

Malak gruffed something unintelligible before he said, 'Enough for today. We need rest.'

'You need rest,' Hansel murmured. 'You're bleeding.'

'It's just a scratch.'

'It's a bite from a wraith,' he snapped.

Eveline ignored them and stared at the wall. She turned over every possibility in her head, revisited every turn, every pull of her gift. She didn't know how long she stood there. A hand touched her shoulder.

'Tomorrow we can figure out what to do next,' Hansel said softly.

She was defeated. Exhausted. Beaten. But his words lulled her back to the present. She gave him a nod, conceding, and turned to find the bedrolls had been set up. Hansel handed her some dried meat, but her stomach was too leaden to eat.

Silently, she laid down, rolling over to face the wall.

What had she missed? How could her gift have been wrong?

'We'll figure it out in the morning,' Hansel said.

But she didn't reply, she was too lost in her thoughts. She didn't know how long it took, but sometime later, the exhaustion finally settled in and pulled her to sleep.

VII

The Crystal Coffin

A hand covered Eveline's mouth and she kicked out instinctively.

There was an *oomph* in the dark and the hand flung from her face. She dived for her blades, but the blankets made her sloppy. Hands clasped around her waist before she could grab anything. She roared, throwing herself backwards. Her head collided with another, the stranger let go, and she rolled, landing on her hip.

The tunnel was dark, and it took a while for her eyes to adjust. Shadows moved through the darkness, too many to count.

'You said this would be easy, Bjorn!' one voice cried.

There was scuffling, a shout, the screech of a blade. A thump echoed on her left as Hansel stepped out of the shadows, halting when his eyes fell to her. Together, they braced for another attack.

The assailants weren't quick, but they were stocky, even if they only looked like they stood about five pixies tall. Another grunt, and Malak roared; it sounded like pain.

'Where are our weapons?' Eveline hissed.

'Taken,' said a new voice. 'You are trespassing.'

Malak winced. Hansel's firm back was pressed against Eveline's, his muscles shifting at the sound of his friend's pain.

'What have you done to him?' He seethed, voice sounding like poison.

Eveline placed her arm on his shaking body, rage coiling inside her gut.

The small space made it difficult to manoeuvre, and considering the depth of the tunnels, Eveline was surprised they'd been ambushed at all. It was why nobody had stayed awake to take watch.

She sniffed the air for magic, finding none.

'He's not dead,' one of the assailants said, 'just mildly wounded.'

Hansel growled.

'Shall we call a truce and talk this out?' Eveline called.

At this point, she wanted out of here. She loathed these tunnels. She missed the sunshine, the smell of spring. She missed the glen, and her father. She didn't want to die in these tunnels, not when she had fifty medallions to take. If they died here, she could never claim her prize. Never claim her vengeance.

'I don't particularly feel like dying tonight, and I'm guessing neither do you,' she said, her voice surprisingly steady.

Silence.

She waited, the wrath of Hansel's gaze slicing into her though she couldn't see it. She opened her mouth to speak, when a small light flickered inside a calloused hand.

'Porchid,' Eveline cried, but the hand pulled her away as soon as Eveline moved.

Porchid's light was a pale white, illuminating her captor's rough features. He stood shorter than Eveline and sported a trimmed, grey beard. He held Porchid by the wings, gentle but steady.

'She's frightened,' Eveline said. 'Let her go.'

'Or what?' the dwarf grunted. 'You call a truce, and now you're threatening us again?' His voice was gravelly, like a rough path through the mountains.

'She's harmless. We all are.'

He chuckled. 'From the weapons we collected, I highly doubt that, little miss. All I see are four strangers sneaking about my mines.' The dwarf held Eveline's stare. 'These are dark times. Odd times. And we happen to find you sneaking about our home. It's too coincidental. Did she send you?'

She?

Eveline's confusion must have been clear on her face because the dwarf faltered. She eyed his fat fingers pinching Porchid's wings.

'Did *who* send us?'

The dwarf looked at Hansel, who's jaw clenched. 'Don't play games,' the dwarf warned. 'You'll lose.'

'Well, if I had the instructions on this so-called game,' Eveline drawled, 'I'm sure I could win, but at this stage I don't know who *she* is, otherwise I wouldn't have asked.'

The huntsman sighed, closing his eyes a moment before he looked at the dwarf. The height was almost comical. Eveline would've laughed if she wasn't so pissed.

Hansel's voice was low when he spoke. 'Skin as white as snow.'

'Lips as red as blood,' quoted the dwarf in front of them.

Eveline's body locked. *Has everybody gone insane?*

'And hair as black as ebony.'

As if in chorus, the strangers' voices echoed as one. 'The fairest of them all. May she reign true.'

The dwarf looked Hansel over with curiosity before he said, 'She's here.'

If someone had told Eveline she'd be following a group of dwarves through a magical wall, she'd have laughed.

The dwarf – Bjorn – had turned after his ominous words and placed his flat palm against the dead end of the tunnel, a smirk on his lips. At first, Eveline thought him unhinged, until it'd rippled.

That's when Eveline wondered for a second time whether the fifty medallions were worth it.

Eveline's gift flared as the dwarves stepped through the wall. She reached out carefully, pausing just before her fingers trailed along the invisible barrier. Sure enough, instead of solid rock, her hand disappeared into its surface, cool and soft.

'At least that explains some things,' Hansel said. She looked back at him, her eyes wide. 'Oh, come on, Eveline. You live in a realm of magic, and you're surprised the wall isn't a wall?'

'That's not—' she started, before he grabbed her hand and pulled her through.

Eveline didn't know what she expected, but it wasn't this. Sunlight cascaded through a forest, a worn path leading from a cave covered in vines. She turned as two dwarves stumbled through, followed by Porchid, and a limping Malak.

Bjorn's grumble came from ahead. 'I don't know how you found your way through that maze, but it brought you here.'

He wore brown leathers, his hair unkempt. His grey and brown beard was trimmed, face younger than she'd expected. He waved impatiently, the other dwarves following without question.

'Seven,' Eveline whispered as the huntsman raised his brows. 'There are seven of them.'

She counted their little heads bobbing after one another. Seven dwarves living in a mine long thought to be empty, with a poisoned princess, and an evil queen chasing them.

What an odd combination of events.

Hansel still gripped Eveline's hand long after they exited the mines.

He'd almost let go, waiting for her to do it first, but she'd only gripped him tighter, her eyes alive with wonder.

Thick, lush moss blended into bright flowers, the ground a rainbow of colour. Honestly, he didn't know where to look first.

Eveline reached out her left hand to a cluster of gold and purple flowers. It broke apart in a bundle of butterflies that flitted around her. She giggled as they lifted her hair, the lighter strands glittering in the sunlight. Her cheeks were flushed, eyes bright, and Hansel couldn't help but smile.

Porchid flew like a hummingbird, finding creatures of the forest who carefully peered at them as they passed. She flew above into the trees, where a flock of silver birds swooped out in a graceful dance. She mimicked their movements, her light glowing gold.

How long had they been in the mines before stumbling into this place, Hansel wondered. A place they would've never found had it not been for Eveline.

Music echoed ahead, and Porchid's pointy ears pricked. She whirled around, tilting her head toward the sound.

'Fairy music,' Eveline murmured.

Porchid hesitated, tentative as she approached the sound. Hansel squeezed Eveline's hand, liking the way it fit in his own.

'How long has it been?' he asked. 'Since Porchid has seen her own kind?'

Eveline shook her head. 'I … I don't know.'

A branch snapped under Malak's feet, though he'd been cautious not to break any of the magical vines. 'Godmother, forgive me,' he whispered. 'It's beautiful, even if it's not designed for one as large as me.'

They followed the dwarves through a tunnel of vines, the rich leaves interweaving together as its ceiling shot to the sky in a pointed arch. Malak continued to hunch, obviously trying to avoid any disastrous encounters.

Contrary to most people's opinions, Malak was short.

With trolls, Malak was considered a child. His years were that of forty, but in troll culture, an adolescent. Despite his gruff appearance with Eveline, Malak had a gentle soul. Something his own kin had shunned him for.

Eventually, the archway broke out into a great forest. The trees were taller, thicker, ancient. Hansel held his breath, magic trickling over his skin.

A dwarf tottered up beside him and winked. 'Older than all the tales, but still as beautiful as a new-born babe.' He smiled, lines crinkling beside his eyes.

Hobbling along the path, the dwarf motioned them forward. Behind the trees' large stumps grew a hedge of great proportions, its thick brush an impenetrable wall. Hansel watched as the dwarves moved through a narrow opening placed carefully along its edge.

Malak sighed. He'd probably have to crawl through. The entrance was tight, but they managed, eventually reaching a secluded grotto. Fresh water filled his senses, the soft sound of the waterfall and the calls of fairy song straight from a story. Verdant grass blanketed the ground, meeting vines of plump berries and the scent of flowers.

There was something whimsical about it, something far away and magical.

And there, lying upon a small island, was a glass casket.

Its diamond-shaped surface glinted in the sun, bouncing light off the water. It gave the illusion of a moving rainbow. Belonging to this place, and yet standing out.

Malak was the first to falter, stumbling towards it without a word, but Hansel knew. This was everything Malak had waited for. What they had sacrificed for.

Eveline released his hand and made her way to the coffin. Her brows furrowed at the girl inside. A princess almost nobody had ever laid eyes on.

Eveline placed her hand on the glass, lost in her thoughts. And despite the Princess, the Queen's orders, or the seven dwarves watching him, Hansel only watched her.

Princess Snow's long dark hair slivered behind her. She lay on white cushions, her dress pressed as if it'd only been ironed that morning. Eveline leaned in closer, noticing the red lips, the princess's cheeks flushed like a pale rose.

She didn't look poisoned, or dead. It resembled more of a deep slumber, as if the princess had laid down for a rest and happened to have never woken. Eveline spied a folded piece of paper in the princess's pale fingers, its edges tattered from it being read so often.

One thing was glaringly obvious: Princess Snow was beautiful, achingly so.

Eveline had earned her fifty medallions ten times over after the mines. Surely earned more than that, with the number of times she'd almost died. The question was if it had been worth it.

Porchid landed on the glass, her ears twitching.

'What do we do now?' she found herself asking the fairy.

Porchid tilted her head, not even a twinkle coming from her as she gave Eveline a knowing look.

'We have to break her curse,' the huntsman said, appearing beside her.

'You say that like we haven't been trying already,' Bjorn grumbled.

'Well, we have something you didn't,' Hansel said, smiling.

'And that would be what, exactly?' said another of the dwarves.

Eveline finally looked up, Hansel nodding towards her. 'We have *her.*'

'So, the Seeker has graced our presence, has she?' started Bjorn.

Hansel was skinning a deer he'd found earlier, listening with keen ears.

Bjorn poked at the fire, urging it to burn as the others roamed, grabbing cooking items and setting up beds.

Eveline stood to Hansel's left, her posture stiff. Since she'd seen the Princess, she'd retreated into herself, going wherever it was she went inside her head. It was surprising, really, how much he wanted to follow, how he wanted to reach out this thumb and smooth the line between her eyebrows.

'I suppose you all think you can break the curse,' Bjorn continued.

'What is the curse, exactly? Maybe we can start from there,' Hansel replied.

Bjorn frowned. 'You don't know?'

He did, of course. Sort of. Hansel had seen her in the library before the incident. He'd even slipped her a note, careful to keep it vague in case another saw it. He'd felt a stir in the air the night before, Myrenna speaking differently about the Princess than usual.

He'd left Snow for fifteen minutes, had only just picked up his sword when one of the servants grabbed him.

What happened next was a rush of quick decisions in a finite amount of time. Enough to get an unconscious princess out of the castle, but not enough for her to avoid the raiders in the mountains. Hansel was grateful he'd found her, but whatever had happened between then and now, the Princess still slumbered.

The dwarf with the cane was the first to respond. 'True love's kiss breaks the curse, as it has always done.'

Bjorn snorted. 'So you say, Bonyx. We have no proof that's what would wake her.'

'So, she's definitely not dead, then?' Eveline asked.

Hansel tried not to cringe at her flat tone.

'No,' Bonyx said, resting his cane on the ground before taking a seat. 'She merely sleeps.'

'Have you tried finding whoever it is?' Eveline asked, focused.

Hansel turned towards the crystal coffin. Malak hadn't left the princess's side since they'd arrived, and when Hansel had tried to coax him to the camp, he'd flatly refused.

'We believe it's Prince Florian, from Carnell,' said a dwarf named Beetle. He was the smallest of all the dwarves. Tiny in comparison, only coming up to Hansel's waist. His cheeks were chubby and his voice just as small as his stature.

All of the dwarves had been named with the letter 'B' except for one, leaving Hansel a little confused.

Hansel was familiar with the prince, if only for the fact he'd visited Bellatorre on occasion with his eleven princely brothers.

Bjorn rolled his eyes.

'You don't agree?' Hansel asked Bjorn.

The dwarf sighed. 'The prince is a cry-baby, not to mention he's twelfth in line for the throne.'

'You call everybody a cry-baby,' replied an older dwarf, sharpening his knives.

'Where is this Prince Florian?' asked Eveline.

Bjorn shrugged. 'That's the problem. He's been missing for weeks.'

Bonyx pointed his cane at her. 'That's where you come in.'

Hansel could see the gears turning in her head, weighing the fifty medallions against finding a lost prince on top of a lost princess. Technically, her bargain was over. The coins were in his travelling pack, ready to be handed over whenever she asked for them. But that was the thing, she hadn't asked for them. Yet.

Eveline hadn't signed up for what came next. The part where Hansel ignored the Queen's orders and didn't return the princess. The part where the Queen would hunt them and surely rip out all their hearts for treason.

Myrenna had let him go for one reason: find the Princess and bring her heart.

He was sickened thinking about it. It was a fool's wish to hope that Snow could live, could rule. If she even wanted to take her place on the throne, there was a rebellion waiting behind her. There would be lives lost, bloodshed. It was enough for him to hesitate.

In his selfishness, a small part of him had hoped Snow had died when she'd eaten that apple pie. That way there was no blood on his hands, and he could return with her heart as the Queen had wished. Even if it partly destroyed him.

What he hadn't bargained for was finding her alive, or finding a cure to the curse. Nor had he bargained for Eveline. A woman who was hard to read, rude, and as blunt as a hammer. She had a sharp mind, sharper ears, and training with her had been some of the most fun he'd had in years. Part of him hoped she wouldn't leave. That she would see this out to do something good. That she would stay for a little longer – with him.

Eveline took a seat beside him, freeing a gilded blade as she picked up the carcass of a rabbit she'd caught. 'My gift could help,' she said, not looking at them.

Was that an offer?

Hansel peered at her, and she shrugged.

'It would help in more ways than you know,' he said, quietly.

He dared not mention the gold medallions. Maybe he could wake the Princess and help her build her army, and

Eveline could help the rebellion. Maybe she wanted more than just gold and whatever it was she was looking for.

As if reading his thoughts, she met his gaze. Her knowing eyes told him she hadn't forgotten, just that she'd chosen the righteous route. Still, Hansel was an optimist. Maybe hope hadn't left the kingdom yet.

Maybe. Just maybe. They could find a happy ending for everyone.

VIII

The Candy Cottage

Eveline bathed in a pool near the back of the grotto. Being the only females, she and Porchid found a safe place where they could strip their clothes to wash off the dust and mud that came from days of trekking underground.

She dipped her feet into the cool water, soaking in the sensation. It was velvet on her skin, the temperature just right.

Porchid perched on a nearby rock, barely dipping her toes in. She'd never been comfortable near water since

Eveline had found her by a creek in the forest, her wings broken and torn. The water would have drowned her had Eveline not found her by the dying light of the sun.

Eveline had been on a job that night, searching for a magical locket. It'd been dropped in the river after the man's wife had jumped to her death. According to the man, the locket still held his wife's essence, and so Eveline had trekked downstream before finding Porchid.

Light almost dimmed, Porchid's first reaction had been to bite Eveline's hand, but Eveline wasn't afraid of pain – she'd had too much of it to shy away.

Eveline had brought her to a fire, gathered fruit for her to eat, and when a small amount of trust had been earned, Porchid allowed her to patch up her wings until they'd found a healer. The fairy hadn't left her side since.

Eveline still didn't know who'd hurt Porchid so badly, but seeing as she didn't speak the fairy tongues and Porchid was not inclined to tell her about it, she let it be.

Since then, Porchid only favoured certain humans but had no bad disposition to any other creatures. Eveline knew of course about fairy hunters – those who captured fairies for money. Some stole them for fairy lanterns, a staple in the Silver City. Others for fashion, like the wings or hair for a brooch. Not many were left in the position, as it provided little income, but some, some still hunted.

Eveline scooped water in her palm and dropped it into a groove in the rock. Porchid twinkled in delight, placing a kiss on the Seeker's cheek before she stepped into the pool. Porchid glowed gold, but Eveline could see the silvery membrane gleaming beneath her skin.

Porchid laughed as Eveline jumped, an octopio grazing her leg. Beneath the water a flock of them illuminated, their faces curious but not menacing.

Octopios were harmless, mostly. They had no stingers, but if you were to find a pregnant one and threaten its home, its ink would burn like acid. These all looked like babes with their pale pink skins and wide black eyes.

When Eveline shifted, they veered away, moving in a kind of a dance.

A rainbow hovered along the cavern roof from the reflection of the coffin. With Hansel, Malak, and the dwarves safely on the other side of the grotto, Eveline hung her clothes out to dry.

The sun gleamed down, reflecting off the blue lapis lazuli Hansel had given her. Eveline had found herself touching it more, the stone calling to her. She ignored it now, dunking her head underwater before scrubbing her hair, attempting to loosen twigs and hard crusted dirt. It was in a worse condition than she thought.

She sighed, and floated for a while, eyes closed. The octopio tickled her but left her alone for the most part.

For the first time in a long time, Eveline found herself content. Almost.

She hadn't signed up to break a curse, only to find a princess. But despite herself, she wasn't ready to leave yet. Wasn't ready to be alone again.

She had direction. A goal.

Vengeance could wait.

Bjorn gruffed something before taking a seat beside Hansel, his eyes narrowed. 'I suppose introductions should be done.'

Eveline and Porchid splashed in the grotto out of sight, their laughter a glorious symphony ringing through the cavern.

'Is it not a little late for that?' Hansel said.

'It's never too late for a bit of manners,' the dwarf grunted. 'Not enough of them round here, anyway.'

The dwarf to his left laughed. 'Bjorn complaining about manners – well, that's something new.'

'All hail Bjorn, the master of manners,' chimed another.

Bjorn grumbled, something Hansel noticed he did a lot.

Bjorn pointed to his companions one by one. 'That old one with the cane is Bonyx, the one with all the weapons is Brufell, Beetle is the small one over there by the blue flowers, and the one by the Princess with your troll is Bronson. Bryn is over by the tree and… where did Rabbit go?'

'Rabbit?' asked Hansel.

Bjorn frowned. 'Rabbit is the seventh member of our lot. He's the silent type, doesn't talk much.'

Hansel blinked as a soft-faced dwarf came around a bush and placed a pile full of fruit near Bjorn.

'He's also a vegetarian,' Bjorn scoffed, but messed the young dwarf's hair in affection.

Rabbit was shy as he assessed Hansel, peering at him under long red lashes before he opened his hand and offered a berry. Hansel took it with thanks, plopping it in his mouth. It was sweet. *Very* sweet. As if he'd eaten a sugar cube. The juice lingered on his tongue, and he grinned. Rabbit snickered and Bjorn scoffed a laugh.

Confused, Hansel's face heated as Bjorn clapped him on the shoulder. 'The berries stain your mouth.' He looked at Hansel's hands. 'And everything else.'

Hansel lifted his hands, finding them stained red. Rabbit popped a berry in his mouth, his own teeth stained like blood as he smiled back at him.

'Is it permanent?' Hansel asked, licking across his gums.

Bjorn handed him a waterskin. 'Not if you wash your mouth out quick enough.'

'The water is free if you want to bathe,' Eveline said, coming around the corner. She had a glow upon her skin Hansel hadn't seen before. Her brown hair looked lighter, clean, the gold threads shimmering under the sunlight. It was so beautiful that Hansel almost missed the nicks on her skin. Some were pink, but most looked old, already silver.

'Are you done staring?' she asked, kicking him out of his reverie.

'Sorry, I just—' but he halted on the words. He was going to ask how she'd obtained the injuries, why she had so many, but it was a personal question. *Too* personal. He closed his mouth before he overstepped, deciding to wash up instead. With his stained hands and dirty clothes, he probably smelt like an ogre.

Malak followed him to the pool, the troll jumping in with a shout of glee. Waves pressed against the shore, the octopio put out. Hansel laughed as he followed suit. The water was cool. A pool of dirt and grime spread around his frame.

Hansel dipped his head under the water, the quiet stilling his thoughts. Despite the sanctuary here, they'd have to leave soon. Myrenna's crows had seen them on the mountain; her eyes everywhere in the realm. With the Princess unconscious, she was vulnerable. He'd have to wake her before the Queen found them. He shuddered at the thought, a vision of her tearing out his heart coming to mind.

He went deeper underwater, where the rocks shadowed the sand. No matter where he went, Myrenna was always there. Her smell of lavender and blood, the way she liked her hair down. Her voice when she whispered into his ear.

He'd known Myrenna long enough to know her temper. He'd picked up the pieces of her tantrums as much as he'd celebrated her wins. She was cruel, yes, but she was also complicated. Not that anyone understood.

Malak loved to use the name the rebellion had given her: the Evil Queen.

But was anyone truly evil? Was someone born that way, or were they made?

He stayed underwater for as long as he could. Until his lungs burned and his chest hurt. Hoping the water would not just wash away the grime, but his traitorous thoughts, too.

Eveline struggled to sleep. The fire crackled low, the blinking stars bright. The dwarves' snores created a chorus in line with Malak, the troll camping by the coffin. It was morbid, really, how attached he was to that thing.

Eveline rolled over, spying Porchid slumbering with an open mouth, a string of drool hanging to a piece of her blue hair.

Brufell, the dwarf constantly sharpening weapons, sat further out, keeping watch. On the other side of the fire was Hansel, poking a stick into the flames.

'Can't sleep?' he asked.

Eveline eyed him, wondering if the man ever slept. She wasn't used to idle talk or spending time in such close quarters with another human. Even after several weeks travelling with him and the troll, there'd always been an end. No expectations to get to know one another. It was a transaction. Once she'd found the Princess, she was to leave and never look back. Except …

Except she'd agreed to help find the Prince.

She considered the repercussions of her decision and began to regret her choice.

Hansel stared at the fire, likely waiting for her response. His eyes held shadows under them. His long lashes and smooth jaw drew her gaze. He was attractive. Would it be so bad if she got to know him?

Her gut clenched, but not in the way she knew it. It clenched as if a thousand of those butterflies she'd found earlier had made a nest in her stomach, and she grimaced.

Fairy Godmother, help her.

'No,' she replied, her voice a little rough.

Needing something to do with her hands, Eveline picked out the blue stone from her pocket and ran it under her thumb. Hansel observed every movement but didn't say anything. They sat in silence for a while, watching Brufell's head bob up, then down, as he shook himself in and out of alertness.

'Maybe I should tell him I'll take over,' Hansel said, getting up.

Eveline wasn't sure why she followed. Maybe she didn't want to be alone. She certainly didn't want to go back to sleep. Not when her dreams were filled with memories she'd rather forget.

Hansel was gazing at the stars as she approached, her palms sweaty.

'I'm sorry,' she said.

He turned towards her, eyebrow raised.

Eveline scratched her neck, avoiding his gaze. 'I know I haven't been… forthcoming,' she fumbled. 'I'm not used to making friends.'

He nodded, which was the best answer he could've given, she realised. He must've sensed her hesitation but remained patient anyway.

'It's okay not to trust,' he said after a while. 'With magic, people are never really what they seem. One thing said, and another done.'

He said it like he knew firsthand. Eveline peered down at him, curious. 'What about you, then?'

'Me? I just try and do my best.'

'Your best?' she asked. 'You always seem so … carefree.'

Hansel chuckled, though she wasn't sure what was so funny. He patted the grass beside him, an invitation to sit.

'I think that, unless you let people in,' he said as she sat, 'you'll forever be stuck inside your own lonely prison. You can't expect trust if you don't give some of your own. I seem carefree because I try to be. I want to be open without being a fool. Not everything is under our control, and sometimes we have to trust our stories are meant for us.'

Eveline said nothing, the words hitting closer to home than he knew.

'In a land where we have so many immortal beings,' Hansel continued, 'it's sometimes hard to remember that we are human. Our lifespan is a blink to those who live long lives.

'Take the sisters Grimm, for example. They seem to age, and yet they return to youth only to age again and continue doing so. They've seen wars raged and kingdoms fall and yet they live on. We don't have that luxury. I decided a long time ago that even if I'm deceived, I'd rather be open to the possibility of finding something real. It would be sad not to experience that kind of magic. Because that's what it is, in a way. Doesn't everyone deserve their own happily ever after?'

Eveline could think of a few people who didn't deserve a happily ever after, the sisters Grimm to name a few.

Still, the question hung in the air. Hansel's voice was charming. She realised, with a guilty pang, she enjoyed listening to him.

'Tell me a story,' she whispered.

Eveline missed stories. She missed the way her father told them, and she liked the way Hansel's voice smoothly tied words together. It was silly, but she didn't want him to stop.

'Okay,' he said, leaning back on the grass. 'Once there was a boy who lived near the edge of the Shadow Forest with his sister and father. Their mother had died a little over a year ago, and they were still finding their way in the world. On the night of her death anniversary—'

Eveline groaned. 'I didn't ask for a story about death anniversaries. How depressing.'

'You asked for a story, and this is what you're getting.'

'Fine,' she grumbled, smiling a little.

'As I was saying,' he drawled, 'On the night of her death anniversary, the three of them took a tribute to her burial site. The boy collected flowers, creating a huge bouquet. The girl made a doll, so cleverly made that even the eyes reflected gold, just like their mother's.'

'And the father?' she asked.

Hansel picked at a patch of grass. 'He took nothing, except for his heart and grief.'

He took a deep breath before continuing. 'When the family went home, they came across a cart where a beautiful young woman was trying to fix its broken wheel.

'The father, being the kind man he was, aided her. But the damage was too extensive. When it was clear more parts were required, the man offered the woman a room. It's not right to leave a woman stranded, after all.'

Eveline snorted, but Hansel ignored her. 'The woman accepted his offer. She cooked them dinner as a thank you, the food beyond anything they'd ever eaten before. When it was time for the woman to leave, the children's father was bereft. Sometime during the night, he had fallen madly in love with the woman, and so they were married.

'For a time, they were happy. But where the man was blind, the children could see. The woman became increasingly jealous of the children and the attention their father gave them. She would give them terrible and dangerous jobs and, when the man was not looking, she would beat and abuse them. When the children tried to tell their father, he would not hear of it, casting off their concerns as nothing but childish lies.

'He then began to change. Where he was once lively and doted on his children, he became solemn and blank, as if his soul were being sucked away piece by piece. The children were fretful of their father's condition, and when they sought help from the neighbouring village, the woman was already a step ahead. She had wooed the villagers, even causing all the men to fawn over her.

'Knowing what the children were up to, she ordered them to go into the forest one day and collect some berries. She wrapped up some bread for them, and a canister of water, telling them the special berries she required were deep within the forest.

'Steeling himself, the young boy took his sister's hand, and they ventured into the Shadow Forest. His sister was a smart girl. Using the breadcrumbs from their lunch, she left a trail to lead them home.

'The two children ventured further and further into the woods where they eventually stumbled upon the berry bush. In their glee, they collected a great pile of them and set on their way back home, only to find the path bare.

'Birds of all shapes had come down and eaten their breadcrumb trail, leaving them lost deep within the forest. When they grew tired and hungry, they stopped and opened their bag of berries. Surely their stepmother wouldn't want them to starve.'

'Sounds like she would,' scoffed Eveline.

'Any other input into my story?' he asked, and she sighed dramatically.

Lifting her fingers, she went to list off the many things about this story she had an opinion on, and he swatted down her hand.

'That was rhetorical.' He shook his head with a laugh, then continued. 'What the children didn't know, was that the berries they'd collected were poisonous.'

'Knew it,' Eveline mumbled.

'When they went to feast upon the deadly fruit, the voice of an elderly woman broke through the trees. She appeared out of nowhere, her black shawl tattered and stained. She warned the children and saved them from death.'

'Why does this story feel like it doesn't have a happy ending?'

'This story will never end if you keep interrupting me.'

Eveline smirked. 'Please continue, grand storyteller.'

Hansel laughed, his voice surrounding her. 'The old woman listened to their plight and told them her cottage was nearby. With starving tummies, the children followed. They didn't question why an elderly woman lived out on her own in the forest. Nor did they question why her cottage was made of candy.'

'Candy?' Eveline rested on her elbows. 'That's ridiculous.'

'Yes, it was made of candy.' Hansel said. 'The children did not question when she gave them a feast, forcing them to eat beyond their means. They did not question when she cackled in the corner and poked at the hot stove.

'Fat and happy, the children fell asleep, and when they woke, found themselves locked in a cage. Turns out, the woman was a witch.' Hansel shook his head at Eveline's smug smirk, a told-you-so on her lips. 'The children were frightened, but the boy's sister was clever. She'd orchestrated herself to become the witch's slave, whilst he remained in the cage, getting force-fed.

'One day, when the witch became her hungriest, she set up the great oven and insisted the little girl check it was burning correctly. The boy knew she was planning to eat him, but his sister had already unlocked his cage, expecting this to happen.

'They waited for the perfect time to flee, and so he stayed in his cage. His sister pretended she did not know what she was checking, and whilst she stood bent in front of the oven, she fooled the witch into showing her.

'Shoving the girl out of the way, the witch bent in front of the oven, and his sister, acting on impulse, pushed her into the great flames.'

'Good,' Eveline replied. But she caught the falter in his voice, how it turned sombre.

'The witch reached out and grabbed her at the last moment, pulling them both into the oven's blaze.

'The boy, screaming in terror, ran from his cage, but it was too late. The witch and his sister had already burned to ashes. He found the axe by the door and, in his despair, set upon hacking the house down. His anger and guilt grew until the boy only saw revenge.

'He decided to kill his stepmother. It had been her who had sent them upon that path. *Her* who had lied to them about the berries.

'Taking great amounts of candy off the house's exterior, the boy spent days winding his way back home, but when he arrived, he found it empty.

'The boy, in his grief, stayed for a while, letting his hatred seethe. He waited for his parents' return, and it wasn't until he ran out of food that he realised he had to do something.

Starving, he used his axe to become a huntsman and, as he travelled, he found out the beautiful woman with the cart was a well-known tale. A tale about a woman who lured in men and sent children to a witch in the forest.'

'Were they ever found? The parents?' Eveline asked.

Hansel's voice cracked, the sound of a broken heart. 'No.'

Eveline blinked and turned to face him. He lay there in stoic silence, letting the awful tale sink in.

She waited a heartbeat before asking what she'd already guessed. 'What was your sister's name?'

He took a deep breath, the exhale long and rough. 'Her name was Gretel.'

IX

The Betrayal and the Briar Rose

The next morning, the eleven of them gathered around a map. It'd already been agreed they would split into groups to cover their bases.

It was decided that Malak, Bonyx, and the little one, Beetle, would remain in the glen to watch over the Princess; Bjorn, Bryn, and Rabbit would visit their cousins at the Peaks of Carfell for any news; and Brufell and Bronson would go north to Troll's Keep. Supposedly, Brufell had a contact there who could help with information on the ash covered forest they'd encountered on the way here.

That left Eveline, Hansel, and Porchid to find the lost prince.

Bjorn showed them a shortcut from the glen that bypassed the wraiths – this one illuminated and well-kept.

Hansel, to Eveline's relief, spoke for most of the journey, telling them stories about the land. Some she'd recognised from the tales her father had told, providing an air of nostalgia. Others, like his own tale with his sister, were brand new.

He told tales of dragons and glass slippers. He spoke of a tower holding a beautiful maiden in a maze and the wickedness of the witch who'd trapped her.

That tale was one Eveline made a point of ignoring.

Sometimes they walked in silence, and sometimes they shared memories from travelling on the road. Eveline told him of the time she found a ribbon that could be shaped into any item of clothing, and a broomstick that could whisk you from one place to another. Porchid would chime in on occasion, puffing herself up on Hansel's shoulders like one of the old heroes.

When Eveline had raised her brow at the fairy, she'd stuck out her tongue, snuggling into Hansel's neck like a puppy. The little flirt.

One evening, after they'd eaten their meal, Eveline shared a story about a soldier and his tinderbox, showing the huntsman the exact location of its constellation.

The journey was nice in a way, calm and smooth. So, it shouldn't have come as a surprise when Hansel quietly gave her a compliment before they fell to sleep that night. 'I love your tales. You come alive when you tell them.'

She thought of her father's vivid and active hands describing giants, magic, and things in the dark. Her eyes stung.

That night, a little piece of her blossomed. Where the wall inside her had mattered before, it didn't matter as much now.

Eveline was content to let it crumble, piece by piece.

A high-pitched scream woke Eveline. She sat up from her bedroll, sleep stuck in her eyes as a murder of crows barrelled from the treetops.

'Stay here,' Eveline warned Porchid.

Hansel shouted as she bolted through the brush, halting at the sight of a woman upon the ground in despair. Her hair lay limp in a veil around her shoulders. Hansel paused at the tree line, holding back Eveline's arm with a tight grip as he gazed towards the sky.

High in the tree was a young girl, no older than fifteen by the looks of her plump, freckled face. Her limp body hung from a rope, which had snapped her fine neck. The creak brought goosebumps to Eveline's skin.

Eveline slid her twin blades out of their sheaths, silent as a cat. The woman sobbed, her hand reaching out as Hansel moved forward to check on her.

But the girl who had been strung up didn't look quite right. It was the way her features sat upon her brow, the way she frayed at the edges of Eveline's vision. Guarding herself, Eveline peered at the corpse.

The woman stopped sobbing.

The swinging corpse groaned as everything stilled in the forest. Hansel went wide eyed as the woman sprung, catching him off guard. He grunted as she palmed his jaw, spinning behind him to catch his throat.

The corpse dissolved into ash as if it was never there, and the woman who'd cried so desperately before now cackled fiercely.

Even with his strength, Hansel could not break her hold. The woman *changed.* Her once strawberry hair turned raven, growing until it fell to the centre of her back. Wrinkled skin turned smooth, her figure slimming to a petite woman.

But those weren't the changes that stole Eveline's breath. It was the colour of her eyes, an amethyst so bright they could only belong to one person.

The Evil Queen.

Myrenna.

Sweat pooled at Eveline's back. Her knives were useless in a fight against magic.

'Picking up strays, huntsman?' Myrenna cooed, her nails sharpened to a point at his throat. 'I asked for a princess, not a merchant's daughter.'

Myrenna's eyes raked over Eveline, assessing her like one would a horse at auction.

She was beautiful, Eveline gave her that, but there was nothing warm about her. Myrenna was all ice and shadows.

'Put him down, witch,' Eveline said, her voice sounding braver than she felt.

Myrenna smirked, a pinprick of blood dripping down Hansel's throat at her touch. Her tongue flicked over the skin, gaze never breaking from Eveline's.

Eveline held back bile at the way the queen smiled.

Hansel's face was pale. He was still, so still that Eveline wasn't sure if magic was involved. Hansel had mentioned the Queen hired him to bring her Snow, but he also said he'd no plan on delivering.

Had the Queen found out? Was she going to kill them?

Warning rippled in the back of Eveline's mind, and she raised her blades. She'd never met the Queen – had never wanted to. The Silver City had been beautiful once, but in the years since Myrenna's rule it had dulled. Most of the jobs Eveline had taken in the city were finding creatures who'd run from captivity, she could only stomach so much.

'I gave you one cycle to find her, and yet you disappear on me,' Myrenna whispered into Hansel's ear. 'Vanishing with no trace left behind. I was beginning to feel abandoned.'

Hansel choked, and Eveline's palms became clammy. She couldn't strike whilst the woman's nails dug into him.

The huntsman clambered for breath, and the Queen's face twisted.

'—Seeker,' he choked.

Myrenna narrowed her eyes, snapping her head towards Eveline. 'Interesting.' She contemplated Eveline. 'If this is indeed the famous Seeker, then I'll finally find what's mine. I'll wager the one hundred medallions twisted your loyalties, dear.'

Eveline wasn't anyone's 'dear', and less so for an evil witch. But with Hansel in danger, she couldn't make any sudden moves.

The Queen lowered her voice, amethyst eyes latching onto Eveline with a new hunger. 'I'll give you the medallions myself, and any riches or resources you require, if you find my prize, Seeker.'

'And if I refuse?' Eveline said.

Myrenna laughed. 'Nobody refuses me.'

Hansel was thrown to the ground as if he weighed nothing. Myrenna shifted before Eveline's eyes until she stood only a breath away. They were so close they could kiss, the smell of lavender and blood ripe on her skin. Eveline cringed inwardly, her blades still raised, one poised towards Myrenna's ribs. They may as well have been toothpicks for all Myrenna cared.

'Remember, child, I could kill you with the sweep of my wrist.' Myrenna smiled coldly, her hand rising slowly. Eveline blinked, bracing herself for the pain when the Queen snapped her fingers.

A scream.

Hansel's back arched like it'd been snapped, bruises lacing along his neck and chin. Blood dribbled from his mouth, his eyes wide.

Eveline couldn't breathe, couldn't focus.

'I will give you two cycles to find the Princess,' Myrenna warned. 'If you do not return her to me, then you'll find me unpleasant.' She paused, her voice velvet as she lowered it. 'Pleasure is his specialty, is it not?'

Eveline understood the meaning, even if it sent a jolt of dark surprise down her back. The Queen gazed at Hansel for a moment, pouting like she had broken a favourite toy before she dissipated into a thousand pieces of black ash.

Hansel lay choking on the ground. If they didn't find a healer soon, he would die. She reached out to touch him, hesitating only a moment before steeling herself. She could be angry later.

He leaned into her as he stood, the bruises deepening before her eyes. 'How did she find us?'

He coughed, blood soaking into his shirt. 'She has eyes everywhere. Her crows. A direct visit is rare, though.'

'Unless it's to see her lover?' she accused.

Hansel stumbled, but Eveline wasn't sure if it was from his injuries or guilt. The rage was there, a sense of betrayal too. The Queen had spoken to Hansel with a familiarity only time spent with someone brought. He wasn't a mere hire off the streets of Roserock, or a random guard plucked from the castle's ranks. He had known her, intimately.

Disgust coursed through Eveline, but she squashed it down. Tears threatened to spill, but she would ask him about it later. Demand an explanation.

Slowly, they stumbled through the forest.

Hansel woke to the sound of a knife clunking on wood.

Eveline stood a few paces away, looking lost in her thoughts as her other knife flew into the trunk. It was a perfect aim.

Hansel shrunk into himself. Eveline wasn't supposed to know about the Queen and the way in which he had… compromised himself to survive. He'd become useful to Myrenna as a guard, and as a lover. It'd saved his life multiple times. He'd never pitied his circumstances, not when it meant he survived without the fear of death or punishment for his friends. But in this moment, it was a heavy cloak of shame. It crawled over him like a nest of ants itching at his skin as he made his way towards Eveline.

Before he'd even moved a step, a knife slid into the bark beside his head. It hurt to flinch. His wounds were deep from Myrenna's nails, but he was no longer bleeding. Eveline had bandaged him in something that smelled like mint.

She stared him down, eyes glittering in a dark rage he hadn't seen before. How could he explain himself? How could he explain he hadn't lied to her, only left out parts of the truth?

He'd told her about his sister. A story only Malak knew, but even that'd been a half truth. He'd left out how he'd stumbled from village to village, trading work for food. Left out when the Queen called for his services, procuring more than just a huntsman or a guard, but a toy.

Myrenna had never hidden her want for him. Didn't need to, not when she always got what she wanted. He'd loathed himself at first, but after a time, he became used to it. Sometimes he even found it pleasant.

The Queen had her moments of vile and ruthless behaviour, but he'd seen the cracks when she revealed a scared, desperate woman. The mirror whispered to Myrenna, tortured her as much as it aided her.

It'd been difficult to break away, but when Myrenna had begun tormenting Snow, a friend, he could not – would not – stay.

He couldn't let Myrenna harm Snow.

He took another step forward. A second knife hit the ground just in front of his foot. His voice cracked. 'Please, let me explain.'

Porchid looked between them, her light switching from blue to white to purple and back again. Hansel begged her with his eyes, trying to show her everything. His guilt, his hatred, his honesty. The fairy clung so tightly to Eveline that her knuckles were white.

'She won't help you,' Eveline said. 'She knows loyalty. Which is something you don't seem to have a concept of.'

'I never meant for it to be this way. I didn't lie, I swear.'

Eveline laughed coldly and his body went rigid. It was an unearthly sound, something that didn't belong within Eveline. 'You swear? You and that clever tongue of yours? And here I was thinking not everybody in this Fairy Godmother's forsaken land was ruined.

'I trusted you and you've just spat it back in my face. Did you think I wouldn't have found out? You've signed my death warrant.' A tear slid down her cheek.

'I trusted you,' she continued, her voice growing rougher with each passing moment. 'You lied to me, you lied to Porchid and you lied to the dwarves. What would your princess say?' She scoffed. 'If that's even what you want. Why not just kill her on the spot and take her heart for your queenly lover? Why not just have us all killed while we slept in that grotto? What's to stop you from spilling all our dirty little secrets to her?'

She breathed heavily. Hansel had never hated himself before now. He always had reasons for what he did, explanations and excuses. But he'd hurt her. For that, he hated himself.

Another tear slid down her cheek, and she picked up her pack. 'You do not get to explain yourself to me, and you do not get the privilege of apologising. You do not get to speak. We will go into that village in a couple of days' time, and we will find Prince Florian and save Snow, and then… then there is nothing stopping me from slicing you into little pieces.'

Hansel nodded, unable to speak. The way her eyes roved over him in disgust pierced him harder than any blade.

As she stormed off towards the path, Porchid passed him with a look of pity.

Nausea rolled off Eveline as she walked.

The way the Queen had crooned at Hansel, leering at him like he was some delicacy.

Why am I here?

The thought was bitter. Why had she agreed to this stupid masquerade in the first place? The Queen wasn't her problem. The Princess wasn't her problem. And the huntsman was *definitely* not her problem.

Chastising herself, Eveline kept well ahead of the huntsman.

Porchid reached up to wipe away a stray tear. If Eveline was being honest, she didn't notice the tears anymore, just the anger. It was a hot poker under her skin, burning and burning.

Eveline resolved she was done after this. All that mattered were the hundred medallions, now she had the

Queen's word for it. Then, she would get back to finding her father's killers.

Porchid looked up at her and pouted.

'You want to keep him, then you can take him,' Eveline said sourly.

Eveline followed Porchid's gaze towards Hansel as he stumbled along the path. His breaths were shallow, his skin pale. Eveline was about to protest about whatever scolding she was due to get when the fairy twinkled and left her shoulder to stay by the huntsman.

'Traitor,' Eveline grumbled.

It was then Eveline noticed the stillness. The utter lack of sound. Just the crunch of a leaf underfoot and the huntsman's wheezing.

'Something's wrong,' Eveline murmured.

The huntsman paused. His face was slick with sweat, the dark shadows under his eyes stark. He swayed, and Porchid let out a squeak as he stumbled.

Eveline barely caught him. 'Hansel?'

He mumbled something incoherent, and between the trees, a whisper echoed over her skin. Her hairs stood on end. Flourishing green turned to grey, ash pooling onto the ground.

And behind it, a slow, slinking fog.

They had to leave, *now*.

Eveline wrapped Hansel's arm over her shoulder. Twigs snapped under their stumbled steps, Eveline grunting. Porchid squealed, flying ahead.

The fog trailed behind them, hissing as it wilted the once verdant grass. The stench of rotten eggs and spoiled flesh burned her nose. She choked.

Where Rumple's fog had been green, this one was a pale grey. It reminded Eveline of ash, the way storm clouds gathered before the rain. But there was something else about it too. Something that raised the hairs on her skin and welcomed her fear.

It wasn't the magic of dreams, but death.

Porchid zipped back to them, puffing, and pointed ahead.

Eveline urged Hansel forward, halting only to readjust her grip as a fallen tree blocked their path. Hansel faltered, her hold slipping as he wavered.

'Hansel?' she asked, receiving nothing but a weak murmur.

Panicked, she heaved a breath and yanked his body as far it could go over the wood. Wary of the fog creeping closer, she ran to his feet and slid them over the other side before slapping his cheeks.

'This is not the time for a nap, Hansel,' she hissed. The fog was gaining.

Hansel's eyes fluttered, his normally warm gaze distant. Eveline placed her arms around his waist. 'I need your help. You won't survive this otherwise.'

Eveline didn't want to think about what that meant. Didn't want to know what she would choose if it came down to him or her.

Her words must have done something because, slowly, Hansel stood. He wasn't steady by any means but at least he was helping.

Porchid twinkled at them to hurry, Eveline grunting with every step.

At the next bend was a sign ravaged by vines.

The Briar Rose

Surely enough, just down the hill was a mill. A river curled around its edge, smoke billowing from the chimney of a cottage. Eveline pushed forward, her voice hoarse as she screamed for help. The fog nipped at their heels, the stench blurring her vision. The world tilted on itself as the backs of her legs burned, life leeching from her veins.

Eveline could barely make out Porchid as she banged on the door. Two figures emerged, both shouting something in a language she didn't understand.

Eveline didn't know how she made it to the cottage. Couldn't remember treading down that hill. But as she passed the threshold, she croaked out a warning. Hansel's body fell with a thump to the floor.

Eveline trembled. Using the last bit of her strength, she peered through the open door as a woman began to chant outside. A language filled with reverence and history. Magic tingled along her skin.

'Great,' Eveline muttered. 'More witches.'

She passed out on the kitchen floor.

X

The Queen and her Dinner Guest

Myrenna and the King of Carnell had played this game for weeks now. He would offer a wedding and she would offer an alternative. Still, he persisted. Myrenna had gone to Carnell for an army, not a husband. She'd already killed one of those and was loathe to have another.

It was like the King had forgotten who she was. He failed to remember the deadly accuracy with which she wielded her powers. How she could slice him like a ripe tomato and feed on his insides.

This time, they sat in the dining room of the castle at Bellatorre, the King taking a carriage two days prior. He was in her home. Her kingdom. And yet, instead of cowering, the oaf of a man clicked his tongue at her refusal.

Myrenna bit down on the cool rage building inside her and smiled sweetly. If her own army wasn't busy fighting in Perridorm she wouldn't have to be at this stupid dinner, nor would she be asking mortal men for help.

She sipped her wine, the only pleasant thing about this whole affair.

The King wore a jacket of velvet teal, and the bald patch on his head peeked from under a slick comb over. His voice reminded her of coal; dry and dusty.

When he thought she wasn't looking, his wandering hands would slide up the servant girl's side. Her young face was plastered with an uncomfortable, pinched smile.

The arrogance of him was astounding.

Myrenna wanted to tear his throat out. The only reason she hadn't done it already was because her mirror had directed her down the diplomatic route. She'd agreed, to an extent. Her plans for Bellatorre were bigger than her own ego.

The King's hands flung in the air as he spoke of the inconvenience of children. He had twelve, of course. Each born from an array of different women. 'It's about options,' he bragged. 'If I am to rule a great kingdom, then why should my country not have the best?'

She sipped from her wine, holding back the retort bubbling to the surface.

'Think of the potential our offspring would bring,' he said, leaning across the table. The chain from his pocket dipped into the soup laid before him.

'With your womb and my dashing looks, our children would be glorious.'

Her smile faltered, the façade slipping through her fingers like water. The fact he'd even addressed her womb, or having an encounter with him, was complete insolence.

The rage she'd been keeping a tight leash on loosened a fraction, the ice of it biting at her bones. Her eyes met the female server, who remained silent at the edge of the room.

'My Queen,' the King purred. 'Our kingdoms united would be powerful beyond measure.'

But Myrenna didn't want a powerful kingdom. She already had one of those. She wanted power itself. Bellatorre had only been a means to an end, a way to access magic far greater than anything ever seen.

He reached his frumpy arms across the table as if to take her hand. The Queen lifted her glass and sipped again, gracefully manoeuvring out of his reach.

She waved to the server. 'It seems the King, in his excitement, has spilled his soup.'

His neck flushed a deep red. Before he could mutter something stupid, Myrenna said, 'Your Majesty, whilst I understand your excitement for our kingdoms'… partnership, I must request you refrain from jumping too far ahead.'

'Of course, of course,' he replied. 'I just adore a good opportunity!'

Myrenna grew tired, her eyes heavy. The partnership between the two kingdoms was in its infancy, the political games still a dance as they learnt each other's strengths and weaknesses. Myrenna may have been selfish, but she was no idiot.

She'd stood in the throne room earlier that week, seething over the Princess' escape, when she approached the gilded mirror. Its bleak surface filled with the familiar outline of the magic within.

'Whilst her heart is what you seek, there lies
another way, so to speak.

'You wish for freedom and a way to break, but
with another kingdom lies an army to take.

'Mirrors four, of black and bone, of silver and
gold and night-blue stone.

'To find the looking glass and the sisters
Grimm, one must always have another in.'

With Perridorm protecting their borders, Myrenna had reached out to Carnell. The king in Maelstrom was a pig but he was useful. His army had been more than valuable, almost doubling her own. Carnell's soldiers were known for their intense training, and she'd seen it firsthand on the borders of Perridorm during battle.

She was powerful, but even she had limits, the well of hers running dry depending on the magic. She couldn't control an entire nation of magical and mortal beings on her own.

The King smacked his lips together and eyed her neck, sneaking a quick wink from across the table. She needed Carnell's support. Without it, she had no hopes of defeating Perridorm or controlling the trade routes.

Not to mention, her mines were running low on recruits. Frankly, she needed the bodies. Especially if she was to find her prize.

The female server rushed over to assist the King as he dribbled more food on his jacket. She was young – perhaps eighteen – and blonde. The King's eyes roamed her bosom.

Myrenna carefully placed her cup of wine down and stood up, to the obvious dismay of the King. Smoothing out her skirts, she locked eyes with him.

'Your Majesty,' she said, her teeth practically grinding at the words. He blinked up at her and she nodded to the servers, excusing them. 'Tonight, I fear we have more pressing matters to discuss than that of a proposed… arrangement.' Her fingers lingered on the table and his eyes set upon hers.

'Yes. Yes. Of course,' he said. 'The matter of your daughter.'

She didn't bother to correct him.

By marriage she logically understood Snow was her stepdaughter, but without the blood relation, Snow may as well have been a stranger. The Princess was an inconvenience, but she played a role in the larger scheme of things.

Snow would be her saving grace. Her own apple pie. Her lifeblood.

The mirror had whispered so.

'Do you have any news?' she asked slowly. Calmly. That same coil wrapped tighter and tighter.

He swiped at his shirt with more furore and mumbled a nonchalant response. 'Dwarves.'

She raised her eyebrow.

'I've had reports the cart in which the Princess travelled was picked up and looted by dwarves. Ugly, hairy, dirty things.'

She waited, but he said no more. 'And?' she asked. Coaxing him. Caressing him.

'And what?' His fat hand grasped the napkin and swiped at the stain on his jacket. He grumbled in frustration. 'She's been found by dwarves. I told you.'

Her patience snapped, like a crack under her skin. He'd told her nothing. Nothing she'd not already known after her beautiful murders and fog dragon had scoped the realm. She knew the dwarves were responsible, but she had yet to find out where they were. Her eye twitched and she took a deep breath.

Straightening her back, she stood tall and proud – the only message a man of his arrogance would understand. 'My patience has limits. Snow remains missing, and you are yet to prove your value with the little information you have given in regard to her whereabouts.'

The King blinked at her, confusion on his face. But, surely, even he wasn't naïve enough to miss the threat in her words, the cold calculation seeping into her voice.

A flush crept up the King's neck as he dropped his napkin. 'We have been nothing but your most trusted ally. Our information has been accurate and more than useful relating to your daughter's location. My Queen, you are sorely mistaken.'

Myrenna looked down at him. 'I do not tolerate when my time is wasted.'

He rolled his eyes and rung a bell. 'And like a typical woman, you let your emotions rule you.'

Myrenna flared her nostrils. 'I do not tolerate when I am insulted.'

He smiled greedily at the serving girl as she re-entered, her fingers shaking as she replaced his dirty napkin.

'I do not tolerate the arrogance of men,' Myrenna said.

The King's hand slowly crept up the girl's back leg and hitched under her skirt. The girl's jolt was the only sign of her discomfort.

'I do not tolerate when I am disregarded.'

The girl shook with terror, her wide eyes shifting to the Queen. 'And I do not tolerate the misconduct towards my staff.'

The King yelped, eyes opened in alarm, and the server skittered back. His hand began to crush inside of itself, each bone slowly crumpling.

Piece by piece.

Myrenna smiled. A cruel, wicked thing.

The King watched his hand in horror. His face paled, pain-etched, and a gloss of sweat covered his brow. Myrenna circled the table and gripped his chin with her manicured fingers. 'I do not tolerate the cowardice of kings. I am not a bug that you can squash.'

The King howled as his elbow shattered, bone protruding from skin.

Myrenna leaned in close, her smell of lavender and blood permeating the air. 'I am not one to be controlled. Displayed as a trophy like the women who bore your children.'

Her voice lowered. Cruel and calculated. 'I tolerate only obedience and power. And I tolerate only those who show usefulness. Neither of which you have granted.'

He ground his teeth as she released him and called over the girl. 'My King, you talk and talk but you never fulfil your promises. Until you do, we're going to take a new approach. One I find highly successful.'

His bones stopped crunching, his breathing shallow. He winced as Myrenna leaned close to his ear, whispering as she would to a lover. 'You are lucky you have twelve heirs who can do the same as you. Carnell will help me find the Princess, or I will crush your kingdom as I have done to your bones.'

His breath hitched and she stepped back.

If dwarves were all he could give, then dwarves she'd find. She would start with the Peaks of Carfell, just north of the Crystal Lake, and when she sent her great beast she would laugh when it obliterated every inch of that worthless colony.

The King's puckered lips tried to say something, but it was garbled under his pain. Myrenna could taste his fear. Could smell the salty stench of his sweat. He was replaceable.

She picked up his goblet, swirling the wine inside as another bone broke, the crack a song to Myrenna's ears.

Snow could hide all she wanted, but Myrenna would find her. She would delve into every crevice, every lake, and every village until she did, and when she found that ungrateful little brat, she'd show her what a true queen was.

One final crack, and the light left the King's eyes.

XI

The Cousins and the Curse

Eveline woke on a small chaise, Porchid sitting on her chest.

It was a relief to see that smile, the glowing gold on her skin a welcome sight. Voices echoed from across the room, and two figures approached with a cup of tea. Eveline groped for her knives and found herself in a nightgown with none of her possessions.

'How do you feel?' the first figure asked.

'Poor dear,' said the other, patting her arm.

Both women wore garish dresses – one was sunset orange, its dusty hues mismatching her pale orange hair, and the second woman wasn't much better, in a yellow outfit which dulled her skin. Both wore their hair in messy buns displaying traces of grey.

Eveline's mouth was dry. The woman in orange handed her a cup and spoke only once Eveline had taken a sip. 'Can you talk?'

'Don't rush her, Fauna,' the other chimed in sweetly.

Eveline reached for more water, wishing it was something stronger, and took in her surroundings. She was inside a cottage. It was small, only the size of a large room without walls.

She panicked for a moment when her eyes set upon the huntsman lying across the way in a bed large enough for two. He was sound asleep; the blood washed off, and his breathing calm. A bandage was wrapped around his neck and shoulder.

Despite his lies, she sighed with relief. If anybody was going to kill him, it was going to be her.

The woman – no, witch – clicked her tongue. 'First, your blasted little fairy has the audacity to come barging through our door. You then bring in a bloodied man and evil magic, and the first thing you do is not thank us but to reach for your weapons?' Her hands sat on her hips. 'You won't find them. Not until my sister and I get a good explanation.'

'She's been through an ordeal,' said the yellow witch. 'Give her time.'

'We don't have the luxury of time, Flora. The mist has gone further than we suspected, and it took a great deal of magic to push it back.'

'I know, Fauna,' said Flora, 'but maybe after some food she'll be more forthcoming?'

Hearing herself being spoken about when she was right there was one of Eveline's pet hates. She tried to lift herself up but failed, the ache in her muscles worse than expected. Her body was covered in bruises, and the scratches from the brush were coated in a balm.

Flora brought over soup and asked Eveline if she could manage it on her own. Porchid watched, her wings fluttering in anticipation.

'We have some for you, too,' said Flora, getting up from her chair and walking back to the kitchen.

Fauna remained standing, staring down at Eveline with unveiled contempt. She stood taller than her sister, and her wiry, thin arms were bony and pale. 'I don't like strangers.'

Hansel groaned from a bed nearby.

Fauna waved her hand in annoyance. 'He's been doing that all day.'

Flora laid down a bowl of berries for Porchid, her pointed teeth already out as she grabbed one. Juice slid down her front, catching in her long hair.

'His wounds were severe,' Flora said. 'He's been given some tea to help him sleep whilst he heals internally.'

Her smile looked genuine, but Fauna – Eveline distrusted her. Her scowl was piercing, her dark eyes cautious and wary.

'Who are you?' Eveline croaked between sips of soup.

'That question is for you to answer first, considering you're in our home,' said Fauna.

Porchid responded in her bell-like tongue.

'Very nice to meet you, Porchid,' replied the yellow witch. 'I'm Flora, and this is my sister, Fauna. We are the good witches of the Briar Rose, and your gracious hosts.'

Fauna snorted in response.

'Eveline,' the Seeker responded, putting down her soup. 'The big lug over there is Hansel.'

'Welcome,' said Flora, clasping her hands.

'And what is it you and your companion are doing in these parts, Eveline?' asked Fauna, moving closer. 'Not many folks are found chased by magic like that, and certainly not while covered in blood.'

Eveline took a moment to consider. 'We were… attacked, and then the black fog came out of nowhere, so we ran. Porchid saw your cottage and went ahead for help.'

It was a vague recounting of events, but these witches were strangers. Eveline might be grateful, but she wasn't naïve.

Turns out, Fauna wasn't either. 'That's only half the story, girl. You want to include the part where you have the evil's stink all over you, and maybe we can go from there.'

Flora reached over and tapped Eveline's hand gently. 'She can be a bit funny sometimes, my sister, but I'm sure you'll come around.' She wrinkled her nose. 'Though she's not wrong about the stink.'

Magic had many smells. Sometimes it was metallic. Other times it was like ripened fruit. It depended on the user. Eveline's magic, though, had no smell. It was more of a feeling. It manifested in a pull to the gut, or a dream.

Rumple's magic had stunk, but she couldn't smell anything remotely like that on herself. She raised her arm, nose crinkling at the stench of blood and grime.

She needed a bath.

'There'll be time for that,' Flora said, addressing the thought Eveline hadn't yet voiced. 'Eat up, and we'll talk more before we get you some hot water.'

It sounded like bliss.

Flora and Fauna had a routine.

For such distinct personalities they moved with swift ease around each other. One would cut the herbs whilst the other cooked. One would gather whilst the other prepared. They bantered easily, swapped hints and tips, but it was the way their bodies shuffled around each other in a graceful dance Eveline noticed most.

The following day, Fauna left for the market, leaving Porchid, Hansel, and Eveline in Flora's care. That suited Eveline just fine – Fauna's sour demeanour did nothing for her own begrudging temper.

When she was well, and after she'd bathed, Eveline did a few laps along the edge of the river. Finding a shallow pond, she decided to train. Flora had kindly returned her belongings, including her knives, giving Eveline a small reprieve from her anger as she threw them into the running water. She targeted the moving fish, testing her accuracy when she noticed one with extra stealth trying to swim away. She'd managed to score three in total before she heard Flora's chirp behind her.

'Hello, dear,' she said. 'Maybe we can take a turn and talk a little?'

Flora held a small basket in her hands, filled with fruits and berries. Eveline was unsure whether it was for their potions or for Porchid's stomach. Falling into step, Flora began speaking without Eveline making a sound. 'My sister and I live very solitary lives, but it wasn't always that way.'

Flora stopped to collect some herbs. 'We used to be part of a regal court with the loveliest king and queen. The queen had problems conceiving, so we stepped up to the throne and offered to help. There were three of us then.'

It took a moment for the information to sink in. Eveline looked down at Flora's fuller figure and imagined a third sister.

Flora smiled fondly. 'Our sister was named Merry. Her speciality was healing. It is a precarious gift, and it can drain you quickly. I have a calming gift, and Fauna's is practicality and reason.' She shook her head, picking up a clump of baby's breath. 'The three of us brewed a great potion for the queen to help her conceive, but we were later advised it was not a physical issue but a curse. After much deliberation, we sought the assistance of our cousins. You may know them as the sisters Grimm.'

Eveline ceased walking. Was this mere coincidence that for a third time in several weeks the sisters Grimm had been mentioned?

Flora paused when she noticed Eveline wasn't following. 'You've heard of them, then?' She waved her hand. 'Of course, you have. They are the creators of the realm. Etched in every story.'

Flora assessed her. 'They were not always bad, our cousins. Their solitude and dark magic twisted them to what you know of them now, and if I'm being honest, we had not considered how deep it ran.'

Eveline wondered why Flora was telling her this and whether her sister had given her approval to do so. Not that her sister dictated her moves, but it seemed like a precarious line to be crossing with strangers who'd come knocking on their door.

'Why are you telling me this?' Eveline asked.

Flora tilted her head. 'My gift not only calms but also senses when others are at war with themselves. I know if my sister and I are to seek the truth from you, then we must also offer a token ourselves.'

Eveline's hand found the smooth, familiar rock inside her pocket, and allowed its comfort to creep over her.

Flora gazed at her like she knew Eveline's wants, her needs. But she didn't know. Nobody did. Eveline wasn't at war with herself. She knew exactly what she wanted. Despite going off-track these last few weeks, she still held firm in her want for revenge. For justice.

Flora picked at a bush with sticky leaves and a hint of white dust, and sniffed it. Seeming happy with it, she began to delicately pluck the leaves one by one.

'What happened next?' Eveline asked, reaching down to help her.

'We were deceived.' She touched Eveline's hand. 'Be gentle with the leaves – much like us, they are fragile.'

Eveline loosened her grip, handing them carefully over.

Flora continued. 'We found our cousins and they agreed to help, much to our surprise. Their only request was to grant a gift upon the babe. It was common practice back then, so we didn't bat an eye. Neither did the King or Queen.

'Our cousins broke the curse, and a young babe was born. She was beautiful, with the chubbiest of cheeks,' said Flora, pinching her own, the basket swaying slightly off her elbow.

Eveline didn't miss the 'was' that came with the statement.

'When the time came, my sisters and I were to bestow a gift of kindness and beauty, so her reign knew only happiness. But before we began, our cousins stormed the throne room and claimed their price. They circled the babe, and the King, in his fear, demanded they be banished, causing our cousins to act rashly.

'For one curse broken they bestowed another, citing that on the babe's sixteenth birthday she would prick the spindle of a spinning wheel and perish.'

The back of Eveline's mind prickled, remembering a similar tale long ago in a small glen involving a crown of lilacs. 'You're talking about Briar Rose.' Flora nodded, and Eveline shook her head. 'Briar Rose didn't die. She only fell asleep.'

'Yes, dear, but that is only because of Merry.'

Eveline picked at her brain to remember the details, but they were fuzzy. If Flora had been alive during Briar Rose's existence, then she had also been alive for the War of Thorns. She twisted to peer at the witch, wondering exactly how old this woman was.

Flora picked up the pace. 'We hid Rose away for a time to avoid the curse – we hid her here, at this mill. It's named after her.'

Flora checked her basket and evenly spread out what she had collected. 'On her sixteenth birthday we tried to keep her safe. All it took was one moment. One spindle and the prick of her finger. It was a tiny little nick, but it was enough.

'Merry, in her sorrow, poured every bit of herself into breaking that curse. She hoped she could keep Rose alive, and in doing so brought upon her own death. Merry did not wake, and neither did the princess, but instead of death the princess merely slumbered.

'Rose slept for years until true love found her. Then she awoke and ruled with a kind and beautiful heart. You would have known her as Queen Rose during the War of Thorns.'

History unravelled in Eveline's mind as she grasped to link the story with the famous queen. Princess Snow, in fact, would be a direct descendant of that line, even if they were separated by several generations.

'Merry was not so fortunate, though. She never returned from that world on the other side.'

A tear slid down Flora's cheek and she wiped it away quickly. 'A truth for a truth, Eveline. That's all we seek.'

The stone in Eveline's pocket grew warm. Flora's eyes were bright, honest, and unnerving. She'd lost a sister. Just as Eveline had lost a father. They both knew grief.

Eveline sighed, took the basket from Flora, and offered her elbow.

A truth for a truth.

It was almost a relief to tell Flora what had happened, a tightness in her chest loosening with each word. She told Flora of her bargain with the huntsman, and of their journey through the mines. She spoke of the sleeping princess, and the meeting with the Queen, right up until the part where Eveline passed out in their doorway.

Flora listened with great attention, nodding when it was appropriate, and never with a judging look. Eventually they ended up back at the house, having explored the entire property. Giving her an encouraging squeeze, Flora looked to Eveline before reaching for the door and said, 'Thank you for your truth. I think we can help.'

Following the woman inside, Eveline noticed Hansel sitting in his bed, a meal eaten at his side.

A truth for a truth.

And maybe a new beginning.

Hansel's head throbbed.

He woke to Eveline and Flora entering the home, their voices hushing as he sat up in bed. Porchid had kept him company, spinning in the air and twinkling in a language he didn't understand. He'd laughed a little, the bruises on his throat catching.

Flora pottered around the house and brought him food, then inclined her head to Eveline and donned her shawl. 'I'm going to meet my sister,' she announced. 'I'll tell her about our talk.'

It was dusk when she left, Porchid at her side for company. Eveline had wasted no time, pulling one of the chairs over to his bed. She didn't speak at first, instead assessing all the places where he'd been injured, landing for a moment on the dark bruises on his neck.

She leaned forward and began to peel off the bandage. He let her.

Hansel remained still, yet every part of his body craved her touch. He leaned in a little as an invitation. If she noticed, she didn't let on.

'I want to get one thing out before you start,' she said, carefully peeling away layer after layer of his bandages. 'You hurt me, and that will take time to forgive. So, do not expect me to do it quickly, but I will at least try to understand.'

He would've nodded if he could.

'I know that I haven't been—that I can be difficult at times. So, I am willing to offer you a truth for a truth.'

She placed the bandage in the bowl by the table. He'd never seen her nervous. Never seen her hands shake or voice waver. She swallowed, dipping her fingers into a container of salve. 'When I lost my father, I lost a little piece of me. I wandered for a while and ran into many wicked things, but after an already somewhat big adventure, I fell into the Cirque Magique.'

He'd heard of Cirque Magique before. They were a travelling circus. Never in one place too long, but they had been around for a while. Madame Viper was the owner.

But it wasn't Viper who drew the crowds, it was the rumours about the seer who travelled with them. A real seer, one who could predict futures with the mere touch of a hand. It was a rare gift. People travelled across kingdoms to see their future.

Eveline's face was grave as she continued to apply the salve, her fingers brushing lightly over his skin. 'I was collected by one of Madame Viper's associates and became what you call a servant of sorts. I'd watch the shows by night and clean by day. Sometimes I collected the tickets and sometimes I sewed the patches on the circus tent. Viper wasn't cruel, exactly, but she wasn't kind, either. The only kind one had been Dante.' She said the name with reverence, emotion thick in her voice. Hansel didn't know whether to feel honoured or jealous knowing about this person.

'Dante was the knife-thrower and tightrope extraordinaire,' Eveline said. 'He would sneak me extra rations, and when it was cold he would give me his extra blankets. After a time, I asked him to train me, and he did, without question.'

That explained her skill, he thought to himself. She procured a new bandage to wrap around his throat.

'After a few years, a plague swept through the circus. Dante didn't survive.' Eveline's voice went quiet. 'But he wasn't the only one who trained me. Lady Nona did too.

'Nona was old, and she struggled with travelling. Where Dante taught me aim and balance, Lady Nona taught me about my gift. She showed me it wasn't mine. That everything I'd seen and done had been at the beckoning of the fates.'

She sat back, pensive. 'When Dante died, I'd never felt so powerless in my life. That's when I decided to run away. To forge my own fate and find the family I had lost.'

Hansel chose his words carefully. 'Is that why you need the medallions?'

'Where my gift fails me, medallions do not.'

He attempted to lift himself up, and Eveline leaned in to help him.

'Is Lady Nona the fortune teller? The seer?' he asked. He'd always wondered if the rumours were true.

She nodded.

Eveline crossed her hands on her lap and patiently waited.

A truth for a truth.

He understood one thing then. This was his chance. His chance to amend, to tell the tale he'd kept close to his heart.

'After what happened with Gretel,' he started, 'I ended up in the nearest village, and begged for a time. I had no money, no food, and no family. I'd seen an advertisement for the Queen's Guard. I was young. It was an opportunity I couldn't pass. The only skill I had was with an axe from chopping trees with my father. My balance was off, my aim terrible, but I had strength in my shoulders, and I focused on that.

'I'd only made it halfway through training before the Queen arrived in search of a new Queen's Guard. There had been rumours about the inconsistency between her guards, and the fact she didn't need one never passed anyone's notice.'

He leaned back into his pillows. 'The strangest thing was the way she looked at us. When guards came forth offering her loyalty, she walked past them like they were a stain on her lovely dress. It was also the day she stopped in front of me.'

He swallowed, taking his time to form the words. Eveline remained still, patient. 'The Queen plucked me from a line of men. From there I had private lessons with a man called Hector. He was a shapeshifter and a strange man. Weathered. Our lessons covered everything from defence, to attack, to patience. His biggest lesson, though, was words. When used in the right way, words can be just as much a weapon as a sword. Words were my ally when I served the Queen.'

Hansel looked at Eveline, wanting her to see, to listen, to feel. 'After a few years, I became friends with the Princess and Malak.'

She furrowed her eyebrows, and he laughed. 'Malak was there as a stable hand, of all things. He's been in love with the Princess since the first day he laid eyes on her, and made an oath to protect her at all costs.'

Eveline didn't say anything, but the animosity was gone. Her lips twitched, like she was about to smile, but she waited, her full focus on him. He wasn't sure how he felt under that gaze, whether it terrified or invigorated him.

'One night, the Queen called me into her chambers,' he said, and her smile faded. 'She asked me to dine with her. She told me stories about her day and childhood, but nothing of real substance. She mainly focused on my training, and took great interest in my sister.

'It was a little bit dreamlike, but I served her in whatever form she required. For a while it was numbing, and then it just … was.'

Eveline's face twisted in disgust. Hansel couldn't blame her, but he wouldn't deny it hurt. It was one thing to work for the Queen, and another to be her confidant.

'Eveline,' he breathed, 'Myrenna would have killed me if I were to refuse. The mornings were for beheadings, and the afternoons were for *her*. It blurred together. The moment it changed was when I saw the Queen leave the throne room. She was mad, raging over whatever the mirror had said. She told me to cut my ties. To never see Snow again. That her time was coming.

'I tried to warn the Princess, leaving her a note, but she took the Queen's bait anyway. I found her later, after a servant found me. After I smuggled Snow out, I lost word of her whereabouts, and the Queen went into a fury. I was ordered to bring back her heart. To kill her.'

Hansel looked up to find Eveline's blank glaze. She took a deep breath through her nostrils.

'Princess Snow is hope in a land so barren of it. I must save her and, in turn, the people. It is not you I have deceived, but Myrenna,' he said. 'I'm sorry. So very sorry.'

Eveline nodded and picked up the chair, placing it neatly by the table without another word.

A truth for a truth, she had said. But she'd given him nothing. No validation. No recognition.

With nothing but emptiness, Eveline walked away, leaving Hansel to wonder whether he should've said nothing at all.

XII

The Mountains of the North

Brufell was a one-minded kind of dwarf, his mission his main priority. In his youth, it'd been to rank first in warfare. During the War of Thorns, it'd been to win the war. During the separation of the clans, it'd been to preserve Parador.

Now, it was the Princess.

His weapons clinked together as he climbed the peak leading north, Bronson close behind. The craggy outlook reached far into the hills, and its grey, rocky surface made the hike difficult.

Brufell had the beginnings of a headache with a slight pinch behind his eyes. Bronson's whistling hadn't ceased since they'd left the grotto and the repetitive tune pierced his ears like needles.

The tips of the mountains penetrated the low-lying cloud, reaching for the hidden land above. The snow was heavy at the peaks, giving way to rock and dust.

The mountains were vast, reaching to the edge of the King's Keep in the north and stretching down into the southern borders of Bellatorre.

Bronson's whistles echoed over the hills as Brufell reached the top, gathering his bearings. Bronson's slow whistle hitched as his breathing lagged from the climb. 'I miss the comforts of home. The smell of Bryn's cooking.'

Brufell noted the soft touch of kohl lining the top of his eyes, and shook his head. 'Home will still be there when we get back.'

'How do you know home will be there?' Bronson asked, a worried expression on his brow.

Brufell squashed the memory of clans dying. The mines falling to ruin. He was old enough that he'd been there for the downfall. Been there for the migration to the Peaks of Carfell. But he was also young enough to not have known the impact or the sheer weight of it all.

Bronson was far younger than him, used to his comforts. He was used to the sounds of the crackling hearth, the stories from Bonyx, and his regular intake of ale. Things they all enjoyed. But where Bonyx and Brufell had seen hardship, the young hadn't. He turned to Bronson, who looked at him expectantly. He could lie of course, but he knew that wasn't a kindness. Kindness lay in knowing what lay ahead regardless of how bad it was. 'I don't,' Brufell said, his voice gruff. 'But we can hope.'

The wind held a chill and Brufell pulled his jacket tight, eyeing the magical forest to the west of the hills.

Brufell raised his arm and squinted. The sun was setting. Nimbly, he lifted his rope and began to attach it to a craggy output when a hurdling screech came from the forest.

'What was that?' Bronson yelped, twisting towards the noise.

Brufell frowned. The trees were alive in the forest, and while he didn't mind a little magic, the kind that grew, mouldered, and bred inside it was the dangerous and sickly kind.

'Best leave it alone,' he said gruffly, securing the knot. He pulled it at it twice, checking it was stable. Brufell leaned over the sharp edge and made his way down. The rope went taut as it held his weight. The climb wouldn't be long, but he'd always had an issue with open spaces and heights. Some of his greatest battles had been fought in large, wide-open plains, but he always preferred the tight, narrow hallways and twists of the mines, the nooks and crevices filled with years of history and secrets.

He'd helped create a great portion of it himself.

It was a dwarf's right to shape part of the mountain, to carve a little piece of your soul and family line into those great halls. His king would've been proud.

If he still lived.

The surface crumbled apart as he made his way down. Bronson followed, though far less gracefully. When they both reached the bottom, Brufell hitched the rope over his shoulder and, with the smallest tug, it came tumbling down.

Frowning again, he looked to the top of the peak. His knot had been too secure for it to unravel the way it had. Brufell slowly made to pick up the rope when he noticed a flash of movement. Tiny, spindly fingers pulled away from the edge. 'We're being followed.'

Bronson paused, eyes wide. 'By who?'

'A stranger. A pixie, maybe.' Brufell guessed.

Either way, it was a problem. If the Queen had sent her followers already, they were in trouble. The grotto had been hidden enough to protect the Princess, to keep the prying eyes of Evil Queen away, but the Seven knew it wouldn't be long until they were discovered.

Brufell eyed the horizon. They were barely halfway to Troll's Keep.

'I thought pixies lived further north,' Bronson said, following his gaze.

Brufell thought the same, but it wasn't the first strange occurrence to happen. Even in Parador the dwarves had sensed the stirrings of change. More creatures coming out of hiding, the war raging on the borders of Perridorm. Parts of the forest withering, maidens disappearing.

The dwarves had found Princess Snow in a mountain pass on the way to see their cousins. It was a narrow pass, with heavy twisted mountains. Its sheer drop deterred most travellers, but it remained a consistent route for those looking to sneak in contraband between the two nations. If the wind or the dangerous terrain didn't get you, the raiders would.

The dwarves had once been a great people but when war had come, their numbers had suffered. When Parador had been destroyed, the dwarves divided. The Seven had remained and the rest settled east. Letters were sent back and forth regularly. The colony had become quite the trading centre, holding a secure spot on the border of Carnell and Bellatorre.

The capital cities lay close by, and whilst the dwarves were left to their own devices, they worked within each kingdom's laws as neutral ground. Though they dwelled in the mountains, they grew a heavy trade in Ivywood, reaching towards the main road between the Silver City and Eastbourne.

A wail echoed along the mountains, leaving Brufell unsettled.

'Come along, Bronson,' he said, forgetting to hide the harshness in his voice.

Brufell's mind wandered, axe in hand. He wondered if the Seeker could find this supposed prince, whether her reputation was an exaggeration. But one thing still gnawed at him: the Prince was just a guess. Sure, love was known to break the greatest of curses, but there was no handbook on curses, no direct cure. Magic was always individual, warped to suit the user.

The dwarves had already tried remedies to wake her. Bonyx and himself had even ventured deep into their libraries for scrolls on cures for ailments and spells. The Seven hadn't dared to ask a healer or a witch in case they were reported to the Queen.

It wasn't until one night when Brufell had been falling asleep on his watch that he was whipped into a tent of red and gold within the deep confines of his dreams. Sage and incense filled its interior with smooth, silky smoke. An older woman stood before him, her long, silver hair waving loosely at her sides. But it was her pale grey eyes he'd remembered most, and the urgency behind them.

'You must listen carefully, dwarf, for I only say this once.'

Her wrinkled hands, speckled by the sun, were firm. He'd barely had a chance to blink when she gasped, a voice not unlike the depths of the caverns pouring from her mouth.

'Mirrors four, of black and bone,
Of silver and gold, and night blue stone
At the dawn of light, with powers three,
A soul will tear and hearts will see,

A gift for giving at the aftermath,
Or a land in ruin of pain and wrath,
When one will stray, another shall gain,
And in blood and loss they will be slain,

When betrayal and love finally mix,
Hearts will shatter as seven become six,
Wood from a tree that's existed an age,
And mirrors of glass in a watery cage,

The theft of a gem and its keeper's revenge,
An obsidian cauldron and the price to avenge,
Shadows of memory, death will reap,
But an act of love will wake her from sleep.'

The woman's hands shook, the skin soft and papery. She licked her lips, worry lurking behind her eyes.

He didn't understand, but there was a heaviness to the air, a stirring of something important. For Brufell, the hardest thing had been deciding on his next few words. Though magic existed, it was a rare thing to be pulled into the business of it.

That dream had lingered long after he'd woken.

And then the Seeker had arrived.

He wasn't one for fate, but he wasn't one to deny it when it came calling, either.

Brufell secured the rope tightly to his pack as they navigated the craggy terrain. He'd sensed the change when they left for the Peaks of Carfell; when he'd received the seer's warning, and when they'd found the Princess.

There was no doubt in his mind that something was coming.

The question was, were they ready for it?

XIII
The Crossing of the Marshes

Flora and Fauna dusted off their kitchen table, revealing a clean, crisp carving of the realm.

Eveline stroked her fingers along the indentation of a river, spotting roads and mountains. The detail was astounding.

Fauna slapped her hand away. 'Don't touch. It'll ruin the spell.'

Hansel snorted, and Eveline poked out her tongue in reply.

The two witches traced the table's lines with a soft powder and brush, delicately following the grooves of the borders and lands.

After a week of rest, Hansel was back on his feet. They'd exchanged only a few tight words. Their truth for a truth still lingered, and she had questions. She refrained despite his offer to answer, simply because it was selfish. He'd answered her concerns. He'd told her of his past, of his relationship to the queen and where his priorities lied. Knowing the rest of it didn't help with their quest or the princess. He wanted to save Snow. Wanted to help her find the rebellion. So, even though it pained her, she kept her interactions minimal and squashed those churning feelings down into the depths of herself.

Fauna smirked. 'Lovers' tiff?'

Eveline grunted in response. She'd grown accustomed to Fauna's looks of displeasure. Occasionally, Eveline envisioned what it would have been like if Merry had survived and what she would've thought of Flora's tale.

The witches picked up a pure white crystal attached to a string and swung it over the dusted table. Where Eveline's gift had failed her, the two good witches had promised to attempt a tracking spell to point them the right direction of the prince. The witches chanted, the powder shifting under the crystal like the sands in a desert. Eveline leaned in, the urge to touch the magic strong. It slithered over the cracks before huddling together over Maelstrom.

The city was a few days' journey away and fell outside the Queen's domain. Whilst the Queen reigned over Bellatorre from her golden throne in the Silver City, Carnell was famously ruled by the twelve princes and their father from Maelstrom.

Fauna brushed some of the powder away to take a closer look and noticed a second pile of powder in the neighbouring hills. 'It's forming a lot of magic in that area.'

Flora fiddled with the indents of the surrounding land and looked to Eveline. 'That's giants' land. You best be careful.'

Fauna snorted. 'Be careful? That's the worst advice I've ever heard.'

'And why would that be the worst advice?'

'It's giants, Flora,' she snapped. 'They'd squish them like bugs regardless of how careful they were. Foul, disgusting creatures.' She wrinkled her nose.

'I've never seen a giant,' Hansel said with wonder.

Eveline looked at him and masked a smile.

'Lucky,' replied Fauna. 'They're downright awful.'

Eveline turned to the two witches. 'Thank you – for everything.'

Flora came round the table and pulled her into a tight hug. 'Come on, Fauna, I know you love hugs!'

'I think not.'

Flora shook her head, and clasped Eveline's cheeks. 'Please do visit when you've saved the poor princess.'

'Yes, but can it be with less of an entrance?' Fauna replied. 'Like, maybe bring a pie instead of a death fog.'

Eveline's lip quirked.

Hansel and Porchid gave their thanks as they left, accepting parcels from the sisters that they'd filled with food and medicine. Eveline almost thanked them again when Flora pulled her to the side.

Flora opened Eveline's palm and placed a slime-covered seed into her hand. 'This is the seed of a Chomping Changer.'

Eveline flinched, almost dropping it, but Flora held her hand firm.

'Why would you have this?' Eveline asked.

Chomping Changers were vicious little plants that ate copious amounts of other plants. Luckily, they were herbivores, but it wouldn't stop them from biting off your fingers due to their disposition.

Flora patted her hand. 'They're misunderstood little critters and can help in sticky situations. Just remember, they will continue to eat until full'—she shrugged—'and you know what happens after that. They can be a good distraction should you need one. Careful to only use it once, as multiples of them can pop from one seed. Just drop it into lush soil with a little bit of water and they'll spring forth.'

With shaking hands, Eveline placed the seed into her coin purse.

The windmill spun at a steady pace, and the river sparkled from the morning light. The parcels were hefty but welcome. The sisters waved from the doorway of the house as Porchid, Hansel and Eveline walked back into the forest.

Leaving the Briar Rose's smoke curling as a farewell behind them.

Porchid spun in circles mid-air, doing backflips whilst they walked.

The path narrowed as they climbed the great hill, the trees thinning. Grass turned to dirt and rock, the dust ever-present on Eveline's skin. The loose stones made it difficult to tread, the three of them moving with more caution than grace.

Eveline snuck a peek at Hansel. His bandages were gone, leaving only a pale shade of pink marking his skin. Breathing heavily, Eveline thought back to his tale with the Queen. It still unsettled her, but was there no end to what you would do for friends? Would she have done that for a friend? To survive?

She looked up at Porchid, who flew ahead between stones and rocks keeping a lookout ahead. Eveline's smile was bitter as she answered her own question.

For Porchid, she would. She would've done it for Dante, too, if she'd had the chance.

She'd been awful to Hansel. He'd shared the truth of what he'd endured. Due to his quick thinking, he'd saved the Princess, had even managed to manipulate the Queen into letting him leave the castle.

But he'd still warmed her bed. How did that make him feel? Had he come to enjoy it? Had he once felt something for the beautiful and wicked queen?

Shame churned in her gut. She'd judged him harshly. Her father would've abhorred her.

Hansel walked up the rocky outcrop without a flicker of discomfort, his powerful form a source of strength. Porchid pointed ahead, forehead sweaty from the amount of flying she'd done. They were almost at the crest, thankfully. Any more climbing and Eveline would start bartering with the sisters Grimm for a set of wings herself.

Hansel hesitated at the top before turning towards her. 'We've hit the marshes.'

Sure enough, the land below was barren, stretching in endless miles of wetlands.

'When you mentioned the marshes,' she said to Hansel, 'I'd envisioned something a little more … Reduced.'

Eveline's eyes settled where the sky met the land, fumes from the marshes' watery depths spiralling towards the clouds. The stench of decay rebounded through her nostrils, and she held up her hand in a pitiful attempt to contain it. She choked, before gulping down some air so she could start assessing how they were to cross. 'That smells disgusting.'

'Smell or not,' Hansel replied, 'we have to find a way across.'

Porchid pointed ahead. There, lying in ruins, were the remains of a rotted bridge.

'Porchid,' Eveline said, 'you know I love you, but I'm not sure if that's the best option.'

'It's our only option.' Hansel grimaced. 'According to Flora and Fauna, this crossing was once a shortcut. If you can believe it, the bridge was a great structure. A main entry point for travellers.'

Eveline stared at the large mass of putrid marsh. She wasn't sure whether the bridge had decayed on its own or if whatever lay beneath the depths of this repulsive place had brought it to ruin.

'Some parts are still intact,' Hansel continued. 'If we tread wisely, we might just make it.'

That was a pretty way of saying it. Some areas wouldn't just require treading lightly; it would require them to take a detour across unstable islands that protruded from the water.

'Eveline?' he asked quietly.

She knew that tone. She wasn't ready to talk yet.

'It's getting dark,' she replied.

Hansel remained on the hill as she walked away, the guilt ever-present. They walked like that for a few hours more, until the moon crested the sky. Unable to see the path clearly, they set up camp.

Hansel sharpened his axe, his biceps moving up and down with a scraping sound. He flinched, a hiss of pain escaping his lips.

'You need to be more careful of your injury,' she said.

Hansel wiped the sweat from his brow, averting her gaze as he replied, 'I'm fine.'

Eveline bristled at the tone but took the hint. But when Hansel hissed again, she snapped. 'Give it here.' she said, pulling the axe from his hands without a complaint. She ignored the pulse of energy that sparked through her fingers at his touch. Carefully, she began honing its edge. She'd have to do her knives, too.

'Eveline?' he whispered.

'I'm not ready.'

They lapsed into silence again.

Daylight was still on their side as they began their rocky descent to meet the marshes' frothing edge. Eveline's nostrils burned as if all the hair inside them were scorching off from the acrid stench.

Hansel didn't look much better. Porchid made her feelings known by flashing a sickly green and glaring at Eveline as if this were her fault at every interval.

From the looks of the map, the marshes weren't that large, but she began to wonder if that was a cruel assumption and if they should have taken the extra days to go around like everybody else. But they'd chosen this route to remain undetected. Neither of them wanted the Queen to visit them again. Eveline eyed the sky, watching for signs of the Queen's murders. She was relieved when she saw it remained clear of birds.

Sections of the bridge were mush, the water uninviting in the way that only black, chunky milk could be. Every now and then Eveline noticed things moving along its waters, reminding her to watch her step.

Hansel was braver than her when it came to the water. Several times he waded through, making himself available to help Eveline cross without having to touch its surface. At first, she'd refused his assistance, but gave in after one of the islands began to sink.

They moved as swiftly as they could, considering the complex path they made, but even though they powered forward, it seemed the more marsh they left behind, the more it kept on stretching in front of them. It was becoming a never-ending landscape of foul, gloomy death.

They stopped for a break on one of the larger parts of the bridge. Eveline's hair stuck to her skin, and she wiped at her brow. The air was thick with moisture, and it was hot despite the grey clouds swarming overhead. If this was the end of winter here, she'd hate to consider what summer was like.

Hansel broke some of their food from the parcels given to them by Flora and Fauna, handing them out like a soldier with rations. He was solemn, always focusing on the waters ahead, the next route to take.

Porchid peered over the bridge's edge, twinkling in concern. She was green, then white, then green again. Nausea and fear. Two emotions Eveline also hadn't seemed to let go of since Roserock.

First, they'd almost frozen to death before falling off a collapsed mountain. They'd been lost in a maze of rock, attacked by dwarves, and found an almost dead princess. Not to mention the black mist or meeting the Evil Queen.

She'd survived, sure, but now they sat in the middle of one of the inhospitable places she'd ever been in her life. The luxuries of a hot bath and a soft bed felt like a dream. One she ached for.

What had they really accomplished, after all?

Sure, they'd found the Princess, but she remained cursed. The only hope lay on a hunch that this Prince Florian could give her a true love's kiss, and even then, it was only a guess. What if they never found him? Or worse, what if they found him, and Snow never woke up?

Eveline's gift tingled upon her skin, a reminder she would find the prince. Even if it was being a little stubborn these days. The gift worked that way. Choosing to seek when it suited itself. Sometimes Eveline found things on her own from years of practice, and other times, without her doing a thing, it pulled her towards something of its own accord.

Lady Nona – the seer at Cirque Magique – had called it a blessing from the fates, said that Eveline had a destiny she couldn't control.

Her time with the troupe seemed all at once an age ago and yesterday – the smell of Lady Nona's incense-infused tent; the harsh snap of Madame Viper's orders; the warmth of Dante's shoulder next to hers as they stargazed.

The night she'd run off had been the worst of her life. Dante had fallen to a sickness, an incurable one that left Viper clipped and angry. Lady Nona hadn't left her quarters much, blaming age and inconvenience, but even she had felt something changing. Before Eveline had visited Dante, the seer had called her to her tent, her foggy eyes sharper than usual.

Over the years, Eveline had attempted to shrug off the seer's words. It hadn't made sense to her then, the words deep but meaningless. They were more an omen than anything.

And yet, she recalled them as if Nona stood right here.

'The theft of a gem and its keeper's revenge,

An obsidian cauldron and the price to avenge,

Shadows of memory, death will reap,

But an act of love will wake her from sleep.'

Eveline palmed the blue stone, careful not to scratch its surface. Fate had a funny way of playing games, of following you no matter how far you ran.

'We should reach the end by sundown,' Hansel said, pulling her from her thoughts. He wiped the sweat from his brow, watching the water with caution as Porchid wandered along its edge.

Porchid's head tilted, and a ripple broke the surface. Eveline barely opened her mouth to warn the fairy when a black tentacle shot from the water.

Hansel yelled; Eveline screamed.

Porchid's wings were a blur as she flailed back, Eveline barely managing to grip her tiny form as Hansel raised his axe. With one swing, he severed the tentacle, black blood spraying across Eveline's face.

The dismembered limb flopped onto the wood of the bridge. Eveline checked Porchid for any injuries before she stood, and Hansel eyed the water for further danger.

'Disgusting,' Eveline hissed.

'The creature is probably starving,' Hansel replied.

'Let it starve,' she snapped.

His golden-brown eyes watched her warily as he began to pack up the food. Good. They were leaving. Eveline had never wanted to leave a place faster. With careful fingers, Eveline eased Porchid into her pocket, a shiver crawling up her spine.

That's when the caws sounded.

Hansel's head snapped to the sky. 'Move. NOW.'

Eveline didn't argue. They ran, dodging a hole in the wood as Hansel pointed towards a shrub. The cries grew louder, the unending sky stretched out before them. She dared a peek behind her, sighting the black cloud rising from the hills.

The Queen's crows.

Eveline was barely off the bridge when Hansel hiked her over his shoulder, jumping over the marshes with swift ease. She clung to him, each muscle rippling with the movement. He panted, while she held her breath.

The cloud of birds rose, the cry piercing when Eveline was thrown behind a shrub. Hansel covered her, his broad form blocking out the light as the murders grew closer.

Both their heartbeats escalated – Hansel's pounding against hers in the close proximity – as the birds flew directly overhead.

Hansel didn't let her go until only silence remained.

Hansel was on edge.

The stench was nauseating; dizziness nagged at the corner of his mind as they fumbled towards the marshes end.

Porchid had been distressed since the tentacle incident and the Queen's murders, so she stayed close. She peered over Eveline's shoulder, checking Hansel was still following.

Eveline stomped just ahead of him, her hair a tangled mess. She'd attempted to run her fingers through it to no avail. Its thickness was too untamed and its slight curl a hazard. Muck and slime coated the front of her clothes, and her patience had long since waned.

They still hadn't spoken about his experience. Still hadn't revealed any other truths. But after being attacked, Hansel didn't want to push. What they needed now was shelter, food, and somewhere to hide for a proper rest.

The marshes eventually evened out; the water receded, and the stumps of land grew more frequent. Their clothes stuck to them for most of the journey, the material itching on their skin with patches of perspiration.

Hansel looked up, brow furrowing as an archway appeared. Beside each pillar was a great stone carving of the old queens, their hands braced towards the horizon. He picked up his pace, glad for an end to this torture. He was trudging along the end of the bridge when Eveline scowled at one of the carvings.

He stopped. 'What is it?'

'Just how many secret places are there?' she asked, quietly. 'There are worlds within worlds, stories within stories.'

He watched her crawl into that place in her mind where he couldn't follow. 'Not everything lasts forever.'

She looked at him with sad eyes before replying. 'No, it doesn't.'

Following the path, they cut through the rocky ground, which veered off into fields of green. They passed travellers and merchants along the road, most of which stared at their muddy forms and kept their distance. They avoided small towns for fear of standing out, and followed the back paths, cutting through farms and properties.

They remained quiet, though it was less uncomfortable now, and just when Hansel thought they'd never stop walking, they crested a hill smothered in daisies only to find grey housing and a swath of chimney smoke.

Maelstrom.

XIV

The Scarats and the Pixie

They were being followed.

Brufell knew it in his bones as they climbed another rocky outcrop days later. They were still a while away from Troll's Keep, but his main focus had been on the forest. The Realm was made up of two major forests: the Shadow Forest, and the Dark Forest. Both foreboding, both dark, and both names completely accurate.

Some referred to them as the beating hearts of the realm, the trees taking up most of the middle land, separating almost every kingdom. Borderlines included the forests, but no royal was stupid enough to claim it. Except for the sisters Grimm, the forest ruled itself.

Because of those reasons, Brufell kept to the edge of the mountains, following the curve further and further north.

Bronson had stopped whistling, growing more nervous with the change in terrain. He occasionally stumbled, his usually combed hair and straight vest in disarray after travelling so far.

The further north they went, the darker the trees became, their thick trunks twisting into one another. A chill came with the wind in this region, one of magic and rot.

This particular area was not used often. Most travellers took the longer, wider route through Carnell and Aurelia, where inns and townsfolk dwelled. But he'd had few options.

That night, they made camp in a small cave. Its opening overlooked the forest, giving them a reprieve from the wind. It was shallow enough to keep them sheltered, which suited Brufell just fine. No pixies and goblins could sneak up on him then.

Brufell opened the packs to divide up dinner. 'Stale bread?' he offered Bronson. 'Or stale bread?'

The options were limitless.

Bronson grumbled something incoherent as he accepted.

Brufell shook his head, checking the pack to plan for the next few days. His fingers trailed over a few slices before he noticed an opened cloth, the second portion of food gone. His cheeks turned red. 'Have you been sneaking food again, Bronson?'

The dwarf stared at him blankly and shook his head.

Brufell grumbled and stared at the nearly empty food pack. He'd specifically packed it himself and knew he'd planned the rations down to perfection for the trip through to the keep.

Scowling he turned to Bronson. 'If I catch you—'

'You won't.' Bronson bristled. 'Cause I haven't.'

Brufell frowned, but gave in. Bronson could be a stubborn pig, and if he was being honest, he had little patience to press the matter. 'I'll take first watch,' he mumbled, settling himself near the cliff.

Bronson murmured behind him, but the old dwarf was focused on the mountains. He understood now why this part of the realm lay shrouded in stories. The silence was unnerving. There were no sounds of owls or birds. Even the wind settled as if it had gone into a slumber. He shifted, uncomfortable.

Bronson hiccupped from his dreamy haze nearby, and Brufell caught movement. He rose to his feet, quiet as a fox when a distinct blue hand peeled open his pack.

Brufell lashed out, grabbing the creature's spindly wrist. It squealed.

'Hello, little thief,' Brufell growled. 'What are you doing so far from home?'

It squeaked in his grip and took a bite of Brufell's hand, drawing blood. He hissed, and the pixie scuttered behind a large rock.

Brufell had not lit a fire – it would have been a beacon to anything crawling in the darkness – but this high, the stars and the low moon provided light. The pixie peered at Brufell as he wrapped his hand in his shirt, shoulders stiff.

Pixies travelled in clans, never alone and separated. It was odd to see only one, and yet that wasn't the real oddity; it was the jarring scar across his eye, and his mottled skin that made Brufell pause.

Tilting his head, he watched as the pixie looked to the bag of stale bread then back to the dwarf. He was hungry. The bread was likely the only food he'd seen in weeks.

'Seen a bit of battle, hey?' Brufell asked, still clutching his hand.

They stared at each other, sizing one another up.

Eventually, the pixie took a tentative step forward, its eye flicking between Bronson's sleeping form and Brufell before it dived for the pack.

Brufell was quicker. He snatched the bag, pulled it into his lap, and wrapped his arms around it with a growl. The pixie dashed behind the rock and looked up at him with his watery eye.

Then the forest cracked.

Brufell whirled at the sound and scanned the forest. It sounded like a whip, the kind for lashing rough skin. The skies were clear, no sign of a storm.

Brufell woke Bronson, the hairs on the back of his neck standing on end. Something wasn't right.

The crack came again, this time louder, harsher. Closer.

Brufell tensed. The mountains were too quiet, the wind too still.

When the third crack hit, the pixie clung to Brufell's pants. The trees moved. Slow at first, then with fervour. Another crack, another crash, then it... Snapped.

The tree closest to them tore from the centre, splitting in two. A thousand beady eyes stared at him from its middle, and as he went for his closest weapon, they blinked again in unison. His stomach dropped.

Bronson took a deep breath in horror. 'Are they—'

'Scarats,' Brufell confirmed.

Brufell's hand closed around his axe when the tree shattered.

Black hairy bodies fell onto the ground, the screech so loud it pierced Brufell's ears. He stood at the edge of the cave, axe raised, as the scarats charged.

Their skinny snouts sniffed as they hurled their way forwards, fighting with one another for dinner.

Bronson stammered but stood firm, raising his own weapons with quiet courage.

They had nowhere to run.

The scarats ran in full force, and when their sharp jagged teeth appeared over the crest of the mountain, Brufell did not hesitate. He slashed the first one, aiming for its maw and neck. Their hairy hides were made of rough skin, an armour that was difficult to penetrate. But their stomachs and heads were not. More and more piled over the edge as he sliced and stabbed, losing count of how many he felled. It seemed with each kill, another came to take its place. Their collective scattering call stifled his thoughts. Brufell was all instinct, all slaughter.

Bronson was panting on his left, his sword hitting true as one went for his neck. Another jumped, Brufell barely missing the blow as Bronson shoved him to the side. His axe went flying at another scarat soaring through the air.

Brufell pulled out his knife and carved it into the stomach of a scarat as another mouth came for him. Before he could reach his axe, the pixie dived and snatched at the scarat's throat, snapping its neck. The pixie growled, blood dripping from its mouth.

Both dwarves were panting. The beasts had slowed down, but they hadn't ceased. The creatures' bodies began to pile upon one another as the rocky crevice was filled with corpses.

Brufell, Bronson, and the pixie hacked and hit and slashed until, finally, *finally*, they remained the only creatures standing.

Bronson puked in the corner, wheezing from either nausea or exertion. Brufell wiped the blood off his face.

The pixie's ears twitched. Another crack rang out from the forest.

Panicked, the pixie yanked his shirt, and pointed to the only path.

'You want us to run?' Brufell asked, and it nodded. 'Where?'

'I think he must know somewhere,' Bronson said, wiping his mouth.

Crack.

If the pixie knew somewhere, then Brufell would take his chances. Without a second thought, the dwarves ran, carrying what they could. The path was narrow and steep. Bronson stumbled behind Brufell as they fought their way through the dark.

The screeches of scarats echoed behind them, the pounding feet unleashing rock from the mountainside. Brufell pulled Bronson forward, urging him to go faster.

His thick feet thumped as they followed the path down. He gripped his sword and axe, palms sweaty when the earth shook, a *snap* crackling across the mountain.

One moment they were running, and the next—

They fell.

Brufell's back hit a slant, the breath knocked out of him as he slid into the earth. It twisted, obscuring the night. His stomach lurched into his throat, the pixie squealing. Brufell braced for the bottom, the pixie clinging onto his beard, when they crashed into the cool surface of water. Dark, eerie silence engulfed him, the weight of his weapons carrying him down.

Down …

Down …

Down …

Brufell struggled, chest tight as he ripped off his pack and loosed his axe. He fought to the surface, grateful for air as he hauled himself over the edge of the pool. The scuttling behind them had ceased, but his wave of relief was short-lived when something slimy touched his leg.

Something else was down here.

'Swim, Bronson!' Brufell bellowed, his voice bounding off rock.

Bronson thrashed towards the shore, kohl bleeding from his eyes as Brufell grabbed his arms and yanked him from the water. A black shape curled around the spot where Bronson had just been, growing larger and larger. Brufell dragged Bronson back, lodging themselves further into the cavern.

The water rippled.

'What is—' but Bronson had no time to finish his sentence as a black hump broke out of the water. A clawed arm shot for the pixie, barely missing the creature as it zipped away.

Brufell's mouth went dry at the sight. It was enormous.

Slowly, the hulking creature raised itself from the pool, its translucent eyes and large nostrils sniffing the air.

Brufell twisted and faced the rock, groping his hands over every surface for a doorway. He was lucky when he found a tiny crevasse, too small for a human but enough for a dwarf. Gasping, he grabbed Bronson's hand and yanked them through, the creature hissing behind them.

The shadow's great body surged as it smashed against the wall's surface, bringing stone and rock from the ceiling. It heaved again, the walls shaking as the dwarves navigated the tight tunnel. Eventually, the sound of the beast faded. Brufell managed to find an opening and stumbled through, his ears ringing as a larger tunnel came into view.

He turned to check on Bronson, who sighed in relief then wobbled. Brufell went to grab for him, only to find himself falling too. Exhaustion coated his bones, his adrenalin depleted.

Bronson laid his hand on his heart. 'Are you okay?'

'No,' Brufell croaked. 'You?'

'I'm alive.'

Brufell could have sworn they were the sweetest words he'd ever heard.

Brufell woke in the dark, muscles sore and head heavy.

He groaned as he sat up, rubbing his eyes. They were in the middle of a wide tunnel, the roof high and jagged. The air was dank, thick, the smell something akin to mould.

The rock was moist, dripping with a substance he was careful not to touch.

The pixie was already awake, pacing the cavern's edge while itching its skin.

Brufell nudged Bronson awake, the dwarf cracking open a kohl-smudged eye. 'I've decided,' Bronson croaked, 'I don't like this adventure business.'

Brufell huffed a laugh. Whilst he and Bronson didn't agree on most things, they agreed on this. Brufell had liked leaving Parador as much as a needle in his eye. Even if it was only wraiths and what remained of the dead, it was still home, and after the war, he didn't get out much.

Brufell grasped Bronson's hand and helped him rise. Bronson nodded towards the pixie. 'What's wrong with it?'

Brufell frowned as the pixie paced, muttering something under its breath like a chant. From what Brufell could gather, it didn't like this place. Neither did he.

The stale air and sulphuric smell reminded him of death. 'We should go,' was all he replied.

Despite the pixie's twitchy behaviour, it followed them. They had no idea what direction to go, and opted for the route that took them furthest from the monster. Somehow, Brufell knew they were going down. It was the way the tunnels wound and twisted, the air becoming thicker.

After what felt like hours, Brufell noticed a fissure in the wall, a trickle of fresh running water carried in the rock. Brufell drank before offering some to Bronson. They followed the water and emerged into a wide cavern.

The pixie fell silent, its gnarled face twisted.

The cavern opened towards the night sky. Pockets were carved into the walls, tiny staircases and ramps all surrounding an illuminated pool of water. Brufell peeked into one of the crevasses, his lips thinning at what he saw inside. A bed, a chair—

They were homes.

He stepped back, the number of homes multiplying as he scanned the cave. The ceiling was dotted with the most glorious stalactites, each one wrapped with wreaths and flowers. Most had wilted, the petals decayed on the ground.

Brufell murmured, 'It's a pixie hovel.'

'More like a city.' Bronson reached out to a small wooden cottage, one of many hanging in waves across the ceiling, and frowned. 'What happened to them?'

The pixie was still. It stared at a broken crib by the water.

Bronson leaned down. 'Was this your home?'

The pixie nodded, balling his hands into fists as he curled into himself. Bronson hushed the pixie and picked it up with care.

'Let's keep moving,' Brufell said, eager to leave.

The next bend was worse.

Brufell paused and issued Bronson a warning before the young dwarf stumbled through. The pixie wailed. Brufell's face only paled.

Hundreds upon hundreds of pixies lay dead, their massacred, shrunken bodies twisted into black corpses. Brufell covered his nose at the reek of death. Somewhere deep inside Brufell, a crack opened. The flash of thousands of deceased bodies laid about the plains and mountains as they bled and fell and screamed. Men, trolls, fairies, pixies. It didn't matter.

More blood.

More deaths.

More funerals.

He navigated the bodies with care, helping Bronson when he faltered. Eventually, the smell of fresh air wafted in, a cave mouth opening into a lush forest.

Daylight had begun to wash over the trees, but they couldn't move yet.

Without a word, Brufell headed towards the trees, picking a bouquet of flowers from the earth. Bronson followed, the three of them sending their own prayers to the Godmother before laying them by the cave.

What was done, was done. For now, the best they could do was remember.

XV

The Prince and the Magic Bean

Maelstrom's smog and dirty streets held a deep stench, filled with poverty and urine. Hansel tried to breathe through his mouth.

He ran his fingers through his dirty hair. He'd need to get it cut, along with the fuzz that had begun to grow along his jawline.

Eveline had gone off to find them an inn, mumbling something about needing a bath. He was to meet her in an hour by the statue of the King, leaving him time to wander the streets. Porchid's tiny hands clasped the top of his shoulder, her head twitching back and forth to keep up with the scuffle of people.

They'd arrived early this morning, when the stalls were setting up. Spring was here, and with it, tourists. Some would leave, of course, travelling towards the coast or to visit family in the smaller villages, but with the rumours of death creeping across the land, more were keen to celebrate and cluster in groups.

Hansel stopped at a vendor and looked down at the array of axes. He curiously picked up a heavily decorated one.

'That's a ceremonial design,' said a man behind the shop's curtain. His grey eyes met Hansel's and looked him up and down.

Hansel assessed the axe closely, noticing engravings of gold with false set jewellery inserted into its hilt. Writing curved up the side, quoting the farewell salute that was given at someone's passing.

Once upon a time you felt life's embrace, may the ever after hold you close.

He shivered. He'd remembered whispering those words over a small makeshift grave, covered with bright daisies from his mother's garden.

Hansel placed it back on the table, a polite smile forming on his lips. 'It's a bit—'

'Ugly?' The man chuckled. 'Rich folk who have no use for an actual axe love them, and they fetch a pretty penny. For you, I'd suggest something up the back here.'

He nodded towards the back of the stall, where an array of weapons was spread out. He had everything from spears to maces; swords and crossbows. Hansel's eyes lingered on a longer axe, the bit a dark silver and its handle wrapped in tight, dark, red leather.

'Ah, good choice,' the man said, pulling it from its hook. 'This one is sturdy and sharp. Its point was carved by a witch who sought revenge from the wood nymphs. It can pierce anything, and even though it looks heavy, it's light as a feather.' He held it towards Hansel. 'Try it out.'

Hansel hadn't been looking to buy a new axe. His current one was not yet old, but he'd been lazy with cleaning it. Eveline had sharpened it for him the other day, leaving it perfectly capable, but bland.

Yet, there was something about the weapon that allured him. It was indeed light, and the balance was exceptional. Its grip was sturdy and comfortable as if it had been made for his very hands. He flipped it with cool ease.

Porchid clapped in excitement, and he smiled. Hansel turned back to the man. 'How much?'

'How long is a piece of thread?' the man said. 'That weapon is worth a king's ransom.'

Hansel frowned.

He wasn't much for bargaining, but even he knew when to be wary of price. The man's smile twitched, a splotch appearing on his neck. Before Hansel could reply, the back curtain fluttered. A boy ran out, frantic as he pulled on his father's shirt.

'What is it?' the man hissed, his eyes only darting to Hansel for a second before turning to the boy.

'It's the cow,' the little boy puffed, 'she's leaking milk all over the floor and nothing I do will help.'

The boy's head was flushed pink, his eyes wide and apologetic.

The man leaned down, his whisper harsh as he pointed at Hansel. He straightened his jacket before speaking. 'I apologise, I must tend to this … problem.' He moved swiftly into the back.

The boy's round face twisted into panic as he turned towards Hansel.

Hansel tapped his foot. 'How much for this axe?'

The boy swallowed, eyeing the curtain before he took in the axe. 'I ain't allowed to make sales, not after I royally botched the other one.'

Hansel raised his brow. 'How did you manage that?'

The boy cautiously looked behind him, and in a hushed tone said, 'I sold our best cow for a couple of magic beans. I've never had a lashing so bad. Oh, Papa was so mad, and now I ain't to make any more sales. I just got to keep you busy until he can come out and sell you that.'

'Well,' Hansel said, 'I don't have magic beans, but I do have coins, which I believe should suffice.'

The boy looked back towards the curtain again, worry creasing his young brow.

'So how much?' Hansel asked again, waiting.

'Umm,' the boy said, his cheeks burning pink again.

Hansel huffed a laugh as he brought out a bag of coins and dropped six gold medallions onto the table. It wasn't a king's ransom as the salesman had wanted, but it was more than what you'd pay for a mere axe.

The boy's eyes widened before he scooped them up and bowed quickly. Hansel shook his head, holding in a laugh as Porchid waved goodbye and the boy bashfully waved back.

When Hansel turned around to look one last time, he caught the father gripping the boy by the ear and rushing him through the curtain. He felt guilty for using the boy like that, but it was also an opportunity he couldn't miss.

He slipped the axe into his straps, the weight welcome. The clock in the square chimed just as Eveline ducked through the crowd and made her way towards them.

Eveline had spent the last hour securing accommodation and avoiding all the hulking guards swarming the marketplace. She'd hidden in the shadows and stayed out of sight, gathering information on the best taverns in town and news on the missing prince.

She felt oddly alone without Porchid on her shoulder, and the crowd had closed in on her more violently than she was used to. She spotted them before they spotted her, and a jolt of jealousy rang through her as she noticed the casual demeanour between the two of them.

People moved carefully around Hansel, his size taking space in the crowds. Eveline scowled as a group of girls giggled nearby, bashfully smiling his way.

Hansel, of course, was oblivious. His sole focus was on the fairy, engaging in whatever twinkling nonsense she was spouting, her sharp teeth on display. Eveline shook her head. Even with his history, he was like a caramel candy: soft on the inside, but all bull on the outside.

Her stomach grumbled as she dipped under the arm of a man who was lifting a small child onto his shoulder. The air was heavy with human life, so different to the barren paths she was used to.

Approaching them both, she noticed the new addition to Hansel's back – a large axe peered over his shoulder, its red leather and silver design beautiful. Anyone with a history of weapons could see it had been made with precision and thought.

Hansel noticed her stare and smiled meekly, as if embarrassed by his purchase. 'I couldn't resist.'

Eveline scoffed, but it was weak. She beckoned them to follow. Beggars stood at the corner, grasping for a scrap of food or coin. Eveline dropped some of their leftover bread into a small boy's hands. He bowed, scattering off around the corner to no doubt feed his friends too. She knew Hansel had noticed, but he didn't say as a word as they rounded the corner toward the One-Eyed Raven.

The tavern's door was a low dip, even for her. Considering the condition of the town itself, the One-Eyed Raven was practically gleaming. Its smoky hues of mood lighting and its velvet carpet had none of the wear and tear of the Skinny Piglet. The tables gleamed a smooth black, carved from a marble surface, and the fireplace was neat and rotund, with the bar in a similar structure.

Hansel dipped behind her, struggling as normal to fit through most doors. The tavern was crowded, but not like outside, and its music was a pleasant, smooth harmony. People chattered about in booths.

Eveline made her way to the barmaid to collect the keys to the room. At this time of year, with the markets and spring celebrations, they'd only had one room left.

Eveline took the keys with a grumble, clamoured up the stairs and took in the room's view. It wasn't large by any means, but nor was it small. It had a double bed with a table for dining and a lounge suite near the fireplace. The windows were round, matching the décor below, providing a view of the street.

She pulled the curtains closed, hating the way her chest constricted at the lone bed.

Hansel laid down his pack, the sound jolting her from her thoughts.

'I'll take the lounge,' he said, making his way over to the other side of the room.

Eveline could offer him the bed; she could take the lounge. Not for the sake of manners, but because she would sleep comfortably on either. It was a benefit to being short. Hansel would barely fit on either, but she was a selfish person, too used to being alone. Too used to not having to consider others.

She did consider him, though, just for a moment. Yet, the words never came.

Dropping her things, Eveline stripped off her knives and headed straight for the washroom, where she knew bliss awaited her.

'Do you think she'll ever speak to me like a normal person again?' Hansel asked Porchid as Eveline washed in the adjoining room. 'Or do you think I'll get the stoic, silent treatment for the next several lifetimes?'

Porchid's glow of orange and gold humour told him she thought the latter.

Eveline hadn't been angry anymore – not since their truth for a truth – but she also hadn't been friendly, either. Not like she'd once been after he'd chipped at those cold walls of hers. She'd been more indifferent, and that, he decided, was far worse.

Gretel had done the same when they'd been at odds. She was cold when upset, lively when happy, and a complete and utter goblin when she lacked enough sleep. He smiled at the memory, almost jolting when there was a knock on the door.

Hansel thanked the barmaid for dinner and laid the platter on the table, dividing up the plants for Porchid. The fairy took one sniff at the butter-laced fruit before squinting in disgust.

Hansel shrugged at her apologetically before finding an apple dug deep into his pack for her. She glowed, hugging the fruit with thanks. Hansel chuckled, but it died as Eveline exited the bathroom, her long hair dripping water as she padded over to the food.

'There's too much butter,' she stated, taking a bite.

'There's no such thing as too much butter,' he replied.

She rolled her eyes. 'The pork is good, at least,' she said, closely inspecting her food.

The clock on the wall ticked loudly, conveniently letting them know about every second that felt like an hour. Eveline chewed and Porchid crunched until something inside Hansel snapped.

'Stop it.' His fork clattered to the table, and he flinched at the sound. It had come out harsher than intended. 'Please, just end this.'

Eveline sat there, startled, with Porchid chewing unceremoniously on her crunchy apple. Eveline tilted her head in that catlike way of hers before placing down her fork.

'Stop pretending you don't care,' Hansel said. 'Stop the niceties and the blank stares and the shrugs. I know you're mad and I know you haven't forgiven me, but I'd rather you yell at me and throw knives at my head than continue being whatever this is.'

He ran his fingers through his hair in frustration, and she smiled that cheeky smile with the hidden joke behind it. He hadn't seen it in weeks, and his heart jumped at its return.

'I have forgiven you,' she said. 'I understand what you had to do, but I'm allowed to be angry at myself, too.'

Hansel paused. 'Why would you be angry with yourself?'

She shrugged. 'For jumping to conclusions. For not letting you speak earlier. I know I can hold things in, and I get lost in it sometimes. Like everybody else, I'm not perfect, and you can be so calm that I forget my actions affect you just as much as yours do to me.'

It was the first time she'd openly admitted his effect on her, and his heart beat a little faster. 'Can we start fresh?' he asked.

Eveline stood up and dusted off her pants before reaching out her hand. 'I'm Eveline Rafter, but I prefer Eve.'

He shook her hand. 'Eve?'

'You have a problem with Eve?'

'No, no,' he said. 'I just never knew.'

'You never asked.'

He choked back a laugh. 'Fair. I'm Hansel.'

She snorted, and moved back towards her chair. 'Tell me about your day, *Hansel.*'

Eve's heart was lighter. It wasn't that anything had changed much, just that it was easier with Hansel, as if she'd taken a lung full of air after drowning.

She felt better than she had in days. She was clean, her hair braided down her back with extra care. She'd been able to take her time for once, the pillows lulling her into a rare deep sleep.

She was invigorated. Almost *hopeful.*

Eve waited in the square as Hansel went to find breakfast. The fountain at her back left a cool spray on her skin, Porchid twinkling beside her in glee. The markets were already busy, despite the early morning. The air smelt of freshly baked bread and newly cut flowers. Eve took the time to just enjoy the moment.

Hansel made his way through the crowd, two bags of berry rolls in his arms. He waved to the little boy who was sweeping the front of the axe stall, the boy waving back, before stopping in front Eve.

'Made a new friend?' Eve asked, grabbing one of the rolls he'd bought.

'He's the boy that sold me the axe yesterday.'

Eve turned, watching the boy hold the broom in front of him. 'Where are his parents?'

Hansel took a bite. 'His dad clipped him yesterday for making the sale. For his sake, I hope the father's busy.'

'And his mother?' she asked.

Hansel shrugged. 'She wasn't there.'

Eve thought back to her own mother, lying sick in her cot as her father pulled together herbs for her medicine. She could smell the spices and unending piles of plants.

'We should go,' Hansel said, pulling her back to the present.

Eve nodded.

The cobblestones made walking difficult, but they trekked through the busy streets. When they finally made it to the palace, they greeted the guards, who led them to a long line of visitors. It was tax time, and lucky for them they'd managed to squeeze onto the list with some quick thinking.

The castle was made of pale stone with a bronzed tile ceiling, pillars extending up to the sky. Shadows stretched across the ground as they waited, the line of people reaching from the bronzed arch entryway into the depths of the city.

The sun's heat pelted onto their skin, the scent of sweaty bodies permeating the air.

Eve moved her toes to keep the blood flowing to her feet, her boredom ripe. Gone was the good mood from this morning, replaced with irritation.

Porchid looked like she was about to turn into a puddle. Eve wiped the sweat off her brow. 'Why is it I always find myself wrapped in one stench or another?'

'The doors are still shut. They were due to open an hour ago,' Hansel complained.

'What's the royal family like?' Eve asked, distracting herself from the burning sun.

Hansel turned his gaze to her, causing her stomach to flip on itself. 'They are interesting.'

'Go on,' Eve enquired.

'The King never married,' Hansel said. 'With twelve sons – Florian being the youngest. Their kingdom holds a large treasure trove and a substantial army. I know Myrenna has traded with them for several years, keeping them on Bellatorre's good side.'

'Get to the good stuff,' she interjected.

Hansel laughed. 'He's had four engagements. Each one ended before the wedding day due to illness or death. Over the years, Myrenna has visited, and there's even been rumours the King plans to wed her.'

'Do you think he killed them?'

Hansel shrugged. 'Maybe.'

Eve snorted. 'Anyone who tries to kill the Evil Queen would be an idiot. Actually, anyone who marries the Evil Queen would be—'

'Hush,' Hansel said, eyeing the nearest guard. 'She's an ally here, remember?'

Eve crossed her arms. 'Any other rumours I should know about?'

Hansel frowned. 'Just one I heard yesterday. The King's eldest son has been in charge since the King went missing a few weeks ago.'

She spun towards him. 'What would Myrenna want from a kingdom missing their King? She has magic.'

'She's building an army, Eve. A big one at that. Why do you think the rebellion is so on-edge?'

'Can she not just *poof* it?' she said, throwing her hands in front of her.

Hansel smirked. 'No. She can't just *poof* an army. Even Myrenna has her limits.'

Eve furrowed her brow. 'Hearts, you mean.'

'Exactly,' Hansel nodded.

When the trumpets blared, Eve's patience was at an all-time low, but she sighed with relief. For now, the line would move, and there seemed to be an end to the agonising heat of the sun.

They finally made it the foyer, its interior a white so bright she'd had to blink. The line snaked forward. Everyone went in with their shoulders high but left with feet dragging. She'd tried to peer through the door when it opened for the people in front, but only managed to glimpse red carpet and a hall that extended far beyond what she could see.

When they reached the doors, the guards took their weapons. They were checked thoroughly, and then the doors opened again.

Eve followed the blood-red carpet down the longest room she'd ever seen. Its ceiling was not as high as expected, but it held small windows with glimpses of the sky at intervals, leaving little squares of light in a neat row along the carpet. White pillars stood on either side, and what she could assume was the throne was a great distance ahead. No wonder they'd waited so long.

Hansel kept pace beside her, his presence a balm.

The throne itself was plain – stone, like the rest of the city – and perched with his legs upon the armrest was the eldest prince of Carnell. He smacked his lips together as sauce from the pork he was eating dribbled down the side of his mouth.

At the introductory announcement, he rolled his eyes as if he wished he was doing anything else, and peered down at them in disdain.

All three of them bowed.

'I've never seen a fairy so attached to a human before,' the prince said, focusing on Porchid. 'And a Riverbell fairy, too. Her wings would catch a lovely price.'

Eve stilled at the comment, but her hands twitched by her side for her blades. Porchid shone a pale white but remained silent.

The Prince smiled, but it was not one of friendliness. 'I dare say they'd look dashing with my lapels for the summer ball in Bellatorre in a few weeks. It would fill my brothers with envy.'

Picking up another slice of meat, he dipped back his head and stuffed it into his mouth.

Porchid slipped to hide behind Eve's back.

Eve blew out a breath and stepped forward. 'Your Majesty, we—'

The Prince held up his hand to silence her. 'You are clearly not from here if you dare speak first. Here we hold traditions, and a woman does not address royalty unless she is addressed first, or unless she is royalty.'

Eve snapped her mouth shut, anger coiling in her gut. She wanted to tell him exactly what she thought about *tradition*; if the guards hadn't taken her weapons, Eve would have surely thrown one into his face after that comment.

Chewing on his meat, the Prince puffed out his chest and looked to Hansel, who bowed politely – though Eve could see the tension in his shoulders.

'Your royal highness,' said Hansel, 'we are here to seek your wisdom and guidance in a royal matter concerning your brother, Prince Florian.'

The Prince laughed, his rotund belly wobbling with him. 'What royal business would a Riverbell fairy, a huntsman, and a *woman* be doing looking for Florian?' He waved hand in Eve's direction. 'I suppose she has a crush on him. Women always want a prince.' He eyed her up and down, the gaze bringing prickles to her skin. 'She could be Florian's type, I suppose. She's pretty enough.'

Eve sneered, a huff of anger escaping her nostrils. Hansel smoothly stepped forward, partially blocking her from view. *This* was not what she had planned on doing with her precious time. She hadn't come here to be insulted nor sold off into marriage to a prince she'd never met. She was the Seeker. A warrior.

Eve took hold of Hansel's elbow and squeezed, *tight*. Hansel shot her a look of warning, a plea in his eyes. It was the only thing holding her back from diving onto the Prince and snapping his thick neck.

'We know he's been missing for a time,' Hansel started. 'Eve here has a gift of retrieving lost things, and with your assistance we may be able to bring him home. I'm sure your family must be concerned for his safety.'

The Prince chortled and sat up straight in his chair. 'Concerned for Florian's safety? Florian doesn't do anything *remotely* dangerous, and the one time he does he goes missing. He's last in line. The boy is useless.'

Eve's brows knitted together. 'You don't want us to bring him home?'

The Prince scowled at her, showing his disgust, but didn't chastise her again. 'Florian is a disgrace.' He leaned forward, gravy still on his chin. 'He's an embarrassment and a weakling. We couldn't care less if he returned, and if he did, I'd hope it was only his head on a platter.'

Eve couldn't believe what he was saying. How could someone be so callous about their younger brother? She had always craved a sibling, and her father had been her world. She knew Hansel felt the same about Gretel and considered that perhaps she'd lucked out when it had come to the family she'd had. Even if they were gone.

'You'd be better off finding my father,' the Prince said. 'Last I heard, Florian was gallivanting out near the farmlands due north. Something about a boy and magic beans and giants.'

Hansel bowed. 'Thank you for your time.'

Before they could leave, the Prince spoke again. 'If you truly wish to serve the kingdom, then bring me those pretty little wings off that fairy you carry.'

Eve froze. The tether she carefully held thinned further.

Eve ground her teeth.

Hansel turned back towards the Prince. 'Your highness, with utmost respect, she is our friend and dear companion. We could not do something to a creature so loyal to us.'

'Then you are wasting my time,' the Prince said, and waved them out.

Eve couldn't remember exiting the room, nor walking through the gates. She was coiled like an asp, about to lunge and spit poison. She had been insulted, disregarded, interrupted, and ignored. The only thing that had gotten her through that encounter was the vision of cutting the Prince into little pieces and feeding him his own flesh. Watch him smack his lips then.

Porchid had already once had her wings almost pilfered for the pursuit of fashion, and if Eve hadn't found her then the fairy would have been left to die by the edge of that creek.

How she'd gotten away, Eve never found out, but it was enough for her that anyone she saw wearing Riverbell wings received her muttered insults.

If only her gift had been curses.

'We need to find the boy from the axe stand,' Hansel said, keeping pace. 'The only magic beans I've ever heard in existence were from him.'

Eve huffed. 'Convenient they were in the same city as us.'

'Most likely thanks to your gift,' he replied.

They made their way to the marketplace, only to find the stall gone. Planks of wood and pieces of cloth lay in disarray, as if they'd left in a hurry.

'Well, hasn't today been mighty helpful,' Eve drawled. 'Now I remember why I hate this place.'

Hansel sifted through the rubble of what had been left behind and looked back at her. 'I think even the citizens hate this place,' he replied. 'They seem to be a miserable bunch.'

'Makes the Queen look like a jester in comparison.'

Hansel snorted.

Eve crossed her arms. 'Do you remember what the boy said, exactly?'

'He mentioned his father had banned him from making sales after he sold one of their cows for some magic beans. I convinced him otherwise and gave him a sum he couldn't refuse before his father came back. It was a quick transaction. The poor kid got clipped on the shoulder as I was walking.'

'So, he didn't mention where they were from or what the beans did?'

Hansel shook his head.

'Maybe his father hadn't believed they were magic?' Eve said, 'What do magic beans do, anyway? Grow giant peaches?'

Hansel chuckled. 'No, not giant peaches, more like stalks that reach the skies. They're a pathway of sorts for the kingdom of giants and dragons. A lot of kingdoms banned them a while back when the giants destroyed crops and the dragons burned the rest.'

'The Prince wasn't too happy after whatever it is that Florian did. Maybe Florian thought he could redeem himself somehow if he found the beans?'

'Maybe,' said Hansel, 'but anyone who deals with giants is asking for trouble.' Hansel paused. 'I guess I should lump us in that category, then, considering the way you're smiling right now?'

Eve's skin tingled, her gift flaring to life. 'Flora and Fauna mentioned giants when they did the spell.'

Hansel raised his brow. 'They did.'

'Then we know exactly where to go.'

Hansel groaned.

XVI

The Tales of an Old Dwarf

Malak carefully placed the narrow leaf on the small structure he'd built, completing a slide into the water's edge. He'd spent the long hours within the grotto killing time, either helping the dwarves or building structures for the fairies.

The youngest dwarf, Beetle, picked berries off the bushes by the trees, eating them as he went. His teeth were stained crimson, and the song he whistled was off key.

The tower of Malak's fairy structure stood roughly three pixies high, its peak held together with vines and twisted roots he'd found dead by the forest. The shamrock-green grass grew around its base, hiding the small steps he'd made from stone which reached to its roof. The slide twisted around its body like a snake and ended with its edge touching the water's gleaming surface.

Malak smiled and caught the glint of tiny hands peeking through the bush.

Butterfly fairies weren't like Riverbell fairies. Whilst Porchid was all slim lines and coloured light, these fairies' bodies were plump, their skin a mix of silver and white. But it was their wings that held the true beauty. They spread wide behind them, a blur of patterns and swirls arrayed in a conjunction of colour and light. One magenta with hints of gold, another with teal lining, the loops and curves of violet twining in ribbons of colour.

Anywhere else they would stand bright and true, but here in the grotto they blended into the mushrooms of wine-red and golden tops, the trees with leaves of summery autumn, the moss that sparkled off the streaming sunlight.

The grotto was its own world, in a way, far from any other and untouched.

Malak only saw the fairies when they wanted to be seen, but as he settled into a routine, they'd become more trusting. One crept out from a boulder, then two, before a group of them studied his creation. Malak smiled in satisfaction.

It was strange, really, building this kind of trust with the fairies. He was a troll, after all. Trolls weren't known for sharing or building things for others. They were more of a brutal people, huddled up north with their traditions. It was precisely why he'd run away in the first place.

Troll's Keep hadn't been his home. The mountains hadn't been his home. Even this calm, beautiful place was not home.

Home was in the castle with his friends. With Hansel and Princess Snow.

He missed caring for the horses, and the way the afternoon light glistened over the gardens. He missed the way Snow would sneak a picnic, or how Hansel would train them both by the barracks.

Malak dipped his hairy toes into the water, letting it soak his feet, the crystal coffin nearby. The octopio bobbed. He gazed at his reflection, his harsh teeth and wide nose hideous.

Sighing, Malak followed an octopio as it glowed near the rocky bottom, illuminating the dark shadow of a cave. He leaned down, trying to get a closer look when Beetle shouted. 'Why couldn't I have gone?'

Malak twisted to find Bonyx by the casket, his cane clutched firmly in his hand. 'You're too young. You're needed here.'

'But I'm always left here,' Beetle replied. 'Always left behind.'

Bonyx lifted his hand. 'Not for long, my boy. You'll be grown soon enough, and you'll wish for your youth once more.'

Malak stared at the casket, hating that he hadn't been able to protect the Princess. When he closed his eyes, he could imagine the long lashes that brushed the tops of her cheeks, the way her lips burned red, the pale creamy skin. He could hear her laugh, the cackle when she'd ridden her horse too fast, the way she shrieked when she was tickled. Snow was beautiful. She'd always been beautiful.

It had been a burden and a relief when she'd befriended him in the castle. Outside of Hansel, she'd been the only one to acknowledge him, to ask about him, to check in.

It was easy to lose his heart to her. To feel a home.

Hansel, Snow, and him.

Malak would have spent a thousand lifetimes in the slavery of the crown if it meant standing next to them. So, he protected. He waited. He prayed.

'What good is youth when I can't do anything about it,' Beetle grumbled.

Bonyx peered down at the younger dwarf, wondering if he'd ever been this vigorous. Beetle had a light about him that couldn't be ignored, a sense of innocence and adventure. Bonyx was too old for those things now, too slow, too creaky.

The word 'old' didn't suit his soul. He preferred to think of himself as 'mature'.

He was a storyteller. A dwarf who'd spent his time in the world and watched. Some of his stories were his own concoctions, and some were taken from the mouths of villagers or spun by children. Some bore witches or dragons or dwarves, others held war or prophecies or monsters. Not all of them had a happy ever after, but not everything in life did.

Beetle kicked at the grass, a shine to his eyes that Bonyx hated bringing forth. The young dwarf missed the calamity of the Seven. It was quiet, but not the calming sort of quiet one found in reading or sitting. It was an uncomforting sort, the kind reserved for waiting or pacing or for unspoken words.

Bonyx couldn't recall if Beetle had ever been away from the others. He was so small himself, and next to Malak he practically looked like a pixie. Whereas Malak had built his structures, Beetle had played warrior. And Bonyx had napped. He needed his naps if he was to function properly. He was already tired, the sun hanging low as afternoon set in. Using his cane, he lowered himself against the crystal coffin and stretched out his legs. He felt a little better.

Stories were his lifeblood. A gift from a very, very old friend.

She who visited his dreams.

He knew of the woman Brufell had seen, for he'd seen her too. She'd been beautiful once. Young. Just as he had been. They'd never met, not in person, but over the course of Bonyx's life they'd become friends.

Bonyx had been lucky; blessed. She had gifted him with something magical: the ability to tell stories, to see things others could not.

The wonder of magic was that it lived in each cell of every living thing. It was neither good nor evil. It neither existed on its own or with other things. It was fluid and unique. Changed by every touch.

'How about a story, little one?' Bonyx asked, tapping the ground beside him.

Beetle grumbled something about silly stories but complied. When the young dwarf was settled, Bonyx looked at the troll. 'And you?'

Malak looked up from the water, eyes wary as he gazed at Bonyx then back to the coffin. 'She always liked stories.'

Bonyx nodded as if this were a universal truth, and cleared his throat. Tonight, he would share a tale from his companion in his dreams. One that had started this adventure by bringing together the misfits and heroes, and now more than ever the truth of sacrifice.

As Malak made himself comfortable and Beetle waited with bated breath, Bonyx began his tale. 'Tonight's story is called *The Father and the Sisters Grimm.*'

XVII
The Beanstalk and its Thorns

Eve's gift led them northwest towards Aurelia.

They'd passed the border this morning, Maelstrom far behind as they crossed through farmland.

Lightning broke through the darkened skies, thunder following in its wake. The people they came across became more estranged, and most carried pickaxes, swords, or homemade weapons. Some mentioned giants, and that the storm appeared several weeks ago but never dissipated.

One thing was clear, though: it stemmed from a town called Hasleholme.

Eve pondered whether it was a magic storm, though it held no colour like the one from her home. She peered at it as they walked, and almost stumbled when Hansel pointed towards the horizon. 'Hasleholme.'

A barricade surrounded the entire town, made of high, carved wood, spikes protruding from its top. Only two guards kept watch, their eyes narrowing as Eve and her companions approached. One was a stout man with a thick, copper moustache. He puffed his chest, his spear raised. 'What business de ye have 'ere?'

The other guard, a much younger version of the first, stepped forward as well. He wore a shirt that had once been white, the stains of dirt turning it brown. Sweat covered both men's armpits. 'What my brother means to say is, we haven't had visitors in weeks. What brings you to Hasleholme?'

The stout man grunted, neither agreeing nor disagreeing.

'We were sent here,' Hansel started.

'Of sorts,' Eve added, biting back a smile. It wasn't a lie, not when her gift had led them here.

'You must be the giant slayer,' the younger guard said. 'You've sure taken your time since the last one went up there.'

Eve paused, about to ask more, when Hansel jumped in. 'Yes, we heard you had a giant problem and came to assist, but there's a rumour your last one was unsuccessful?'

Eve hid her smirk. *What a little liar.*

Hansel had taken a gamble asking about the last slayer. If it was the Prince, they'd take any information they could get. Her gift was rarely wrong, but at this rate she couldn't tell if she was following the Prince's trail or the beans.

The stout man nodded and lowered his spear. 'We bin waiting for ya. Last one was too pretty. Knew he wasn't up for it.'

'He didn't seem like the type, ya know?' the brother said. 'But considering we'd never had an infestation like this before, we didn't know what a giant slayer looked like. You both look more the part, that's for sure, although I'm unsure how a fairy would be of assistance.'

Porchid bristled.

'I suppose you're looking for a place to crash for the night?'

'That would be very kind,' Hansel replied.

The younger man waved them through the gates. 'Rumour is magic beans were sold around here to a boy, who planted them by old man Crocker's fields. Just that way,' the guard said, pointing over the curve of a hill.

Dark clouds twisted into one another, and the hot, moist wind was sucked into the growing vortex.

'Enormous stalk grew on the poor bloke's farm, and we've had giants for weeks attempting to come down it. Haven't seen any dragons yet, thank the cauldron. But no matter what we do, we can't cut it or kill it. It's impenetrable. So, you lot are welcome, as long as you get it down.'

The man with the moustache shook his head. 'Bin a downright mess.'

Eve peered into the distance, attempting to see the vine, but it was too dark.

'Is all ye got those small knives, miss?' he asked, keeping stride with Eve, 'Giants be needing a bigger weapon than that.'

'I assure you, mister …?'

'Pickles,' he said, puffing up his chest again.

'I assure you, Mister Pickles, that these are more than enough.'

His whiskers crumpled as he scoffed at her, but she chose to ignore him. She had more weapons on her than he knew. The smooth pebble in her pocket gave her strength, and if all else failed, she had the gift from Flora and Fauna.

'Last fellow went with only his wits, and we thought he was crazy,' the guard in front of Hansel said. 'He was dressed like a peacock and his laugh was too forced. Looked more like a Prince than a giant slayer.' He turned. 'I'm Archie, by the way.' He shook Eve's hand, grip firm.

The town was more of a meeting place, sparce with only three buildings as its central hub. A general store, a post office, and an inn. The main road was narrow, linking to cottages that spread off in no apparent direction.

'The wall was built as a precaution after a mishap with a giant a few weeks ago,' Archie said. 'The town hall and school got the worst of it. Now all that's left is debris.'

Archie explained that after the last slayer came to town, he'd caused such a stir and raised the hopes of everyone. That was until the first day passed, then the next, until weeks had gone.

'We've tried to cut and burn the vine,' Archie continued, 'but it's impenetrable. Its hide is covered with thorns, and no matter what blade is used we can't break its skin.' He shook his head. 'It's as big as a field. Old man Crocker is beside himself and with the missing villagers it's only got worse.'

As they walked towards the tavern, Eve's skin tingled. She peered into the storm-lit sky, wondering if it was her nerves or gift pulling her at the seams. When it was this strong, it was difficult to tell.

One thing she did know was that the Prince was up there.

Whether he was alive or not was another story.

Eve paused at the crest of the hill in the early light, assessing the vines structure. Archie hadn't been kidding when he'd mentioned its size.

The vine wasn't one whole, but hundreds of black tendrils wrapping around themselves to create a thick, giant structure that reached into the clouds. The thorns were just as big, their points so sharp that even the lightest touch would slash through the skin like parchment.

Hansel scoped out the area, wandering around the trunk with a focus she'd only ever seen in training. 'It won't be easy to climb.'

Eve shuddered at the thought. The height almost made her crawl into a ball. She wandered around the trunk of the vine and found no way to penetrate it.

There were gaps in places, tiny holes that Porchid managed to squeeze through before zipping back out. Eve watched with a pale face. The vine seemed taller with every minute.

She could do this. Right?

But the words were weak. She swallowed down the bite of terror and focused on the fairy. Porchid lit up the centre, revealing it to be hollowed-out. The issue was getting inside.

Eve's fingers twitched, the stone growing warm in her pocket. She hissed as it burned her side and pulled it out. A glow flickered from within.

'What the—'

It vibrated, a pulse thrumming in her palm, and the vine responded. Eve took a hesitant step back, a thorn barely scraping her arm, the vine shifting until a doorway appeared.

Magic will be the death of me.

Eve stepped through the opening, with Porchid close behind. Hansel followed her lead, a whimper escaping Archie's lips as the vines closed behind them.

Eve finally dared to look up. They stood in what resembled the eye of a tornado. Hansel squeezed her shoulder in that reassuring way of his, the warmth of his hand far more soothing than she cared to admit. 'My gift is going crazy,' she whispered. 'Prince Florian is here somewhere, but I don't know how far.'

Archie blinked and lowered his sword. 'Prince Florian?'

Eve nodded. 'Yes, your giant slayer and the Prince are one and the same.'

'But he—'

'Better not ask too many questions, Archie,' Hansel said, patting the man's back.

Little nuggets and branches protruded from the vine's walls in a makeshift stairwell following the outer circle of the structure towards the sky. The thorns were smaller here but just as deadly.

With a sharp intake of breath, Eve began to climb.

Hansel stayed close, as if he would catch her should she fall. Eve remembered the mountains, the way she had saved him from the fall and how he had saved her from a panic attack. The green on the vine was slashed with pink, and a tower flashed before her eyes. Her breath hitched for a moment.

'I'm with you,' Hansel said.

Those three words may as well have been poetry to her ears. She took another step. 'Don't let me fall.'

When he didn't reply, she turned around only to find Hansel softly smiling at her. 'Never.'

Eve stayed far enough from the thorns to not cause damage, but close enough to the walls to miss the drop off the edge. It was like walking on a tightrope, precarious, except this time there was no net to catch her.

For hours they climbed, their breaths becoming forced, not only from exertion but from the thinned air. Porchid twinkled encouragement. Eve didn't dare to check their progress. Archie remained silent as they climbed.

Eventually, after what felt like hours, something shifted. It was as if they'd crossed a barrier of some kind, leaving Eve's lungs fuller, her reflexes sharper. Perhaps they had crossed worlds. Magic might linger in everything but Eve had never pretended to understand it.

The moisture of the clouds shrouded the group's steps, and they took more caution as the branches became slick with condensation.

Eve stopped for a break and nodded towards Porchid, sending her to scout. Her legs burned, and her lungs were shot. Despite the cold, each of them dripped with sweat.

Porchid returned, uncertain, her nailbed chewed to the quick in her mouth. Her light flickered white before glowing blue. Eve knew those colours: fear and sadness.

Eve swallowed down her own terror. Ahead lay the coiling black surface of a portal.

'Ready?' Hansel asked.

She wasn't.

'Yes,' she replied instead.

XVIII
The Trolls and their Keep

Bronson used sign language to communicate with the pixie. He was rusty from lack of use, but it was enough to figure out the gist. Small words at first, then sentences. It reminded Bronson of music, the way the symbols could be read outside of the known language of speech. Music was beauty, and Bronson had always loved beautiful things.

Brufell didn't speak much after the cave – not that he spoke much anyway. But Bronson never liked the sound of silence. When he wasn't with the pixie, he whistled or combed his hair. His steps were a beat, distracting him from the ache in his legs.

They reached the end of the forest where grass met the towers of Troll's Keep, and Bronson stopped whistling.

A stone wall stretched further than the eye could see. Smoke billowed from mismatched houses. At the entrance stood two grand statues carved in granite. Bronson couldn't help but stare at them with wide eyes. As one might expect, they were trolls, but they were swathed in lush clothing. The granite statues were that of a female and a male standing with brute swords and spears, their knuckles encased in iron spikes.

Troll's Keep bowed to no one, despite their city being located between Ashenfell and Aurelia. They had their own ruling monarchy, their own political system, their own religion.

Brufell pulled forward his cape, tucked the pixie away, and traipsed down the hill, Bronson in tow. The guards at the bottom greeted them with curt nods as Bronson took out their paperwork. One of the trolls leered at their size, a booger stringing from his right nostril.

He jumped when the other shouted, 'Open the gates!'

Brufell huffed something under his breath as he yanked Bronson forward, dragging him onto a dirt path that slowly turned to pavement. Mighty houses stood tall, with strong stone, and arched doorways. The streets were clean, with children playing games.

The trolls were a small but mighty race, believing in strength, loyalty, and companionship. They didn't interbreed. Their proud species ran true of troll blood.

That was until the war.

Bronson remembered the stories from Bonyx, the way the old dwarf compared trolls to dwarves in that respect. Even the strongest of the dwarf lines had shunned those who had mixed. Called it the filtered blood. A weak blood.

Lot of good that did when their king died.

Bronson caught his reflection in a shop window and smoothed down his hair, hating the way dirt crusted his fingers. He became distracted by something shining in the window. Trinkets of sorts, all made from the materials of the realm. There were jewels from the mines, silver from the north. The silks were from the east, made from an expert hand. The shape of what he supposed to be a petite troll mounted and fashioned in the windowsill.

Brufell called out, but when Bronson turned, his shoulder was bumped. A troll woman halted, her long eyelashes dark against her green skin. He jolted, expecting a yell, but she winked at him instead.

Bronson shuddered, then bolted for Brufell. Sure, Bronson missed females, but he missed the female dwarves from the mines before the war. The ones who lived in the deep canyons of the caves. They'd spoken in a smooth manner, words rolling off their tongues in seductive and naughty ways.

He smiled at the memory, and Brufell whacked his arm. 'You need to get your head checked.'

Bronson held back a laugh and followed Brufell with a skip in his step. He halted when he saw a cart shrouded in the skin of a large creature. The grill smelled of fresh meat, the smoke curling towards the sky. Bronson handed over a few coins before thrusting a leg of meat into Bronson's hands. Grease spilled on his fingers, the taste remnant of the Seven's cooking in the grotto.

It brought back fond memories, ones of him lounging by the water and humming tunes. Bonyx telling tales while Bryn invented something new.

Brufell grunted when he took a bite, but he didn't grumble which Bronson took as a good sign. They made their way through the crowded streets, the curved paths steering up the slant of a hill. Though Brufell wasn't one for talking, Bronson was positive he'd said something about having a contact in Troll's Keep, though he couldn't figure out who. The rest of the Seven could barely keep secrets, but the two oldest were silent. Both Brufell and Bonyx had been alive for the war, and any mention of that past turned them both into vaults.

It was exceedingly annoying in Bronson's eyes.

Brufell slowed when they turned into a quieter street, eventually halting before a red house trimmed with green. The thick, rimmed windows were covered in muck and grime from years of neglect.

Brufell paused at the door, his frown deepening.

Bronson counted to ten before he asked, 'Are we going to knock?'

'I'm still thinking about it,' Brufell grumbled.

Bronson peered over the old dwarf's shoulders. 'Will they be home?'

'Bo is always home.'

'Then what's the problem?'

Brufell scowled at the door. 'I haven't seen him in a long time.'

Was Brufell *nervous?*

The older dwarf's fingers tapped on his hilt, a twitch that was unfamiliar. Put him on a battlefield and he'd sever a man's head with ease; put him in front of an old friend and he apparently fell to pieces.

Bronson rolled his eyes and knocked thrice.

When there was no response, Bronson knocked again.

Brufell's brows knitted, a look that had been focused on Bronson on many occasions.

'Maybe we should—'

Brufell tilted the door handle. Oddly enough, it clicked open. The pixie was the first to move, flying inside without a backwards glance.

Bronson stepped over the entryway.

The hall smelt of mildew and mould. Its once ornate wallpaper was cracking and peeling. Bronson stopped to peer at the bizarre collections of items along the way. A sword mounted, a shelf with curious plants. He touched a statue of a troll before a clang echoed from deeper inside and made him jump. Brufell shoved past him, moving through the halls like this was a second home.

When they reached a room near the back, Brufell paused in the doorway and shook his head. Bronson peeked over his shoulder to find an old dwarf swinging a giant pot at the pixie's head.

Brufell grunted his hello. 'Still kicking, I see.'

The pot clanged to the floor and a wide grin spread over the old dwarf's face. 'Coming from the dwarf who looks like he was spat out after a bad meal.'

There was a pause, something Bronson couldn't quite decipher. Then both dwarves gripped each other in an embrace.

'You look old, Bo,' Brufell said.

Bo chuckled. 'So do you.'

Bronson sipped from his cup and cringed at the sour taste. Bo made moonshine. By the Godmother, it was potent.

Brufell and Bo had been playing catch up for hours now, and Bronson had long grown bored.

Why Bo had chosen to move to Troll's Keep baffled him. The trolls were ugly creatures. They praised strength over beauty, and to be honest, he didn't like how much they spat.

Bronson looked to the table, where the pixie prodded at a wanted poster for the Princess. His spindly fingers ran down Snow's face in curiosity before he twisted towards Bronson and made a sign with his hands.

Bronson smiled. 'I agree. She is beautiful.'

'Are we befriending pixies now?' Bo asked as he entered the room. 'Last I'd heard they were one of the biggest pests in the mountains.'

'Well, they won't be now,' Bronson replied, a hint of venom in his voice. He'd been thinking about the caverns for days. So many of them gone. Parents still clutching children in a desperate escape, leaving just their little companion on his own. It'd only been one colony, though. Surely the others had survived. Surely their new friend would have somewhere to go from here. Right?

The pixie flinched under his gaze, as if he knew exactly where Bronson's thoughts had roamed.

'I'm sorry for what happened to you.'

The pixie scrubbed its mouth and moved to the lounge where Brufell sat. Brufell moved his elbow to make room for him as he settled on the armrest.

Bo took a sip of his drink, keen eyes watching the whole interaction. He turned to Brufell. 'What exactly did you find?'

'Death,' Brufell replied.

'Their bodies were shrivelled and decayed,' Bronson clarified, 'as if the life and magic had been sucked right out of them.'

Brufell stifled a swallow of moonshine. 'It's part of why we've come. There are strange things happening. We hoped you'd heard something of it.'

Bo leaned back in his chair. 'Here I thought it was to visit an old friend.' When Brufell didn't reply, Bo sighed. 'I don't know much.'

Bronson's shoulders slumped. Had they trekked this whole way and faced those awful creatures for nothing?

'What I do know is that dark things are crawling,' Bo continued. 'There's been talk of the forest coming alive again. A troll gone here and there, rumblings in the night, and a dark space that sits above the trees. It moves sometimes. I don't know what it is, but it's not good for business.'

Something trickled in the back of Bronson's mind – a tale Bonyx had told one night.

'What does it look like?'

Bo frowned. 'It's a heavy fog, dark, but it moves. Not in the way you or I know how a fog moves, but sort of with an intention, as if directed. We saw it leave for the mountains the other night and then it was back the next day.'

A shiver ran up Bronson's spine. He turned to Brufell. 'Could it be the same thing?'

Brufell looked contemplative. 'I don't know. That same mist hasn't been in existence since the war.'

'But the pixie colony …' Bronson replied. 'They had similar symptoms to what the fog does, right?'

The pixie tapped Bronson's shoulders, eyes watery, and signed. Bronson translated. 'He says a black smoke entered their cave, one with teeth that smelt like fire. It ate everyone inside with a mere touch.' When neither of the elder dwarves responded he asked, 'What does it mean if the fog has returned?'

Bo shuffled on his seat. 'Nothing good.'

'It means,' Brufell said solemnly, 'death is coming.'

XIX

The Giants and the Piper

Damp mist coated Porchid's wings, weighing her down as she broke through the portal into a land of grey. It was as if a filter had been placed on her eyes, stilting the colours on the mismatched buildings and the junk on the ground.

Porchid flittered between the shadows and counted her breaths. Her coloured light was a beacon, so she had to tread carefully. There'd been no sign of life except for the roar from a great beast echoing through the darkness.

On occasion, she passed a giant, the floor rumbling with every step. She squeezed between key holes and windows, under floors, and through cracks.

Eventually, she landed upon a windowsill, where a boiling pot bubbled with the scent of cumin and paprika.

She could taste her own fear, the way it dried her tongue and whispered doubts. She had to remind herself to keep counting, that she was more than her wings – she was the saviour of a princess. Eve and Hansel would be waiting for her, relying on her. She couldn't let them down.

A sob broke through the sound of the boiling pot along with a smell that was uniquely human. Porchid's nose twitched with it. She worked her way through the crack of the window. Her steps were silent, her breath held as she peered around the edge of a flowerpot. The wilted leaves provided cover, but it didn't cease the tremble of her fingers or the way her heart felt like it was going to burst from her chest.

Porchid counted two giants and—

A house elf?

The creature shuffled about the room. His ears were sharp and pointed, his lanky limbs holding a broom too big. His knobbly knees buckled as he swept the floor, collecting the soot from the fireplace.

Elves were strange creatures: short, even by dwarven standards, and they certainly didn't dwell in the realm of giants. Porchid tilted her head as the elf huffed a sigh.

Flattening her wings, Porchid searched the room until she found a cage made of twisted wood. Inside sat a human, his face covered in blood and dirt, his golden hair tangled and matted. The sash he wore was torn, and one of his shoes was missing. From the expensive embroidery on his jacket, Porchid guessed it was the Prince.

Heavy footsteps echoed across the room. Porchid flitted back into hiding, wings squeezed in tight to avoid being seen.

A female giant hummed, the sound bringing goosebumps to her skin. The heat from the pot was stifling. A drop of sweat ran down the back of her neck.

One glance in her direction, and she'd be caught, squished like a bug.

Porchid flinched when the giant snapped at someone else in the room. 'Shut up.'

Porchid braved a look, finding a male giant grumbling nearby. The female had brown, weathered skin. Her elbows were pointy, and her collarbones were sharp. Skin sagged off her thin limbs, reminding Porchid of those farm birds she despised.

'Stay out of me way when I'm cooking,' the female giant said, sweeping the elf to the side when his broom got too close. There was a crack as the elf hit the fireplace. The giant cackled and began to cut a carrot.

Porchid waited for the elf to move. When he didn't, she shuffled on her feet. He could be harmed – or worse, dead. Holding back a twinkle of annoyance, Porchid waited for her chance and shot across the room as the giant's back was turned.

She ducked behind a bucket, the elf a stone's throw away. Before she could twinkle, the elf popped open a calculating eye.

Without a word, the elf propped himself up and dodged behind the bucket, his finger pointed at Porchid. 'Silly little fairy, I could see you from the fireplace.'

His skin held a greenish tinge, his wrinkles stained with grime. 'What are you doing here?'

She bit her lip, unsure of how to say it.

He raised his brow. 'Well?'

Porchid huffed, then spoke, her twinkle harsher than normal.

'I see,' he mused. Uncertainty crossed his face. 'Well, you best be saying goodbye to him. He's stuck in that cage. Your friends also better not be human, because supper is almost ready.'

Porchid wasn't exactly sure what that meant until the elf pointed towards the stove. The female giant had plucked a different cage from the shelf, an old human man shivering inside. The giant smacked her lips.

The human wailed as the giant dipped him into her boiling stew and began to turn the pot. Her humming drowned out his screams.

Bile crept up Porchid's throat, and the elf shook his head. 'Get out of here before you're seen.'

The elf returned to sweeping while Porchid shot towards the window. She was about to climb through the crack when her wings cramped. She squeaked, arse in the air when a fist smashed into frame.

'Stupid bugs,' a male voice grumbled.

Wide eyed, Porchid turned to find the male giant staring down at her. She trembled.

Forgetting to breathe, she flattened her wings and pushed, barely managing to get free. The giant bellowed out a curse, the sound echoing through the dark streets.

Porchid was already gone.

Eve stared at the portal for so long that her vision blurred. For all she knew, it could have been ten minutes or ten hours. How long had it been? How long should they wait?

Porchid was her best friend. Her confidant. And she was alone.

Eve clenched her fists, trying to expel some of her nervous energy. Hansel shuffled behind her, but she didn't dare look back. It was enough to know she sat in the sky, the vine the only thing holding them there. The thought made bile rise to her throat.

When the portal flashed, Eve jumped. Hansel gripped her arm before she could fall, his chest against her back. But for once, it wasn't his strong grip she focused on but the fairy who'd crashed into her chest.

The fairy was wild, her hands and voice too fast.

Eve frowned, trying to keep up but failing. 'Porchid, slow down.'

Porchid huffed, her skin glowing white. Something had spooked her.

'Tell us what happened,' Eve said gently.

Eve tried and failed to understand her twinkle when Hansel chimed in. 'Did you find the Prince?'

She nodded frantically.

'Is he alive?' Eve asked.

'What about the giants?' Archie piped in.

Porchid motioned with her hands, slower this time, as they asked her questions with yes-or-no answers. She gestured towards her mouth as if she was eating something and pointed at them all. Confused, Eve shook her head. Porchid tried to mime biting one of them and rubbed her tummy.

Eve frowned. 'They're eating the villagers?'

Porchid nodded.

'Ugh' Archie choked, his face ashen. 'I think I'm going to be sick.'

Eve went a bit green herself. 'What is it with everyone in the realm wanting to eat hearts, or lungs, or people? I feel like we're a food speciality.'

'We've always been a source of food for giants,' said Hansel.

'Doesn't make it any less disgusting.'

Hansel's scent of pine and wood surrounded Eve as he squatted beside her. 'What's the plan?'

If Eve was being honest, she hadn't really thought this far ahead. In fact, she never thought that far ahead. Most of the items she'd searched for in the past had been relatively easy to find. When she did get into a pickle, it was usually a human or a creature that succumbed to her knives' sharp edges and her quick aim.

Giants were a different breed altogether. Her twin knives would do nothing against their thick hides, and when they'd become the food source, stealth and swiftness would be their only ally.

Archie vomited over the side of the branch they were on, Porchid turning green at the sight. Eve wondered why he'd even come.

Hansel waited with focused eyes, his body coiled for a fight. His leathers strained against his tight muscles, and Eve tried not to stare as she thought of a plan.

Perhaps a distraction was the answer. And what better distraction than a creature who bloomed colour in a world of grey?

'Porchid,' Eve said, 'listen closely.'

Eve pulled at her cloak, thankful for the haze covering their tracks as they navigated the realm of giants. Hansel warmed her back and Porchid was wrapped in a dark cloth to hide her light.

Archie had remained behind to guard the entrance. He'd looked ready to be sick again and took little convincing as the three of them set off through the top of the vine.

To Eve's surprise, the giants' homes didn't look large or grand. More like a shamble of bits and bobs mixed to make a home. She didn't know if she pitied them or was impressed with the use of resources.

They paused when a roar echoed over the buildings. Orange flashed through the sky – the only speck of colour, coming from dragon fire.

Eve shivered. She'd never seen a dragon, though her father's tales had featured many. Some had been fierce, some greedy, some terrifying. But on occasion there would be a story where the dragon helped the hero. Eve wondered how many of the stories were true.

When they reached the house, the humming of a woman cascaded through the open window above. Eve wrinkled her nose at the scent of cumin and burning flesh. One look at Porchid confirmed they were in the right place.

Eve made her way around the edge of the house, managing to find an opening that reminded her of a mouse hole. She was careful to avoid the walls as she snuck inside and led them through the narrow passageway.

Thick cobwebs crossed the walls; most were easy to navigate except the few that required Eve's knives to cut a way through. Eve wasn't overly fond of spiders, but with the giants nearby she couldn't be picky with her fears. If all of them came down, she'd be unable to focus.

Light pierced one end of the entryway and they followed it, eventually coming out near the edge of a fireplace. Eve paused in the entryway and took in the home.

It was only one room, the inside just as jumbled as the outside. It held two large beds, parallel to each other against the far wall. In the centre, a long kitchen table was cluttered with an array of materials, but where her eyes veered was to the walls. Where you would normally find pictures or paint were shelves spread out haphazardly. Objects of all shapes and sizes lay strewn across their space, including pots of half dead plants.

And there, hidden near the centre, was a row of cages.

When Archie said the giants had taken liberty when venturing down, he hadn't been kidding. Eve counted six humans.

The voices of the giants were heavy, coming out in a deep rumble, as if something underground had been disturbed. Eve had to strain her ears to understand.

A large male giant was sitting on a makeshift metal stool by the centre table. It groaned under his weight.

'I ain't lyin', it was a fairy,' he said, his knife and fork at the ready. 'No bug glows like that.'

The pot over the fire spilled over, water hissing on the burning logs. Eve stepped back as the female giant walked over to check on it. 'We've spoken about your fanciful ideas, Bogart. Tell me why there'd be a fairy here, of all places.'

Hansel pulled Eve further back into the wall as the giant walked past. His hand was warm on her skin, burning through to her core.

The giant picked up the pot, kicking soot up in her wake. Eve wrinkled her nose, a sneeze crawling up her throat. Hansel clasped his hand over her mouth just as she sneezed.

Both of them froze in place.

But it was only the elf near the table that looked in their direction.

Eve's eyes watered.

Hansel stepped back as soon as it was clear. 'That was close,' he whispered.

Too close.

But Eve was distracted. She took a tentative step forward and leaned down, rubbing the soot between her fingers. Her lips curved as an idea formed.

She quickly collected a pile before stepping back into the shadows. Holding back another sneeze, Eve quickly smothered Porchid in the soot, dulling the colours of her light. Next, she wiped it over her face and neck. Hansel followed suit.

Before she finished, Hansel came closer and touched her wrist. She stilled. His smile was shy as he lifted a chunk of leftover soot in his hand.

Eve swallowed. His touch warmed her skin to the point of boiling. She licked her lips, then gave him a nod.

He was careful as he stroked her skin, ensuring she was concealed from head to foot. She usually hated being touched, especially when she was covered in so many scars. They were memories, battle wounds, but they also reminded her of darker times. Times when she'd been weak or trapped or alone.

Hansel's touch wasn't soft, but neither was it hard. His calloused hands were strong and brought goosebumps to her skin.

Hansel smiled softly when he was done and focused back on the giants. Eve tried to get her head back in the game, but it was difficult when the touch of his hands still lingered on her skin.

Flecks of ash fell from Porchid's wings. It wasn't ideal, but it would have to do.

The giant woman placed the slosh of soup on the table, and Bogart slurped it with glee. Eve held back a shiver as the reminder of what he was eating crawled over her.

'First, the so-called vine over in the south, you claim, and now a fairy? What has gotten into you?' the female giant chided. 'They haven't existed in lifetimes, Bogart. Wherever do you get these ideas?'

Bogart focused on his dinner like a scolded child, almost sulking. The female lifted bones from her spoon with her cracked, yellow nails. She sucked at the bones with the same vigour as the Prince in Carnell had on his throne.

She smacked her lips. 'I'd almost believe you because of the humans. I don't know how you found them, but you did.'

Whimpers and the sound of someone vomiting rose from the cage on the high shelf. The giants ignored them.

Eve ushered Porchid forward, the fairy taking deep breaths. When the fairy was ready, she zipped through the house with stealth, using the clutter to hide her from unwanted eyes. When she reached the house elf, Eve blew out the breath she'd been holding.

He was their ticket to freedom, whether he knew it or not.

The elf was currently sitting on a shelf of ingredients. Tiny ropes lay about, and he used them to climb and shuffle around the space. He was placing the lid on the pepper jar when Porchid caught his eye, and in a blink he'd disappeared with her behind the jar.

Eve fingered the cool stone in her pocket. She turned when she felt Hansel's gaze, her cheeks flaming.

A large clock chimed six times as Porchid slid from behind the jar. The elf reappeared beside the giants as if he'd never been gone and wiped a spot on the table. Eve reached out to grab Porchid just as she shot towards them and held her.

Bogart looked towards the upturned soot and squinted. 'Myrtle? Is there a winda open?'

Myrtle rolled her eyes. 'Honestly, Bogart, does it matter?' The skin on her arms wobbled as she plucked a bone from her tooth and tossed it onto the floor.

The elf collected and swept the remains into a large garbage bag. His face was placid, undeterred. Eve wondered how he could stand it. Elves had a history of falling into slavery. Most of the time it passed through lineage, and unless an object of true ownership was returned to them, they were doomed to serve whoever held their counterpart.

The elf made his way to the door to take out the trash. Hansel and Eve followed him outside.

The elf was already waiting by a large rubbish bin as they arrived. Hands on hips, he scowled at Porchid, who was perched on Eve's shoulder. 'Stupid little fairy. You may as well have brought them on a platter. The masters would have adored that.'

Now the elf was closer, Eve could see the lines on his face. His greenish-grey skin and knobbly knees told her he was old, but there was nothing weak about him. His eyes were cunning, his body nimbler than he looked.

'We need your help,' she said, leaving no room for argument in her tone.

'You definitely need help. But I'm no witch healer and have no training in brain trauma. Are you crazy?' he hissed. 'I don't have time for this.'

Eve was about to tell him he had plenty of time to place a stick up his arse when Hansel stepped forward. 'If you help us, we can help you. Don't you want freedom?'

The elf scoffed with half a laugh. 'I've been here for fifty-odd years, I know every nook and cranny of this house. Don't you think if I could have set myself free, I would have done so by now?' He lifted his arms in exasperation. 'Do you lot have a death wish?'

Eve met Hansel's eyes and an idea stirred. 'Is it true that to free an elf, an item of personal value is the price of freedom?'

The elf looked at her sceptically, then nodded. 'Yes, but my flute has been hidden for years. If it was anywhere in this house, I would have found it by now.'

Eve smiled crookedly, placing her hands on her hips. 'What if I told you I could find your flute?'

'I'd say you're insane. But I'm listening.'

'Finding things is my speciality. A gift.'

His eyes narrowed. 'Like magic?'

When she gave him a sharp nod, he eyed her over, assessing her like one would a fine cow. 'You find my flute, and I'll help you do whatever you ask.'

'So, the cost of their freedom is simply the cost of yours?' Hansel asked.

'Not bright, is he?' the elf asked.

Eve reached out her hand. 'Mr Elf, we have a deal. I'll find your flute if you help us break out our friends.'

He remained sceptical but grabbed her hand in a firm shake anyway. 'It's Pip,' he said. 'The name's Pip.'

They met later when the giants had fallen asleep.

The moon lay hidden behind the grey mists, and the temperature had dropped by several degrees. Eve's arms were dotted with goosebumps as she hugged herself, trying to keep in any warmth she could. It wasn't just the temperature of this place that left her cold but the feeling of it. Between the heavy silence and the dragon roars, she was on edge.

'Why are they so important, anyway?' Pip asked. 'Are they worth risking giants?'

A grumble reverberated through the mists, and they all looked towards the mountains with the sleeping dragons.

'Let's just say we have no other choice,' Eve replied, trying to remind herself of the medallions she'd receive once this was all over.

'You always have a choice,' he grumbled. 'My choice would be to not be a slave, so here I am, risking my skin with the first free humans I've seen in five decades.'

She looked at his leathery skin, then into his dark eyes. What had he gone through, to end up here with giants, sweeping the dust and soot and bones of their victims?

'Tell us what you know about the cages,' she said.

The elf pulled out a pipe and began to fill it with freshly cut leaves. His pouch was brown leather, engraved with the pointed ears of the elves and a flute.

'Is that the flute?' Hansel asked before Eve could.

He pulled out a match. 'You lot have a lot of questions. Didn't do your homework before you came here, did you?'

The pipe lit in a small, dull flame, and smoke swirled around them as he puffed on its stem. 'The giants have been here for millennia, and a few decades ago magic beans were declared redundant by the royalty across the entire realm. After the wars, the giants weren't needed anymore, and instead of being a military asset, they became a pest. Crops grew thin, and food was scarce enough as it is. They have tempers, you see, and when they get hungry, or don't get something they want, they go … rogue.

'When the King banished them to above, it was a land of useless things. Sort of like a massive garbage dump. With the giants banished, the land below locked out all exits with the beans.'

He took another puff and paused before he continued. 'Back in my youth, I was … let's say, ambitious. I had a skill with the flute, you see, and with that flute I could call upon anyone I wished. Sort of like a trance. Adults were a bit tricky, but children were easy.'

Eve squirmed.

'I worked for a man who was known as the Dream Weaver, and when I would call upon the children, he could weave their dreams.'

The Dream Weaver was also known as Rumpelstiltskin.

Eve held back her shiver at the memory of the other creature stroking his spindle.

Pip continued. 'Children were best – their imagination is limitless. I was rolling in coin, there was no challenge I wouldn't undertake. But my pride grew, and so did my resolute belief in my capabilities. I moved up from children and went out on my own. First, adult humans, then the fairies, then the mermaids, and so on. When I'd perfected all species, I found myself curious about giants.'

'And you called us crazy?' Hansel murmured. 'Everybody knows giants are dangerous.'

'Then why did you come, smartarse?' Pip snapped.

'What happened next?' Eve asked, her patience thin.

'I happened on some magic beans, and I scaled the vine to conquer a giant.' he replied, 'When I stumbled upon Bogart, he was playing in the garden. He was a child then, and merely mistook me for a toy. I dodged him for a time and played him different tunes, some high and some low to ascertain what note would do the trick, but I failed.

'When Bogart finally found me intolerable, he became enraged and flung me halfway across the garden. By the time I'd turned around, Bogart had my flute in his hand.

'My pride had placed me in that situation, and for the first time I found my body doing things against my will. It took to his demands like a master with his puppets. When he asked, I found myself doing the dishes. When he wanted a magic trick, I'd do a magic trick. And when he asked me to sweep, I would indeed pick up the broom and sweep.'

He shook his head, disgusted. 'Even after centuries of warning from ancestor to ancestor, I didn't listen. After four generations of freed elves, I had given up my free will by waving that flute around as if it were just a mere trinket. Fifty years I've been looking for that flute, and for fifty years I've been here. Obedient in every sense of the word. So, yes, girl, if you can find what I cannot, then I'll help you free your silly little friends.'

Eve narrowed her eyes. She wasn't against violence, not when she dabbled in it so often herself but there were limits. Was she just tricking one monster to free another?

'Did they die?' she asked, venom dripping into her voice.

'Did who die?'

'The children,' she hissed. 'When you lured them to the Dream Weaver?'

'Ah, so you know the Dream Weaver.' He smirked. 'Rumple can be hideous at times, but I swear that most children returned home the next morning. Whether they were the same was another thing. Does that satisfy your conscience?'

She didn't miss the word 'most', but they were running out of time. If they succeeded, she'd need to clarify.

She didn't know why it bothered her so much. Months ago, she would have made a bargain for coin or information without a second thought if it got her closer to the sisters Grimm, but after Hansel and the Princess, she'd started to guess at the complications and repercussions of her actions.

Hansel asked her a question, and she blinked. 'Huh?'

He shook his head in exasperation. 'I really wish I knew where you went inside that head of yours.'

She turned before he'd notice her blush again. That was twice in one night. When had she become so self-conscious?

'How do we get inside the cages?' she asked, changing the topic.

Pip blew out a smoke ring. It curled in the still air around them, and she followed its movements. 'There's a special key Myrtle keeps around her neck. She won't let Bogart near it because he's an idiot, but she never takes it off.'

'Okay,' said Hansel, 'so, if I have this right, we just need to steal the key directly from a sleeping giant, free the prisoners without making a sound, find your flute, and flee before they wake?'

'Without dying,' Pip added.

'Without dying,' Hansel repeated.

Eve sucked in a breath. 'Sums it up nicely, actually.'

XX

The Broken Dream Weaver

Myrenna dragged her eyes over the female dwarf shivering on the red carpet. Her red braid was frayed at the edges and her dress covered in mud. A dwarf child clung to her with pudgy hands, his wide, terrified eyes darting around the room.

Myrenna could feel it now. That closeness to the end.

She could practically taste the Princess already and smiled. The thought of her warm, tender heart beating in her hand filled her with excitement. Where others had failed, her beast had not.

Most had survived the attack, either by moving further underground or by being escorted to her own mines in the south. The eastern dwarven colonies weren't as grand as the ones at Parador, but that didn't mean the dwarves didn't hold the required skills.

She'd needed more hands, anyway. The mines in the south had become stagnant, no closer to finding the prize she sought. Her army had grown with the alliance from Carnell, but she still had nothing to show for it with the battles on the Perridorm border.

She needed more time. More power. More control.

She'd set upon the Peaks of Carfell in haste once she'd taken the king in Carnell. If the dwarves wanted to meddle with royals, then she would unleash not just a queen, but a monster.

The dwarf lifted her chin in defiance as the Queen raised herself from the dais. The Tinker's spindly hands held the dwarf's throat. 'Where is the Princess?'

It was third time she'd asked. Three times too many.

The dwarf stared back, silent. Myrenna hissed through her teeth.

The pull from her hair pins had given her a headache, leaving her with little patience. 'Enough.' She turned towards her guards. 'Bring him in.'

The doors opened, and her guards brought forth a gangly creature covered in a tattered shift. The dwarf gasped, and a cruel smile crossed over the Queen's face.

The new arrival had been an elf once, but whatever he was now had been contorted by the magic he wielded. He'd been easy to weasel out after Myrenna had broken down his empire piece by piece. He'd never stood a chance.

Myrenna always got what she wanted. She wanted the spindle, so she stole it. She wanted its weaver, so she stole him. Rumple had fought at first, his own pride and ego a fortifying wall, until the Tinker had broken him down. Her Tinker was useful that way, if not a little unsettling.

Rumple had lost a considerable amount of weight since he'd arrived, but his eyes remained focused. He was old, but he was also selfish, and even though those eyes threatened Myrenna with every ounce of his being, she stared back in challenge.

The red-headed dwarf still clutched at her young as they dragged him before her. Myrenna's closest guard took out the spindle, its delicate wooden frame balanced between his hands. Myrenna took it.

Rumpelstiltskin's face crumpled.

'We all know how this goes,' Myrenna began. 'We've been here before, and I promise you it will not be any different.'

She stepped forward, met Rumple, and lifted the small wooden object. His eyes darted to the female dwarf, who trembled.

'Cooperate,' Myrenna said, 'and we can all live happily ever after. Don't, and there will be repercussions.'

The Dream Weaver edged away from her, defiance still hidden within his skinny body. Myrenna smiled at the challenge. She would crack him, and when she did, she would use his considerable skills to draw out what she wanted.

The dwarves were simpler. A child and the promise of a threat were enough for them to comply. She just had to figure out how much was truth and how much was fabrication. If the spindle did as she hoped, the dream would give her what she needed.

She asked questions but received no answers. It seemed brutality remained her closest companion.

'Fine,' Myrenna drawled, and waved over the grinning Tinker. 'Play with them.'

That night, from the confines of the throne room, the castle only heard screams.

XXI
The Keys of Giants

The snores of the giants reminded Eve of a lion Madame Viper had once captured for the Cirque Magique. Its mane had been a glorious burgundy-orange, and when he would roar it was as if he were singing to the sky.

Eve had loved that lion.

She'd been given strict instructions to train him for one of the acts, but when she'd finally taken him to Madame Viper it was not praise she was given, but punishment.

Madame Viper had locked her in the cage with the lion then left her there.

The first lesson Eve learnt was that no matter how much you train a beast, you cannot befriend it. She was attacked when hunger set in, claws raking down her side, before Dante had set her free. Lady Nona had patched her up.

Eve reached to her side as she remembered the hot, harsh cuts bared open to the air. The memory of their sting sometimes caught her off guard, as painful as the day she received them. Though, they weren't her first set of scars. Nor her last.

Madame Viper had promptly killed the lion the next morning and bought a new cub as a replacement. Eve had cried for days, for the lion and the burial he never had. Another carcass pushed off the side of the cart with a heavy thump, no more than an inconvenience as the circus moved to the next location.

She remembered staring at the lion's corpse as they rode away.

A similar roar came from the two parallel beds the giants laid upon. Myrtle wore a long nightgown filled with layers of frills and lace.

Bogart hadn't bothered to change, his body spread like an eagle in his suspenders and loose pants. A dribble of saliva ran down his chin.

Pip had warned them that Myrtle was a light sleeper, so the trick was to pinch the key when the clock struck ten, to block out any sound when the time came.

That was Hansel's goal, though.

Eve's was to find the flute.

She called on her gift in the hope of it deciding to be of some assistance. It didn't always come when she called, but she hoped if it had led to the Princess and Prince, then surely this was just another piece of the puzzle. Porchid's job was to hush the prisoners and wait.

Eve took a few steps, then swiftly ran towards the centre of the room. A familiar tug pulled at her chest, a warmth spreading through her bones. It grew hotter near the giants. She cursed under her breath. Knowing her luck, it would be with the big smelly male who'd taken it.

Pip waited by the shelf, and Eve wondered if his heart was hammering like her own. She wished to the Fairy Godmother they wouldn't be able to hear her.

She tiptoed towards the bed on the right, the shadow of Hansel doing the same on the left. The chime of the clock was due in a few minutes, and she focused on the tug of her gift. Hitching her knees onto the post, she deftly made her way up to the mattress and lightly tapped her foot, testing its movement. It didn't spring back.

Hopefully, her light weight would be a countermeasure. She thought of Hansel's large size and wondered if he could do the same.

The tug led her towards Bogart's body. His arm was splayed around his face, and his huffs of stale breath lifted into the air. Eve crinkled her nose at the smell and the bone caught between his wide-gapped teeth.

She paused every time he breathed, the mattress shifting with the inhale and exhale of his breath.

The warmth in her chest burned as she neared his wrist. He wore a makeshift watch, the wristband made of wood and aluminium. The face was large and round, its thick, wide body plucking at a hair on his skin.

Eve treaded carefully, pausing to eye the other bed where Hansel crouched on the bedside table. The necklace delved deep into Myrtle's chest, and she stifled a laugh.

Out of all the places to be caught, inside her bosom was a nice little touch.

The watch glinted against the low burning lamps as Eve grew closer, her chest almost thrumming. Squinting, she made out a latch. She couldn't see the flute, but her gift could feel it. From the looks of the watch, it was possible there was a hidden compartment.

Eve smirked. They were close now.

The clock clicked over, and the first chime rang—

Ding.

She took her chance and dived forward.

Ding.

She clasped the latch, pulling at its rusted hinges.

Ding.

Eve heaved at the weight as the giant's breath hitched.

Ding.

Bogart's arm began to rise, twisting Eve through air. She collided with the adjoining wall and slid down its surface.

Ding.

Eve blinked off her stupor as Bogart blew out a breath, his saliva landing on her leathers.

Ding.

She hurtled back to her feet, lifting the wristwatch's surface.

Ding.

Her heart leapt when she found a slim, silver flute lying inside.

Ding.

Bogart shuffled and swung his arm onto the edge of the mattress, where Hansel stood with a key, his face pale and arms raised.

Ding.

Eve stilled as Myrtle sat up in bed and stared at the two of them.

XXII

The Dragon in the Mist

Bronson loved shopping.

After the window he'd seen in Troll's Keep the day before, he'd expected a tailor to make him something as extravagant. Except, when he'd entered and asked about a shirt, the troll had stared him down, only to laugh at his small size. The mood had been set from there.

He paused in a window and fixed his hair, his kohl-lined eyes bringing out the gold in his irises. He huffed as he carried several bags from the practical list of necessities

Brufell had given him. The warrior clearly knew how to ruin a trip that was supposed to be a little fun.

With the weight of the packages, he dawdled down the street. Having finished early, he decided to make his way to the local tavern to taste something better than Bo's awful moonshine.

The two older dwarves had gone to meet a contact outside the city about the mysterious black fog. Bronson didn't know how any of it related to the Princess, but he'd make a wager it involved the Queen. He'd always happily avoided the mishaps of others, but after the Seven found the Princess, he'd been dragged into a mess he couldn't escape.

Beetle had been whiny when he'd been told to remain at the grotto, and if Bronson hadn't been older, he would have happily traded places. Swimming in the pool with a berry-infused facemask sounded far more appealing than being surrounded by trolls and chased by scarats.

Though, if Bronson was being honest, he'd felt the changes too.

The wraiths had been more disturbing than usual, waking from old sleeps and acting strange. Then the Seven's cousins hadn't responded in the east, even after several letters had been sent. Finding the Princess abandoned on the dangerous crossing near the Peaks of Carfell was the cherry on the top.

Bronson wondered what else Bjorn and the others had found there. He would have much preferred the familiar route to his cousin's home instead.

Bronson was halted as a heavy-set troll stopped in front of him. Bronson stared down at his disgusting hairy toes. They were covered in grime, his feet in desperate need of a pedicure. When Bronson finally looked up, a troll leered at him, his large belly rounded in a suit of silk. The troll chewed on what Bronson suspected was tobacco, the spit falling in his direction. Bronson sighed. He really hated when they did that.

'Hello, little dwarf,' the troll sneered.

'Can I help you?' Bronson asked.

The troll grinned wider, but it set off the hairs on the back of Bronson's neck. 'You can, actually.'

Bronson realised his mistake too late. Two large trolls grabbed him from behind and pulled a bag roughly over his head.

One minute he'd been on the main cobblestone road. The next, a sharp blow to his skull knocked him out cold.

Brufell followed Bo towards a farm on the outskirts of Troll's Keep. The cart rumbled under them, the horse slow and ancient. Its brown mane was matted, its skin covered in patches of flies and shedding skin.

Bo claimed his contact may have vital information in relation to the strange occurrences.

Because the trip took up the whole afternoon, the pixie had been left at the house, wanting to be alone, and Bronson had gone shopping. Brufell had given him an extensive list of food items, new packs, and weapons. He'd hoped the list would keep the young dwarf out of trouble whilst he and Bo were gone. Troll's Keep was a large city, after all, and Bronson hadn't the experience with open winding roads or the bustle of people.

They crested a hill, a cottage appearing in the distance. When they slowed to a stop, Brufell helped Bo down before handing him his cane.

'Have you thought about upgrading?' Brufell asked as he held Bo's elbow, helping him stand.

'Upgrading?' Bo scoffed. 'This horse is as loyal as they come.' He patted the horse's hide in affection.

The farmhouse was a round double storey home, made in stone and covered with moss. Trinkets hung from the porch, clinking in the wind.

'Homely, don't you think?' Bo asked, a tilt to his lip.

The house, as Bo had said, sat on the northern edge of the Shadow Forest. It held a foreboding presence that Brufell would not call homely at all. The forest was so close he could feel it watching. Hidden eyes. Hidden magic. Hidden beasts. All out for blood.

He didn't like it.

The porch creaked as a stomping sound came from inside and someone yanked open the door. A troll with pale green skin and a long nightgown peered down at them. The smell of body odour and sweat leaked from inside, causing Brufell to wrinkle his nose.

Bo smiled. 'I was hoping you'd be home.'

The troll looked down his nose at the dwarf and his cane. 'I'm always home.'

Bo chuckled. 'One day you may surprise me.'

'Not likely,' he gruffed, before nodding to Brufell. 'You know, I don't like strangers. Why is he here?'

Brufell shuffled uncomfortably but remained silent. On the way here, the old dwarf had forewarned him about

Ryker. The troll deeply distrusted everyone. Including his own kind.

'He can be trusted,' Bo said calmly, shifting his cane. 'This is my somewhat nephew.' Bo waved his hand in Brufell's direction.

Ryker stared at him and narrowed his eyes. His nose flared as if he was sniffing Brufell for lies, before he grunted and stepped aside. 'We're not due for boulders for another week. Is it cancelled?'

Boulders was a game of chance. Dice balanced on a lightweight stone carved with the old runes of trolls. The aim was to roll them and gain two of the same pair. If you rolled the same pair, then you gained no points. First person to gain fifty points lost. It was a game of gambling – something Bo had sworn off, considering his history with the dwarves. He'd been exiled from the colony after stealing money and cheating to pay back debts.

Brufell frowned, but Bo didn't miss a beat. 'No, no. We're still on to play.'

Bo took a seat in a worn chair next to the fireplace. He placed his cane carefully on its edge. 'We're just here to visit.'

Ryker narrowed his eyes again. 'No good comes from visitors and strangers.' To make a point, Ryker glared at Brufell.

'How about some tea?' Bo suggested politely.

The troll rolled his eyes but went to the kitchen anyway and began to boil a pot. Bo motioned to the seat beside him, and Brufell took it, even if he struggled. He had to jump a little to reach it, and looked to Bo with his cane.

'Boulders better not be cancelled,' Ryker mumbled, clearly uncomfortable with their surprise visit.

Bo chuckled as the troll placed down their chipped mugs and sat on the opposite lounge. It groaned under his weight.

Brufell shuffled and stared at a lone whisker coming from the large mole on the troll's chin. If Bronson were here, he'd insist he pluck it out.

'How have you been?' Bo asked, taking a sip from his cup. The liquid was supposed to be tea, but it resembled mud. Brufell placed his down, thinking he'd rather something stronger. *Much stronger.*

'Same as last week,' Ryker replied dryly.

Bo graciously nodded, leaving Brufell to scowl.

He loathed small talk. It was aimless and time wasting.

'Are you still hunting?' Bo asked.

The troll huffed. 'Caught a couple of rabbits this morning, but they were off.'

'Oh? How so?' Bo enquired, sipping at his tea again.

Brufell caught where this was going. According to Bo, Ryker wasn't one for questions. Bo had warned Brufell that subtlety worked best. Another skill Brufell failed at.

Ryker narrowed his eyes but continued. 'They looked fine, except for the teeth. And the pelts smelt funny when I skinned them. Like rotting meat. Had to throw them out.'

'Do you think it's related to what you mentioned last week?' asked Bo.

Ryker grumbled, ignorant as to where this conversation was going. 'Probably. The mist has been moving an awful lot lately and I don't like it. Ruining the meat and disturbing my quiet. Those noises keep me up at night.'

No wonder Bo hadn't known much. Getting details from the troll was like a mouse trying to move a brick wall.

Bo placed down his tea and leaned forward, resting his right hand on his knee. 'I wish I could say this was a friendly visit, Ryker, but you see, my nephew here requires information regarding the black fog, and we're hoping you'd be able to help?'

Ryker's watery, distrusting eyes shifted to the dwarf. 'Why does he want to know?'

Bo shrugged casually. 'Well, as you know, I originally hail from the great mines of Parador, and my nephew has informed me of some strange things happening within the mountains. A shift in the wind, of sorts.'

Brufell noted the lack of information regarding the Princess. He took a sip of his muddied tea, feigning politeness.

Bo continued. 'I remember last week you mentioned the fog, and it came to my nephew's attention that he'd seen it moving within the Mountains of Eyrie. We were hoping you could enlighten us on some of these … odd occurrences.'

Ryker sniffed, and lifted his sleeve to wipe his nose. The whisker moved as he spoke. 'I don't know what's happening,' he admitted. 'Most of it you already know. The fog moves, and where it goes it sucks out the life of whatever it touches, magic and all. The realm is made of magic, and without magic there is no life. I don't know what to tell you. It vanishes and then it returns. Sometimes for a day and sometimes for a week, but it always reverts to that same spot. Just over the ridge there at the back of the house.'

Brufell looked to Bo, who nodded. Permission to speak. 'When was the last time it moved?'

'Two days ago,' Ryker answered. 'Came back this morning.'

'Can you show it to us?' Brufell asked.

It was a leap, but one he hoped would pay off. Ryker contemplated the question and nodded. The tight hold on Brufell's chest released a little.

They followed Ryker to the back of the property towards a silo standing alone by the grass line. They climbed to the top, the wind caressing Brufell's beard. He breathed it in, taking in the long dark stretches of the land. Puffing behind him, Ryker pointed towards the dark forest. Far in the distance lay a large shadowy mass, lingering over an open section of the trees.

Brufell sucked in his breath. The shadow moved like a pond. Still, yet continually shifting. He barely made out the small ripple of an elongated shape. A crack, and the black mist shifted. From its depths came a thin, elongated body, its wings spread wide as it shot for the sky. A cry rang out, raising the hairs on Brufell's arms before it dove back into the mist.

'It's a dragon,' Brufell whispered. He tried to gauge how it came into existence. Had the pixies been a target of this beast, or had they been in the way of whoever controlled it?

Bo was silent, his beard flapping in the wind.

Ryker looked down at them and gruffed, 'Not something you can hunt.'

Brufell's stomach churned. His instincts had been right. Something had brought this animal into the realm, and someone controlled its strings.

XXIII

The Fate of Freewill

The spindle cracked.

Myrenna lifted the wooden figure and inspected it closely.

Over the last few weeks, Rumple had weakened. His proud nature was a shadow of its once furious glory, but it brought her no relief. He was receding into his mind, becoming lost, which did nothing to help her.

Myrenna lifted the magnifying glass and peered at the spindle to assess its damage.

'It's not broken,' the Tinker said from the shadows. His voice crawled over her skin. 'Only bending.'

Myrenna frowned. She'd wanted to break Rumple. Breaking him meant breaking the spindle and breaking apart the dreams lingering inside. One did not work without the other, and where she'd planned to woo Rumple with sugar she'd been met with sheer determination.

The spindle only worked when he'd coax it. It bent to nobody else's will. Despite her efforts, it remained the creature's possession, and it frustrated her to no end. She needed a dream, and she needed it desperately.

The dwarf woman was wallowing in the pits of the dungeon, calling for her kin, but the Queen had not yielded. The dream had to be surrendered, and it required permission. It had to be seduced. Freely given to the weaver.

Which meant Rumple was in control. No matter how long she spent staring at the spindle under a microscope, in her hands it was a wooden figurine. Its power bowed only for the one master it had ever known.

The mirror had chastised her for Rumpelstiltskin's capture. It'd called her imprudent. Foolish.

'When honey is used, people will freely sacrifice as asked. But with thorns, it is forced upon them, and they sour with each task.'

Myrenna disagreed. Regardless of whether she'd wooed Rumple to her side or not, he was selfish. Pain was the only language they both understood.

The Tinker plucked the spindle from her hands and placed it delicately on the bench top, his tools spread out around him in organised chaos.

'Can you bend it to my will?' Myrenna asked.

The Tinker bowed. 'I will certainly try.'

Her lip twitched at the way he didn't crumple under her gaze. She didn't know if she hated it or not. He was odd, after all.

She was stressed, the tension in her neck pulled too tight.

The mirror had never steered her wrong before, but perhaps like all things, it wasn't as omnipotent as it seemed. Whilst it provided her with power, it wasn't always helpful, and pulling information from it was like pulling teeth.

But Myrenna was her own woman with her own plans. She wanted freedom. Control. Power. In this, she was determined to prevail.

'Keep me updated.'

The Tinker bowed lower. 'Of course, Your Majesty.'

XXIV

The Chomping Changers

Hansel knew fear.

He'd felt it as his sister fell into the witch's fire. He'd felt it when he lay in an alley with only hunger as a companion. He'd felt it when the Queen had picked him out from a line of soldiers and taken him to her bed.

And he felt it now as Myrtle opened her eyes just when he pulled the key from her chest.

It'd been too easy.

He'd waited on the bedside table, ready to act when the clock chimed ten. He'd watched the slumbering giant as her snores reverberated throughout the room, as Eve scouted along the mattress with the grace of a dancer and waited. He knew he'd have to be quick. Once he got the key, it was merely a case of transporting it to Porchid and Pip, who would set the waiting prisoners free.

When the clock chimed the first time, Hansel shot to the side of the bed where Myrtle lay, the key swallowed by the flesh of her bosom. Her skin rippled as she heaved a sigh, a smile tickling her mouth at whatever dream she was having. Hansel was too high on adrenaline to notice anything else as he fortified his fears. Encouraging himself towards her chest.

He waited till she exhaled, and lightly touched the chain wrapped around her neck. Each chime echoed like the thunk of an axe as he tugged the key, pixie by pixie. Her breathing remained steady. Every inch of his body was aware of Eve's movements, of the way Myrtle sighed, and of the stillness of the prisoners.

When he finally slid the key from between Myrtle's curves, he sucked in a breath. The key was smaller than anticipated. Its carved shape was etched with scorpions, scarats, and spiders. It was an ugly thing, made of bone and patches of glue.

Myrtle groaned in her sleep, the puff of air from her lips blowing his hair back in disarray. Hansel winced at a pinch on his skin – his finger was caught in the chain.

Piece by piece, the key came into view, and when the ninth chime hit, Myrtle began to turn, pulling him with her.

One moment he'd been free, and the next his face was planted on top of her chest.

Hansel froze.

At least the key was in his grasp.

His triumphant smile faltered as he turned to find Myrtle's eyes open, staring at his body splayed on top of her.

Hansel didn't hesitate. He dived.

With a roll, he was up, running towards the edge of the bed. Before he could jump, the mattress bounced. Hansel soared into the air, his grip tight on the key. He landed with a crack, something snapping near his hip. He turned to face the giant.

Myrtle sat on her bed, eyes focused. Hansel raised his arms in surrender.

Yes, Hansel had felt fear before.

But it was nothing compared to the fierce rage of the giant staring down at him.

Eve raised her arms and peered to the shelf where everyone had frozen.

The last chime reverberated throughout the room as they waited for Myrtle to act. Her face swelled and puffed, before she released in an ear-piercing shriek.

Eve covered her ears as the scream cut through the room.

Bogart was up in seconds, his drool leaving a pool of saliva on the cushion. Pots exploded, the window cracked, and Bogart turned towards the intruders.

Eve was upon Hansel in moments. A grunt escaped his lips as she snatched the key and sprinted towards the shelves.

Pip's eyes were wide as Eve scrambled up the rope, hoping Hansel was close behind. At the top, Eve shoved the key into Pip's open arms. He moved in short rapid bursts, opening each lock with a clink.

Porchid had the pleasure of distracting the giants. Eve barely noted the fairy as she flitted around an agitated Bogart. His heavy arms swung in tired movements as she poked and prodded. A roar shook the room as Bogart tripped over the blanket. The shelves trembled.

Pip unlocked the cages with ease, and each human headed for the ropes.

When the last of them had crossed over the ledge, Eve followed, swinging herself down. She counted her breaths, refusing to look down, and focused on the rope as it cut into her palms and burned her skin.

Too fast, too fast, she thought.

Bogart's arm came swinging above her and smashed the shelf into pieces.

Faster, faster.

Pain lashed up her arms. Hansel had already pushed the others towards the exit and waited for her at the bottom. He caught her before she hit the ground and tugged her forward to run for the hole embedded into the fireplace wall.

Eve had barely stepped over the threshold when she paused. Something held her back, a need. Eve turned as Bogart charged. A foot smashed onto the brick, the soot turning the world white. Eve coughed up dust as the last of the prisoners rushed through.

Bogart leered down, gaps in his teeth where the hanging bones penetrated. Eve met the gaze head on, a war in their eyes.

Hansel gripped her hand. 'Eve.'

But she wouldn't break Bogart's stare. Wouldn't be the first to back down from his hungry gaze. He thought he'd won.

She knew Myrtle was behind them – they'd only have seconds. She would only have seconds. When Bogart's head leaned down to get closer, his breath hot and sticky, Eve's fingers trailed her knives.

Hansel's warning voice echoed in her ear again. 'Eveline.'

She ignored him.

Eve was sick of being pushed around. Sick of being threatened to become food. Sick of being played for a fool by creatures in this land who felt like they could do whatever they wanted. She was not a meal, and she wasn't someone's plaything.

She gripped the hilts of her daggers, the familiar handles a balm. She honed in on the giant's eyes, and the world turned silent.

Myrtle came tumbling forward, her screech piercing through the haze as Eve inhaled. Her first blade flew with ease, the gilded hilt glowing in the light as it impaled Bogart's eye.

Exhaling, she flipped the second blade, and with a precision Dante would have been proud of, the blade hit his second eye, sinking with a sick, sucking noise.

'My eyes!' Bogart roared.

'Where is that useless elf?' Myrtle bellowed. 'My key! Bring back my key!'

Debris came tumbling down as the wall fell under the pressure of Bogart ripping away the brick.

Eve grabbed Hansel's hand and fled. They slid through the gap under Bogart's howls of pain and tumbled through the opening. Cobwebs clung to their clothes. They turned a corner, only for the web to catch their feet. Eve fell forward as Hansel gripped her hand. They tumbled, and pain shot up her side, Hansel wrapping her in his arms. When they finally stopped rolling, all Eve could hear was the thrum of her heart and the ringing in her ears.

Hansel's golden-brown eyes were inches away. They touched nose to nose, only a breath between them. Eve licked her lips, Hansel's eyes flickering down to the movement. The walls shook and Eve jerked back. She writhed, the webs growing tighter when Pip appeared. He tore at the web, freeing their arms enough for Eve to twist and thrust the flute towards him. The elf glowed as it touched his skin.

With no time to think, Eve tore through the last of the webbing and helped Hansel up. He was about to speak when Pip placed his mouth around the instrument and began to play.

The tune was haunting. Slow and melodic.

A collective scuttling filled every nook of the wall. From the darkness came a flash of beady eyes.

Eve took an involuntary step back and hit Hansel's hard chest. His hand found hers in the dark. Her breath locked in her chest as a set of eight limbs scuttled into the light. It was huge, something straight out of the nightmares of children. Hansel squeezed her hand, just as clammy as her own.

The tune on the flute tilted, hitting a higher pitch. Suddenly, the hall was filled with spiders, each one black with fathomless eyes. Pip picked up the pace, a smile on lips when the spiders charged. Hansel wrapped Eve in his arms as the spiders shot past, avoiding them as they stampeded through the cracks and empty passages and into the giant's chamber.

Myrtle shrieked as the spiders exploded through the fireplace, fangs out. She grasped at them as they clung to her skin, sucking and biting and scratching. Eve's eyes widened in horror as blood began to seep from the giant's body. One spider crawled into Myrtle's mouth.

Bogart was no better. He slammed his foot down, trying to stomp the creatures, but they were too fast. They scampered up his pants, slinking under his clothes and coming out from his collar. Bogart screamed, the blood in his eyes already clotting.

Pip continued to play his flute, hitting another high note, and the spiders became deadly. Their bites held poison. Black veins protruded along the giants' skin. It spread like a disease, consuming the two giants in seconds.

It was horrifying.

And strangely beautiful.

Pip halted his song. 'We need to run.'

Hansel moved first, pulling Eve through the tunnel and out into the mists. A stitch pierced her side, her steps faltering. Hansel didn't slow, his own breath ragged as they aimed for the portal.

Archie screamed at them, but she couldn't hear him over the rumble of feet. Eve dared a glance back, only to regret it instantly.

Myrtle stumbled from the house, screeching out, 'Humans!'

Other giants came to her call, their hounding feet close behind.

Eve crashed through the portal, screaming, 'Move!'

Running was easier said than done. The stumps provided little in the way of a smooth path, and with the height, Eve was dizzy. They were wounded and shaken, adrenalin the only thing keeping them going.

The vine around them shook. Eve snapped her head up to find a giant crawling through the portal. His eyes focused on them with rage. Eve urged her feet forward, stumbling when her next step missed a stump. Porchid clung to her shirt with a scream.

The vine groaned as more giants entered the realm. Thorns shook, the vine bending from the newly added weight. Eve was thrown to the side, narrowly missing a thorn. Hansel shouted from below, but she was too far behind him, her fear slowing her down. She swallowed back bile as the vine shook again.

She could see the ground now, though she was still high up.

Hansel helped an older woman navigate the branches, eyes wide as he looked back at Eve. Eve shook her head: Hansel was where he needed to be.

She at least had Porchid by her side but there was no way they would make it. No way to close the distance before the giants were upon them. Without her knives she was useless, her small size nothing but a hindrance as giants tore through the portal. Leaves and greenery fell from above.

There was nothing she could do, no weapons she could wield. Except … Eve slid her hand into her left pocket and brought out the slimy seed. Would the ground have enough moisture? She hoped so.

The entire vine groaned again, tilting so much she was afraid it would snap. The giants were gaining ground, but the others were so close to the bottom. She took a breath, waiting until the last second to drop the seed.

Her heart belted in her chest as the eye of a giant peered through the branches to the interior of the vine.

Myrtle.

Eve screamed as Myrtle tore at the plant. She had little care of the thorns. Blood pooled on her palms and the vine shivered with every attack. Eve held onto the stump and snuck a peek at the ground.

'Come on, come on, come on,' she repeated, ducking to avoid a falling thorn.

Suddenly the entire plant shifted as if its roots had unstuck. Eve screamed as she was thrown to the side, her fingers barely grazing a section of the vine. A wail echoed from below, halting the giant just enough for Eve to run.

She skidded down the vine, skipping a few branches at a time. Thorns bit into her clothes and skin. The sounds of the giants and the chompers silenced the rest of the world. Dust filtered up from below, resembling a tornado. Eve noted the flash of sharp teeth.

The Chomping Changers' bulging eyes sat upon a gaping mouth, their bodies made of roots. They ate so fast and so ravenously that Eve understood Flora's warning when handing her the seed.

They munched and chewed and spat, growing with each meal. The vine groaned in protest, and a snap echoed from somewhere below. A sharp crack, and the vine shuddered.

Eve dropped.

Reaching out her arms, she caught a branch as the vine began to fall. The screams of the giants reverberated through her body.

She was still too far. The drop would kill her.

She could no longer see the prisoners or Hansel, and even though fear gripped her, there was relief. At least he was safe.

Thorns broke from above, shrieking past her head like a javelin. The branch underneath her cracked, and the slope of the vine became more like a slide than a well.

Porchid winced and Eve shoved her into the safety of her pocket. She looked down at her branch, fear turning into an idea. With a jump, the branch snapped under her weight. Before she knew it, she was sliding.

Eve clung to the branch with bleeding nails, shifting her weight to dodge the oncoming carnage and thorns.

Porchid screamed as the thorns slashed the branch, tearing through its exterior with every bump. Its density lessened the further she slid. Her thighs burned as she dodged another thorn.

Debris fell around her. The shadow of a giant, falling to his doom.

The Chomping Changers gnashed at the vine, their forms growing into the size of horses. One hissed from her right as she passed, its bulging body jumping straight for her. Eve dived, and the branch she'd been riding smashed into the Changer's face.

The wind tore past her ears and she braced herself for the hard ground. From this height she wasn't sure if she would die or simply break some bones.

Some people compared falling to flying. Eve compared it to nightmares. She whispered under her breath – a prayer or an apology, she didn't know.

All she realised was that the ground was softer than anticipated. Louder.

A grunt echoed in her ears as her body was caught, Hansel taking the brunt of her landing.

Hansel wrapped his arms around Eve and carried her through a break in the roots. His chest heaved against her, and his limbs shook as she clutched his shirt. Part of her wanted to never let go, the other part was too weak to fight it.

Above, the storm swirled in an angry haze, the last of the giants trying to fight against its thrashing. A crack rang through the air.

The storm exploded.

The Chomping Changers continued eating until they were the size of the giants themselves. Eve could have sworn they'd twitched and twisted and shook before exploding into a thousand pieces of green, sticky mud.

Eve's head pounded. Pain shot up her spine. The thump of Hansel's feet was heavy and determined. She tried to speak, but no words came out. She managed to look down, and saw blood. It seemed she hadn't missed the thorns after all.

The vine fell like a whip, rolling into itself as it collided with the ground. The earth shook on impact. The storm contracted as it boiled and churned.

Eve squinted as a shadow cast itself over the greens of the field. Through the portal came a giant beast, its pearlescent wings wide against the sky as it roared.

The last thing Eve saw were the blank grey eyes of Myrtle, her body sprawled at all angles.

She blacked out.

XXV

The Trickle of Doubt

The Dream Weaver broke on the night of the full moon.

Myrenna's Tinker was a talented man, his fingers the creator and medic for not only objects but also the living. What he could build, he could also break.

His experiments had been questionable in other kingdoms, and where he'd been shunned, Myrenna had welcomed him with open arms. He was useful. Even if he was a little unsettling.

The light of the full pale moon slid over the Silver City. Myrenna wrapped her cloak around herself. The aerie above the castle was cold this time of year, winter still thawing from the lake. The birds flew from alcove to alcove, biting at each other. Some of her murders dozed here, others flew across the kingdom in search of threats.

The huntsman and Seeker had yet to be found, though.

For now, she had Rumple and the spindle.

It'd taken days, but eventually Rumple had ceded, giving her the dream she sought.

Myrenna took a breath, letting the cool air clear her head. There was a lot to unpack, a lot to plan. The dream had shown her flashes of the dwarves in the colony in the east. The swift tunnels of Parador and an old dwarf with grey eyes. She'd seen a broken cart and the sleeping Princess. A glade with silver moss and the gleam of a deep blue pool.

The dream had been broken upon the dwarf's scream.

The Queen had barely spoken before the dwarven woman lashed out, colliding with Myrenna and crunching her against the pillar. Myrenna had touched her face, wiping the drop of blood that had fallen, before the guards had rushed in and pulled the thrashing dwarf off her.

A cold sort of anger had overtaken her then, something akin to an unrivalled winter.

But it'd been the spit at Myrenna's feet that'd been the dwarf's true undoing. Myrenna had targeted the child first, the flick of her wrist cracking the child's neck. The mother barely had time to scream before her neck found the same fate.

That was all it took. A mere swish, and it was as if they'd never been.

Myrenna looked down at her hands. Free from blood but coated all the same. She didn't usually handle the direct deaths of conspirators or prisoners – she reserved that for her generals – but unique times called for unique measures.

The aftermath was what troubled her. She'd killed more times than she could count, a necessity to reach her goals, but still her body and mind never failed to recede into that pool of guilt. She breathed through her nostrils in long, slow breaths, a calming technique she learnt long ago for when rage and fury took control.

After the kill, Myrenna had screamed in rage and ripped back the velvet curtain in the throne room, slashed at it like some uncontrollable animal. And when she was done, she'd crawled to the gilded mirror, clutching at the carpet's edge as angry, hot tears threatened to drown her. 'Mirror, mirror on the wall, am I not the fairest of them all?'

The mirror shimmered, and its surface of molten gold transformed into a silky voice. *'The fairest queen – of that you are, but folly you make, and you'll go far. Without the heart that you desire; your soul is doomed to burn in fire.'*

Myrenna begged then. Anything but another riddle, another rhyme. 'Mirror, mirror, do I not do as you please? Do I not follow your guidance? Do I not deserve my own happy ending?'

The liquid surface melted as she looked upon her reflection. The mirror's voice edged through the hollow room. *'Your fickle mind and selfish desire are the bars to your cage. Without her heart your fears will come, with blackened ash and age.'*

Despite the power it had given her, she hated it. *Loathed* it. It was her prison and her freedom. Her companion and her enemy.

Myrenna stared towards the star-speckled sky and sucked her teeth. She'd found where the Princess slept, and she'd almost found that prized possession deep within her mines.

But as she stood in the aerie, the birds biting at each other for food, she questioned herself. Where she had been once so sure of victory, Myrenna now felt a trickle of doubt.

XXVI

The Ties Between Fates

Hansel carried an unconscious Seeker towards the village, his heart almost bursting through his chest. His ribs ached; possibly a broken bone or severe bruising when he'd caught Eve inside the vine.

A baffled Mr Pickles directed the escaped villagers to the inn, where the town healer waited. Porchid flew ahead, scattering the onlookers as a blood-covered Hansel ran.

He'd never seen anything like it. Eve had snapped that branch without an ounce of delay and had skidded down the vine's interior like she'd been the wind itself, wild and untamed.

Once he'd gotten the villagers out, he'd run straight back there. Not a shred of fear had been in him when he went for her. It was Eve; she was it. The all-consuming thought took over his body and he moved without direction.

When he'd fought his way past the Chompers, she'd been so high up the vine he'd begun to climb. And when Eve had fallen, his heart ceased to beat.

She'd been a force like nothing he had ever known. She dodged with swift movements, her hair flying in the wind like a queen riding into battle. She'd been terrifying, glorious.

Three days later, Hansel sat in the main room of the inn. The barkeep had been especially kind, letting Hansel sip on free ale as his knee ticked under the table. Supposedly, the barkeep's wife had been one of the captives. Hansel had fought off his gifts of money and land when he eventually bargained for a hot meal and ale instead.

The local healer spent the last day or so patching Eve's wounds. They were extensive – some broken bones, a few lacerations from the thorns. Though Hansel had washed, he swore he could still see her blood on him.

The healer had stipulated minimal visitors, Porchid being the only one allowed to stay. The fairy slept by her side, seemingly afraid to touch her. Her small light was pale in comparison to her vivid and wild nature.

Time moved as slow as an hourglass with unlimited sand. Hansel fiddled with his cup. The survivors sprawled out throughout the main sitting room. They didn't speak much, most of them lost in their own world.

Hansel peeked up from his glass, eyeing the golden Prince by the window. He hadn't been what Hansel expected. He had a small, sharp chin, with a scattering of freckles across his cheeks. His long fingers fiddled with the feather of the hat he held in his hands. The Prince was pensive, the rash on his neck inflamed despite the healer's remedies. He sneezed more often than he spoke, an opposing contrast to his brother in Maelstrom.

Hansel wondered if he could indeed break the curse and wake Snow. Compared to the Prince, Snow was fire – alive and energetic and free. Florian somehow seemed trapped, quiet, and contemplative.

The Prince wiped his nose on the sleeve of his tattered jacket and caught Hansel watching him. Hansel looked away.

Besides resting at the inn, he'd mostly helped the villagers with the burials. The clean-up from the vine was a heady task, but therapeutic. He'd always needed to move his hands, to be useful.

He'd at least managed to visit the markets, mostly collecting food. Yesterday, he'd come across a blacksmith, where he made a request for something special.

The bench below him groaned as Pip sat down. 'For a bunch of people determined to save your so-called friend, you don't look so *friendly.*' Pip wiggled his fingers at the Prince.

'We need him,' Hansel replied.

Pip sniffed the air. 'As a deterrent to the outside?'

Hansel held back a laugh. 'I know what he seems like, but he's more important than you realise.'

The Prince wiped his nose on his sleeve again, another sneeze escaping his lips.

Hansel sighed. 'Believe it or not, he may be the saviour of the realm.'

Pip snorted and took another puff of his already lit pipe. 'If anyone was to be a saviour of any realm, it'd be that girl of yours upstairs.'

Hansel smiled.

The clip of a bag sounded from the hallway and Hansel's head perked up. The healer walked in with his blue silk jacket and eyed Hansel.

Hansel sprung up from his seat, his body was tense, nerves coiled from waiting for days.

'She's awake,' the healer said flatly.

Hansel moved so fast the table wobbled, and Pip chuckled. Hansel looked at him and the elf waved him away. His heart thrummed in his chest – whether from relief or anxiety he couldn't tell.

He ran up the stairs only to halt at the door, his outstretched hand inches from the handle.

Did she want to see him? What condition would she be in?

Questions swirled in his head as his breath hitched. He'd never know if he didn't try.

The room was lit by a lone candle on the bedside table. Porchid sat swinging her legs off the ledge and waved as he entered.

Eve sat in bed, a slip sliding off her shoulder to reveal bare skin. Hansel's cheeks flamed at the sight, but he didn't look away. Couldn't if he tried.

She was alive. Awake. *Whole.*

He rubbed his chest. The tightness he'd been carrying lifted as she met his gaze.

From the day Hansel had met Eve, a match had been lit. The spark slowly setting fire to whatever walls lay between them.

Her eyes were bright. There were bandages wrapped with clean precision around her arms. But it was the smile, the one that slowly spread over her face at the sight of him, that was his undoing.

In that moment, the fuse hit its mark inside his heart. And it exploded into a thousand fireworks.

XXVII
The Wrath of a Royal

Beetle's head bobbed as sleep threatened to consume him.

He hated being on watch. Hated how dull it was to sit here. Hated how boring the grotto was.

He missed the others. Missed Bjorn's grumbles, and the sharpening of Brufell's knives. He missed Bronson's singing and Bryn's creations. He even missed Rabbit's silence, the way he spoke with only his expression.

He sighed. Malak's snoring was the only sound left coming from the sleepy grotto. The troll lay sprawled by the coffin. Bonyx was close by, the old dwarf snuggled under a thick blanket.

Beetle rubbed at his nose, a huff on his lips as he tore a leaf. It was entirely unfair that he remained here. Sure, he understood why he couldn't go with Brufell and Bronson. The journey was treacherous, the trolls unhinged. Even Malak hadn't gone. Something about leaving or burning bridges. Beetle had zoned out long before that, too put out by the fact he couldn't go with the others.

Bjorn, Bryn, and Rabbit.

All they were doing was heading to the colony in the east. He'd been there at least three times with the Seven over the years. Couldn't Rabbit have stayed? He would have melted into this silence perfectly.

Silence and waiting. Two things Beetle decided he dreaded.

He dropped his leaf and picked up another. The green veins reminded him of miniature roads. He imagined travelling down those roads, finding a hidden object to destroy a great evil.

He'd always dreamed of going on a quest. Coming home as the hero. All the females in the east begging to be his wife. Brave, they would call him. Handsome. Gallant. He imagined a crowd bellowing his name, and when Parador became a hub of life again, they would carve him in great stone, his figure left to guard over the grand halls.

He jolted when a roaring crack ran through the grotto. Leaf forgotten, Beetle eyed the forest.

Perhaps he'd imagined it. His boredom did that sometimes – made him believe that something had happened when it hadn't. Sleep built in his eyes, and he rubbed them again.

A twig snapped, and the hairs on the back of his neck stood on end. The moon shone bright, casting a pale glow on the grass. The brushes and moss blinked, their lights shutting off as the slow, oncoming mist of shadow crept through the crevice of the brush.

He scrambled back, his mouth dry. The fog slithered through the trees, a hush falling over the grotto. In its wake was ash and death.

He had to wake the others.

The fog nipped at his heels as he tripped over a root. He scrambled up, his feet unsteady as he reached Bonyx and Malak. His voice cracked as he shouted them awake. Malak held his club in hand, eyes wide as the fog circled over the grotto, the ferns curling into themselves.

'What is it?' Bonyx asked, his cane in hand.

'It came from nowhere,' Beetle stammered.

Bonyx ushered him to the side. 'Stand behind me.'

Beetle had no idea what to do – his axe remained in the fog. A sweat permeated his brow. He backed away as the fog shrivelled the hedge, opening a gaping wound in the wall. The forest beyond loomed, the grotto too open, too vulnerable.

Malak reached towards the fog and Beetle shouted, but the warning was too late. The troll hissed as it burned his hand. 'We need to run.'

Malak sprinted for the coffin and hacked at the crystal with his club. The fog grew darker, thickening. A crack rang out as Malak severed the lid, and he pulled the princess free with his thick arms. He lifted her body over his shoulders.

Whispers from the fog kissed Beetle's skin. He stilled at the sound.

'You need to run, little one,' Bonyx yelled, grabbing his sleeve.

But Beetle already knew it was too late. They'd never planned this far. Never considered something would come.

As the flutter of a thousand wings broke through the trees – the fairies collecting themselves – the fog bulged. And the Evil Queen stepped out of the shadows.

XXVIII

The Calling of an Arena

Bronson's head was pushed deep into freezing water.

A hard grip tore at his hair, pulling him up, then under, again and again.

He sputtered, wheezing as his head was pulled back. There was a chuckle, and the bag was ripped off, exposing a stone floor speckled with scratches and dirt. He looked around and caught the pale glint of iron bars.

The troll in the silk suit adjusted his stance, checking his pocket watch before he shoved a plate of food with his foot. 'You, dwarf, have been selected for glory.'

Glory?

Bronson blinked water out of his eyes, his breath loud in the dark.

'I run a lucrative business,' the troll said, smoothing a hand over his hair. 'When I see an opportunity, I take it.'

A crowd roared in the distance, the ground vibrating. He tried to gather his bearings and failed miserably when the troll leaned down. He leered at Bronson like a treat, his buck teeth and bright eyes more of a warning. 'You, my handsome dwarf, are that opportunity.'

Bronson remained silent, waiting for the medallion to drop.

'You are to be my bait, my crowning glory, my victor! With a man of your stature, you'll succeed where others have not.'

Bronson's head pounded. Was he dreaming? He had no response besides that of a mumbled, 'What?'

The troll clapped. 'I've registered you for the third round. It's time to go. Up! Up!'

He was hauled to his feet by two trolls he hadn't noticed, their calloused hands rough on his skin. He wobbled but managed to stand as a piece of bread was shoved in his mouth. Another roar echoed above them, and Bronson's eyes widened.

Brufell is going to kill me.

He was alone with trolls, the shopping long discarded on the sidewalk. He'd had one job, one responsibility, and he'd been *kidnapped.* He had no time to think as a grate along the side wall opened, the trolls heaving him out. He looked over his shoulder.

The troll in silk was beaming. But it only brought bile to Bronson's mouth. Whatever this was, he already knew he wouldn't like it.

Brufell and Bo returned to the house and found it empty.

The pixie lay in a food coma on the kitchen table, surrounded in crumbs. His unscarred eye was half-closed from gluttonous glee.

Brufell plucked him from the table, brow raised. 'Where's the young one?'

The pixie shrugged and Brufell scowled. Something he felt he'd been doing a lot of lately.

'Has he not returned?' Bo asked.

It was after dusk. Bronson should've made it home long before they'd returned.

Bo placed his canc by the door. 'Where did you say Bronson went today?'

'Shopping,' Brufell replied. 'I gave him an extensive list so he wasn't dawdling off. Food, weapons, that kind of thing.'

'Weapons?' Bo asked.

Something akin to dread settled in his stomach, a warning he couldn't shake. They were in Troll's Keep, a city filled with violence, and Bronson was alone. His voice was steady as spoke, but his fingers shook. 'Of course, we need them to get home.'

Bo's face turned grave.

'What is it?'

'You won't like it.'

Brufell pulled free his axe, a growl in his throat. 'What did you do?'

Bo was smart enough to back away. 'Personally, nothing. Though I run a business you may not approve of.'

Brufell stepped back. 'Gambling?'

'Of a sort.' Bo replied carefully. 'I think I know where he is.'

Brufell waited for the dwarf to explain, to wave off his concerns and tell him Bronson was safe. Instead, Bo picked up his cane and headed towards the door. 'If he entered downtown, there's a good chance he's been picked up.'

Brufell gripped his axe. 'What do you mean "picked up"?'

'I should have considered it this morning when you sent him out,' Bo said, looking to his left and deciding their direction. 'I blended in due to age and usefulness, with knowledge of the forest and mountains, but Bronson would be an easy target.'

The words didn't soothe Brufell, they only prodded him. Fear curled inside his heart; Bo's tone was too dark to mean anything but danger. But his words didn't make sense.

'An easy target for what?' Brufell asked, failing to hide his irritation.

Bo turned to him with a look of pity. 'For an old troll tradition.'

The crowd roared as Bronson was shoved onto a pit.

Bright lights burned into his skin, and gritty sand stuck to his clothes. He raised his hand above his eyes to focus, only to find rows upon rows of trolls. The crowd was stifling, their clothes too vivid, their voices too blurred. They screamed in synchronicity, the words lost as they clapped.

Bronson shook. The sand sucked at his boots as he hesitantly stepped forward. He was met with another roar.

The screech of the silk-suited troll came rolling over the crowd. 'Welcome, welcome. What an honour it is to be here tonight!'

The crowd whooped. The troll's voice chuckled at the reaction. 'Tonight, we have something special in store for you. I'd like to introduce our first volunteer …'

The troll paused as someone whispered in his ear. Bronson wasn't sure how his voice had been amplified, but it rang in his ears all the same.

'*… I didn't get his name.*'

'*Make up his name …*'

'Mr Eyeliner,' the announcer called.

The crowd thundered and Bronson's ears dulled. The ground was littered with mismatched weaponry. Spots of old blood stained the sand. He blinked at the grinding sound of a grate opening.

Bronson didn't want to look up, didn't want to meet whoever was on the other side. But his body had other ideas. Slowly, Bronson raised his eyes as his competitor appeared.

Bronson swallowed as the largest troll he'd ever seen stepped into the arena.

He was a great hulk of a beast. His arms were tattooed in the old language, covering his biceps in what Bronson assumed were his clan colours. His hair was matted and long, and his calves were so chiselled Bronson crumbled a little under the thought of what they could do.

This was Brufell's skill, not his.

His was singing and listening to Bonyx and chasing after Rabbit. He instantly regretted dodging Bjorn's lessons on self-defence. Regretted not taking up an axe to mine, or a sword to wield.

He had no chance. None. Not even a speck.

He wasn't even fast, so running was off the cards.

The troll raised his arms, and the screams of the arena pounded into Bronson's skull. He was dead. Royally, and utterly dead.

This was worse than Bjorn telling him off, worse than their trek through the barren hills, and worse than the scarats.

Bronson pissed his pants.

Bo's walking stick clattered on the road as he heaved himself forward towards a large stadium near the centre of town.

The last of the sun settled, leaving the city's bright lights to burn into the dark sky around its structure. The roaring crowd could be heard from streets away.

Brufell gripped his axe, knuckles white with anticipation. If it was a dwarf they wanted in the arena, then a dwarf was what they would get.

Bo had explained in no uncertain terms that this was where Bronson would be. The troll culture expanded not just to troll-only combat, but to that of other creatures. It was hugely popular and worked on a *volunteer* basis. Except, volunteer was a loose term. There was no way Bronson would ever volunteer for such an exercise.

Bronson was not a warrior. The pixie was more of a warrior than the young dwarf.

Bo's back remained straight regardless of his age or height, and he strolled into the stadium as if he were in the ruling family himself. The guards at the door didn't blink as they entered, instead bowing as Bo passed.

Brufell didn't care to know how many times Bo had entered this arena, and he didn't particularly want to know if the old dwarf enjoyed it. He'd seen enough blood in his life that watching it for sport was not an activity he was interested in.

The light flared in front of them as they entered the stands. Troll after troll lined the arena, yelling at the spectacle. Their hands clapped as the most hideous troll Brufell had ever seen entered the sand pit below.

Bo pointed ahead and said something, but the words were lost to Brufell.

Brufell moved, his instincts taking over as he lunged down the stairs and over the railing into the next level of onlookers. Only a few stopped to stare, caution crossing their features as Brufell shot past them.

He didn't think. Didn't stop. Didn't hear.

All he could focus on was the dwarf below with the wet-stained pants. That was his cousin down there. One of the Seven.

The troll lunged, swung his spiked mace through the air, missing Bronson by a hair's breadth. Bronson's roll to the side was clumsy, but Brufell smiled with pride at the dwarf's attempt as he dodged the second blow.

Brufell reached the first row and jumped. He rolled as he landed on the sand, using his axe for momentum. A roar escaped his lips as he charged, and the crowd echoed.

XXIX

The Breaker and the Curse

The feather in Prince Florian's hand fell in little fluffs and hit the sticky floor of the tavern. His skin still itched, but the stern healer had slapped him when he'd gone to scratch, leaving him to sit in itchy discomfort.

He'd been without medication for weeks now, but he'd known that would be the case when he left Carnell. Did his family even notice his absence?

He was the youngest of twelve, but he may as well be invisible.

Useless.

The word ripped open his chest.

The big man with the axes and the attractive girl had come into the giant's home and accomplished what he could not. If it was jewels and riches they desired for his rescue, then they were going to be sorely disappointed. The last time he'd been home, his family had a dinner in his honour. Dinner that had been served with a side of insult, a dash of disappointment, and a large dose of pointing out Florian's flaws.

He'd never really said much when it came to his family's favourite game of targeting him. His father had lost any sort of kindness when his mother had left. Despite being last in line, his father had been one for tradition – another silly word used for 'old beliefs'.

As a child he'd tried to meet his father's expectations, had even picked up a training sword until the wood had splintered in his hand. When he did the training exercises out in the gardens, his hay fever would flare, and when they took him to stay in the barracks, the insects left their mark with large, bulging blisters.

'Useless' his father would say. And that hadn't even begun to cover the creative array of nicknames he'd endured.

Florian had wondered more than once if his father even remembered his name. He'd remembered the eldest, of course. Angus. He was always the favourite. Sure, he could hold a sword and swing with the best, but the last few years had simply been food and women.

The hat Florian held had been a gift from his mother. She had been the only one to encourage his reading, to accept his quiet nature and meek personality.

But he had strengths too. He scored highest in their schooling and devoured the texts in the grand library. He knew theory, not practice.

He'd snapped at the dinner when his father had advised they were all to be wed. Each prince was to provide something of value, a way to woo the maidens entering the castle. His brothers had prepared battle trophies, and when Florian had presented his works on plants, his father had thrown it into the fire.

Sometimes, he could still smell the burning parchment.

'A scholar is no son of mine.' The King had seethed. 'Until you bring something of value, you will not bear my name.'

Florian had understood the meaning. He would be cast out with no title, no name, no lineage. Maelstrom wasn't a city you wanted to live in without connections.

Desperate, Florian had left. He'd heard about whispers of magic beans and a vine of thorns that opened a portal to the land of the giants.

It was a long shot, but he was a gifted tracker. He knew all the foliage, the trails, the skills. It was just putting it into practice where it troubled him.

He hadn't wanted glory or a grand trophy. He'd simply hoped to not get sick and prove he had indeed ventured into the land of the giants.

But he'd been naïve. Useless.

One step into that land and a giant's hand had lifted him up so fast he hadn't had time to scream. He was locked in a cage – half the village imprisoned by that point – and that was when Florian had begun to watch them be eaten one by one.

Another section of his feather hit the floor. The barkeep wiped down the bar as the huntsman and elf sat at the table near the hallway. Florian had caught him staring once or twice, his curiosity barely hidden.

He continued to watch the feather's pieces fall, imagining it was his head when he returned to his father with nothing.

Eve ached as she placed on her leathers, the material too tight on her bruised skin.

She'd asked to speak with the Prince. Her gift had led them to him, but she didn't know if that was because the dwarves had set their search to find him or whether her gift knew he was the one they needed to find.

She'd only just managed to sit on the edge of the bed when a knock at the door interrupted her. 'Come in,' she called, her voice croaky from lack of use.

Florian stood in the doorway, eyeing the room like a startled mouse before Eve gestured towards a wooden chair.

His back was hunched, as if he was trying to look smaller. His wilted feather left a trail on the ground. His eyes darted about the room, taking in every detail, before they landed on her. His deep-brown stare assessed her from top to bottom, and he nodded in acknowledgment.

Eve tilted her head. She'd figured the prince would be … *more*.

He took a seat in the chair across from her, splaying his fingers across his knees.

'Hello,' she said, attempting to break the silence.

'Hello,' he replied quietly.

His voice was soft, the accent of Carnell more of a lilt than the harsh sound of his brother. His knee twitched, propping up and down in a nervous habit.

Eve shuffled on the bed, avoiding a bruise on her thigh. 'You look well, considering your … ordeal.'

He stared at her blankly.

'Did you want something to drink?'

'No, thank you,' was all he replied.

At least he was polite.

'My name is Eve Rafter, but you may also know me as the Seeker. You are Prince Florian?' she asked.

He nodded.

By the Godmother, it was like pulling teeth. 'I know this may seem forward, but—'

'He won't give you gold.'

Eve raised her brow.

The Prince's cheeks bloomed red, a stutter escaping before he looked at his feet. 'He won't give you gold. Not for me. He'll chop my head off instead. I'm useless to you.'

She pondered this a moment and remembered his brother's responses to their questions on his whereabouts.

He's an embarrassment and a weakling. We couldn't care less if he returned, and if he did, I'd hope it was only his head on a platter.

'It's not gold we're after,' she replied softly. 'Not exactly.'

She leaned over to grab the jug of water, her mouth suddenly dry. She could feel Florian's stare. The way he twitched at any sudden movements reminded her of a fox. 'It's complicated,' Eve said, 'but essentially we need to wake a sleeping princess.'

Florian blinked. 'Snow? She's alive?'

So, he knew who she was then. That at least answered one question she had.

'Kind of,' Eve said, and took a sip from her glass. 'Maybe it's best if I start from the beginning.'

Eve started by telling him of her gift and the bargain she'd made with Hansel. She spoke about the mines and the Seven dwarves, the coffin with the princess. She told him of the curse and her visit to Maelstrom before freeing him from the giants.

When Eve finished, she sat back. It was almost a relief to tell the story, to share some of the weight with someone else. She'd only been hired to find the royals, perhaps now they could take over.

Florian fiddled with his hat, his neck flaring red. There was something endearing about him, the way his body reacted to his emotions.

Eve leaned forward and placed her arms on her knees. 'We know you have history with Snow. There seems to be an assumption – theory may be the better word – that she was affectionate to you. That you might be her true love's kiss and wake her.'

'Kiss?' he squeaked. He rubbed his neck and stared at a spot on the wall, his breath shallow. 'I'm afraid I'm not who you're looking for.'

He fiddled with his hands, another nervous gesture. 'Snow was – is – beautiful. She's alive and adventurous. But I … I only knew her a little.'

Eve frowned. *What did he mean he wasn't who she was looking for?*

'Would you at least try?' she asked.

'I do not wish to go home,' Florian said, before considering his next words, 'but I do wish to make a difference.'

'So, you'll go?' Eve asked.

'I'll go,' he agreed. 'But I can't promise I'm what you think I am.'

This she already knew, but she nodded.

Florian quietly stood. 'I hope I'm what you want me to be, for I cannot bear to be another disappointment.'

Eve opened her mouth to respond, but he'd already closed the door.

XXX

The Huntsman and his Seeker

The air at the Mountains of Eyrie cooled Hansel's skin, a reprieve from the heat already blooming up north. The mismatched group had left Hasleholme days ago. There'd been no sign of the Queen's crows, no soldiers littering the roads. The ease of the journey unsettled him.

Pip kept pace despite his short legs, whistling a tune, the smell of tobacco and mint permeating the air.

Hansel peered down at the elf and asked the question that'd been eating at him for days. 'Why'd you come?'

Pip blew out smoke from his pipe. 'I came because I have nowhere else to go.'

The thought was dreary.

'You could return to Rumple,' Hansel said, and Pip snorted.

'I'd rather find another giant, thanks.'

Hansel raised his brow, but the elf didn't elaborate. They walked in silence, the hills flashing pockets of green. As spring came to fruition, the snow partially melted, leaving space for the flowers to bloom.

Porchid wiped at her wings in careful movements on his shoulder. Since the ash of the giant's den, she'd been almost obsessed with rubbing them clean. She caught him looking and blushed, turning away.

Eve's laughter echoed over the hills as she shared a skin of water with Florian. Her injuries had been healing well, the scars turning pink. Occasionally, Hansel applied balm to her back, to help with those she couldn't reach. She gave him soft smiles, the tentative kind when they were alone. Sometimes they shared stories or hopes or dreams.

But those times were rare. With the Prince and the elf now in tow, the group was loud, the path too easy. If Hansel was being honest with himself, he'd been in a mood.

Doubt flickered in his chest, not just about the Queen's eyes but at Florian's capability to wake Snow. He also worried about Eve, what it meant. What they meant.

Did she still want the gold, or had his companionship become something more? Did he want her to stay?

These were new feelings, ones he wasn't sure how to grasp. All he knew was that when he slept, she was in his dreams. He'd had less nightmares since Rosewood, less worry, less anxiety. But he'd also had more. More training, more stargazing, more laughs.

It was as if leaving the castle had awoken him somehow, opened his eyes to look at the world beyond the Silver City, beyond Myrenna.

The sky turned a sheen of purple and grey, the shadows growing as twilight fell.

'We should set up camp here,' Hansel announced.

The space was as good as any, the trees still thick enough to hide them from the crows should they come.

'I'll go scout,' Eve said, dropping her pack.

Florian went for wood, Pip and Porchid setting up the bedrolls. Hansel hunted, bringing back a rabbit to the fire blazing in the hearth. He taught Florian how to peel the skin, the prince shy but eager, and left them to cook.

Eve stood by the ridge of the mountain, a lone figure in the world. She shivered as darkness finally descended. Hansel quickly grabbed a shawl before he made his way over, his boots crunching on the dry grass.

Her hair blew in the breeze, loose strands escaping her braid. They wrapped across her face like a mask.

'What will you do when Snow wakes?' she asked as he placed the shawl on her shoulders.

Hansel took a breath. He pictured Snow's pale skin and long black hair inside the coffin, so cold compared to the princess he knew. He thought of her smile, the way she cackled when she won and ran through the gardens.

Snow was beautiful, yes. But it was the kind of soft beauty found in stories, the way one would compare a flower arrangement. He peered down at Eve, noting her pointed nose and sharp cheekbones.

Eve was different in so many ways. She wasn't the storybook kind of beauty, but a honed blade. She was small and delicate, but her scars were a sign of a warrior, not a princess. Eve's beauty lay in the thick locks of brown hair and her deep all-seeing eyes. It lay in the way she saw the world, the way she trusted and hoped and spoke.

She was not innocent or guilty, but raw and unrefined.

'We will go on,' he said, unsure how to answer. 'Make a better world.'

Her long lashes lifted as she looked at him, the real question behind her eyes. *What will you do? Where will you go? What happens next?*

Truthfully, Hansel didn't know what came after waking the Princess. He'd considered the rebellion. Marcellus had had some dealings with them in the past – smuggled goods on their behalf. He supposed the Skinny Piglet would be next.

The moon was bright tonight, leaving the land in a silver glow. It made Eve's skin look like porcelain. Of its own accord, his hand grazed the side of her cheek. Her face was soft, flushed from the cold. And for a small moment, she leaned in.

His breath hitched, the touch gentle. He stroked the edge of her jaw, and her eyes closed. A loose breath escaped her lips.

The wind was cold, but he didn't notice it wearing his leathers. It was heat and want and desire consuming him now. She was an enigma, a current that pulled you out to sea, or a stroke of lightning mid-storm.

When she opened her eyes again, she sucked in a breath. She licked her lips, Hansel following the movement with a heavy-lidded gaze.

'Did you come over here for a reason?' she asked, a little breathless.

He blinked, remembering how close the others were near the fire.

'I …' Hansel started. He'd come over here for a reason, but now that it was nigh, his palms went clammy.

Hansel fumbled for his pocket, needing to move his hands, and pulled out a wrapped parcel. It wasn't pretty by any means – the ratty cloth the only thing he could find on the road. But it wasn't the wrapping he was worried about – not truly; it was what he had inside.

Eve eyed the package carefully, her face neutral. Hansel swallowed his nausea, hoping he hadn't crossed a line. The gift had been bought on a whim, a moment of weakness when he'd caught Eve reaching for a weapon that was no longer there.

His hands trembled as he handed Eve a parcel. There was a sparkle in her eyes as she accepted it. He swallowed, motioning for her to open it. He wasn't sure his words even worked.

Her hands were rough, warm, and calloused. Years of training, focus, and resilience honing a skill others struggled to master. She made quick work of the wrapping and opened the box to reveal a set of twin blades.

She sucked in a breath. They weren't unlike her old ones – the hilt was gold – but now with a red encrusted ruby. She faltered, her eyes meeting his in question.

'I thought you might need them – you know, after you lost yours and all. With the giants.' His words fell out in a jumbled mess. 'And now you have some, see. Just a little different. I couldn't get exactly the same, but I thought you'd enjoy the ruby, and I wasn't sure if you had a preference, but I got a good deal, and, well, you were sick, and the blacksmith in Hasleholme was happy to—'

Eve grabbed him by the jaw and kissed him.

For a moment he froze, his arms locking at his sides before he sunk into her touch. There was nothing soft about the kiss, nor graceful, nor tentative. It was a bolt of lightning to his skin, her mouth hot on his.

He eased in his tongue, one hand on her waist and another in her hair. Despite the hard edges, she was soft, pliable. She smelt of lilac and grass. He pulled her closer. Suddenly he needed her everywhere.

And then she was gone, the wind biting his skin.

She'd pulled away, her cheeks flushed and eyes bright. Hansel panted, already wanting to pull her back, to take more. But he held himself back as she shyly glanced away.

His heart was thrumming, his breaths loud in the quiet night.

Eve's hand rested on his chest as she swallowed, her fingers trailing down as she glanced at the ruby encrusted blades.

She licked her lips again. 'I never thanked you.'

'For what?' he asked, still out of breath.

She laughed, the sound light. She dropped her hand but didn't go far as she sidled into him. It was a relief. He wasn't sure if he'd let her leave even if she tried.

'For hiring me. For bringing me out of my shell.'

Hansel wrapped his arms around her, her head resting on his chest. 'You could have done all those things yourself.'

'But I'd be fifty medallions poorer if I did.'

'Ah, I see.' Hansel chuckled. 'It was about the money.'

She shuffled to look up at him, her eyes serious. 'It's about more than the money.'

Hansel pulled her closer, the words hanging on the wind. He should've asked what she meant, pressed about what came next, but for the moment he didn't want to. He just wanted to hold her as they stargazed.

So, Hansel did.

XXXI

The Troll and his Courage

Malak raised his club as Myrenna stepped from the shadows, the fog twisting into the shape of a beast. Scales flickered in and out of the mist, teeth gnashing as it encircled its queen.

A wall of fairies lined the grotto, their wings beating as they guarded the dwarves. Beetle shook, tears trailing down his cheeks.

Bonyx was stalwart in the face of danger, the end of his cane a blade, his eyes furious. Time went still as black smoke crept from the Queen's hands, her magic building into living, breathing death. That was the only way Malak could think to describe it. His palms were clammy, the taste of fear thick on his tongue.

Myrenna licked her lips as if she could taste it too. 'Fight or die.'

Malak barely had time to blink before the fairies screamed, charging towards the Queen in a mass of sharp teeth and wings. They swarmed, beating down on her with a veracity that surprised him.

'Get behind me,' Malak shouted to Bonyx, the old dwarf conceding. The coffin was shattered, the princess hidden away. It was the best Malak could have done with the circumstances. It was temporary, given the power of that fog and Myrenna's magic.

Snow wouldn't be safe for long.

Blood dripped from Myrenna's arm as she raised it high and snapped her wrist. The crack of a hundred necks echoed through the grotto. Bonyx screamed as she used her magic again, more fairies falling with vacant eyes.

Malak bellowed as he ran for the beast, club raised. But the dragon was ready for him.

Claws raked through the fog, their sharp edge barely missing Malak. He stood on unsteady feet as the grotto rose in temperature.

Malak shouted but the sound was drowned out by the rumble of the dragon's throat, purple fire building in its stomach.

We're all going to die.

Malak shouted a warning and Bonyx rolled as flames engulfed the grotto, licking at the grass and fairies with heavy fumes. Malak blinked away the sting of smoke as Bonyx raised his own sword and swung.

His blade rebounded off the dragon's hide.

Myrenna cackled, the sound chilling Malak to his bones. Before he could swing again the dragon shot into the air and crashed into the pool. The water steamed and bubbled along the surface. Then bulged.

Malak swore and sprinted for the dwarves. He threw them over his shoulders and held tight. Beetle wailed as Malak shot for the gnarled trees, their roots offering protection.

A roar echoed from behind him as a wave of water crested over the grotto.

Pain lashed Malak's side as he was thrown into the ground, the grip of the dwarves digging into his skin. He held tight as the grotto flooded, the wave drowning every inch. He smashed against the tree but refused to let go. The water belted him, surging and flowing until finally it receded.

Malak sputtered out a curse as he stood, checking the dwarves for injuries. Beetle was pale but alive. Bonyx coughed, cane still in hand when heat seared Malak's back.

He turned, the dragon rearing its head.

Fog enveloped them.

Myrenna emerged, her amethyst eyes glinting.

The bodies of the fairies littered the grotto, some as still as the frozen ground, others twitching with little life.

'Find her,' the Queen ordered. Her dragon receded with a whimper.

Myrenna's lip curled as she stepped towards Malak. 'My, my, how Snow's standards have fallen.' She kicked Malak's stomach and he dropped. 'Once it was a prince, or a huntsman, but now'—she *tsked*—'now it's a troll.'

Malak pushed himself onto his knees, his fists turning white on his club. He ignored the burn in his lungs, the fear crawling under his skin and stood. He was not built for battle. Or bravery. Or sacrifice. But Snow had nobody left to protect her. Nobody but him.

The Queen watched with a cruel smirk. 'She will break you. Just as I will break you.'

Malak held his ground. His breathing remained steady, though his heart thrummed inside his chest. He would not go gently.

A sob broke from Beetle, and Bonyx murmured something. The old dwarf was brave, but he was weak, and Beetle was too small; too young. Malak was all they had.

The Queen sneered. Malak had seen that look before, the one where he was judged as pathetic. He'd seen it at Troll's Keep, in the way the nobles or other children looked at him. But it didn't matter. None of it mattered without Snow.

He'd made an oath. And by the Godmother he would keep it.

A voice that was not his own came forth as he said, 'Snow is not yours to take. Not whilst I remain here to protect her.'

Myrenna cackled, and the fog closed in, reaching into every space, every crevice. The Princess flashed in his mind. They would find her if he didn't stop them.

Myrenna raised her arm, about to flick her wrist, when Malak charged. He swung his club, the Queen hissing as she dodged his attack.

She was fast. Malak used his momentum to turn back, swinging his club one way and gripping her wrist with the other. The sharp ends of her nails swiped his chest and he gasped.

Bonyx came from behind and swung his cane, only for Myrenna to twist and throw him back. Bonyx crashed into the rose bush, the thorns drawing blood.

Malak used the distraction and swung again, narrowly missing as she vanished into the fog.

His breath was ragged, eyes darting every which way. The hairs on his arms stood up as Myrenna's voice slinked across the grotto, coming from nowhere and everywhere at once: 'I want what is mine.'

A shadow appeared on Malak's left, and he dived on instinct. It darted past him, something sharp digging into his calf. He was covered in blood, his knees cracking on the grass.

Myrenna materialised on his right and slashed his face. He howled. Blood coated his eyes. The tingle of his toes and the ache of his muscles told him his energy was waning.

Myrenna landed a hit to his chest, a bone snapping, and he tumbled.

Malak wheezed as the Queen stood over him, her anger palpable. 'Where. Is. She?'

It didn't matter how many times she asked, Malak wouldn't give Snow up. Couldn't. Not when so much was at stake. Not when he had made an oath. She was his friend. His princess.

He would protect her. He would remain, and he would endure.

Myrenna's voice rose in frustration. 'Where is she?'

But he did not waver.

She cut him again.

Through his bloody gaze, he looked towards the dwarves. Beetle pulled at Bonyx's unconscious body. Tears stained his cheeks, dirt and blood encrusted on his skin.

'TELL ME!' Myrenna screamed.

Her magic hit Malak like a blow to the head. He was thrown to the side, his breath shallow. 'She is not yours to take.'

Stay awake, he told himself. *Endure. Protect.*

Beetle's efforts were fruitless: Bonyx did not wake.

The Queen hissed. Her pacing burned a path into the ground. The fog bulged in response to her anger, wrapping around the grotto. Grass withered and plants shrivelled as the life was sucked from every living thing.

Malak could only watch as the fog dragon came back empty handed, the Queen's skin turning red.

'Grab the dwarves,' she snarled.

The misty beast reached its great talons forward.

Malak gurgled on his blood and spat. He didn't know where the pain began or ended. It pulsed through him like a ribbed blade.

But the Queen didn't move towards him. Didn't even look as the dragon went for the dwarves.

First, Beetle fell; the dragon gripping both dwarves in his talons. Malak tried to lift an arm, but pain shot through his torso, his head. He dropped into the dirt, ears ringing as the Queen, her beast, and the dwarves disappeared into the shadows.

XXXII
The Betrayal of Kin

Brufell's rage was a sight to behold.

Bronson dodged the spiked mace in a futile attempt to run but tripped and fell instead. The troll's stench – like a garbage pit on a hot day – was overwhelming as Bronson crawled away.

Brufell yelled a war cry, his axe raised and collided with the troll in a clang. The dwarf parried, knocking the troll's weapon with ease and grace, as if he wasn't as old as time itself.

Bronson's mouth was full of sand, and his limbs were shaking violently. He peered into the stands and found Bo's face grave and unwavering. The onlookers jeered in his direction, but where everyone was shoulder to shoulder, a large space around the dwarf remained, as if he stood in his own bubble.

Sand sprayed, and Bronson lifted his arm, the lights jarring his sight. Brufell blocked an attack, then dove. He swung his axe straight into the thigh of the troll.

The troll roared as his knee hit the sand with a thud. Brufell lifted his hand for the next swing when the troll pushed off his back leg and tackled him into the ground. They rolled, all teeth and claws and blood.

Brufell needed help. Despite his skills, the troll was too large. With a weapon, maybe, but in hand-to-hand the old dwarf was done for.

Bronson found a spear discarded a few pixies away and scrambled forward. There was nothing graceful about his movements, nothing that would get him in the hall of fame, but it didn't matter. Brufell was his guardian, his tutor, his mentor. Without him, Bronson would be a mess.

As his palm wrapped around the spear, everything became as clear as glass. He twisted towards the troll and homed in. This fight was now between him, the troll, and Brufell's life.

Brufell went to dodge, but the troll's hulking body landed on his legs, and he cried out in pain.

Bronson's legs moved of their own volition, the spear raised over his head as he screamed. The troll still had Brufell pinned and was reaching for his head when Bronson jumped and brought the spear down.

And sank it into the troll's neck.

Blood splattered, covering Bronson from head to toe. The troll teetered, his gurgle lost to the sounds of the crowd.

Bronson wheezed, the taste of blood leaking into his mouth. The world was red, the smell metallic. His stomach lurched as he realised what he'd done. He spewed.

The buzzing in his head was louder than the crowd.

At some point, Brufell must have clawed over to clutch his chin. The old dwarf's eyes were wild, and proud. He gave Bronson a lopsided grin and said, 'Good job.'

Bronson couldn't do anything but nod. Couldn't do anything but keep his breathing steady.

Brufell latched onto Bronson's elbow and pulled him to his feet.

The last thing Bronson remembered was the looming gate opening before he succumbed to darkness.

It was a miracle they were alive.

Brufell assessed Bronson's wounds in a back room, checking for anything life-threatening. The troll's blood still covered Bronson's shaking body but there didn't seem to be anything immediate to tend to. Satisfied his cousin wasn't about to die, Brufell blew out a breath.

Bo was involved with this bloodshed, involved in the bets and the battle and the money. He'd originally left the colony for his debts, and yet here he was running a fighting ring with 'volunteers'.

Brufell barely had time to process it before the sound of clicking heels came down the hallway. Bo appeared, cane in hand.

'I'd hoped you wouldn't be involved,' Bo said almost sadly. 'It's not something I wished for you to see.'

Bronson heaved again on the stone floor.

Brufell whirled towards Bo. 'What in the Fairy Godmother's name do you think you're playing at?'

The old dwarf remained calm. 'I saw an opportunity. One that came with power and fortune.'

'An opportunity?' Brufell hissed. 'It's a bloodbath.'

'Yes,' Bo admitted, 'but one the trolls adore. It allows the underdogs to build a better life for themselves. You were always an avid supporter of the underdog, Brufell.'

'Do you not think we've had enough bloodshed?' asked Brufell, exhausted.

Bo gripped Brufell's arm in that fond, familiar way. 'Yes. But it is not I who calls for it. I am simply the one who thought to control it.'

Brufell stepped back. This was not what he had in mind when visiting Troll's Keep. He wanted to go home. He wanted the quiet halls of Parador and his companions. He wanted the fairy grotto and the crystal coffin and a nice cup of ale.

'We'll leave in the morning,' Brufell said flatly.

The old dwarf nodded. 'I think that would be best.'

A chasm had opened between Bo and Brufell as they said their goodbyes.

There were no jokes or friendly banter. No memories reminisced on, or drinks of ale shared.

Bronson shuffled under the awkwardness, his body sore from the day before. The pixie hovered by his side, watching with a twitch as the cart was finally loaded.

This time they'd take the road home. It was less treacherous and didn't have scarats.

Brufell climbed into the cart and picked up the reins. They'd cut through the mountain's path to Butter Pond before stopping in Ellendale on the way to their cousins'. If the Seeker and the huntsman had indeed been successful in awakening the Princess, then they'd need a plan. And allies.

Otherwise, they were all dead.

XXXIII

The Apple Pie's Curse

Eve led the group along a grassy path through the ancient trees. Pip's whistle carried on the wind, and Florian dragged his fingers along one of the giant roots.

No butterflies greeted them this time. No fairies. Eve moved with caution, new blades in her palms.

She gazed warily at Hansel. He frowned and pulled his axe free from its holster. 'Something is off.'

She sensed it too.

Eve hurried her pace, her heart picking up speed with each step until she was running, the world a haze. She reached the hedge. Where it'd been luscious and green before they left, it was now ripped apart, the colours bleached and black. The sight was like a festering wound.

Eve didn't stop. She dodged a branch, crashing her way through the underbrush. What she found was dry rock and ash. Long, deep indents scarred the ground, and the smell of death hung like a cloud. The crystal coffin lay fractured, and corpses of the fairies frozen in death were littered about. Her mouth went dry.

'Check the area for survivors,' Hansel yelled.

Eve followed the debris to the bank where she'd bathed with Porchid. The bodies of the octopios were sprawled along the rocky bottom. Tears pricked her eyes, and dread settled over her shoulders.

The grotto was no longer a haven. It was a graveyard.

Her eyes lingered over the bodies, heart cracking in her chest. The bottom of the chasm where the water once remained was silt and rock. But it was neither of those things that caught her gaze.

There, lying in a cave that would have been hidden by the falls, was a green foot. Hansel yelled out another order, but Eve was already climbing into the chasm.

'Eve!' Hansel called.

She navigated the rock formations, coming upon the cave with a heavy weariness. She entered slowly, finding Malak wrapped around a thin body. His club was discarded nearby, his skin mottled with blood and burns.

How long have they been here?

'Eveline!' Hansel yelled again.

But she was too far gone. Too afraid. Too determined.

Eve scooted forward, squeezing in through the gap with a grunt.

Despite the tight entrance, the cave was enormous inside. Gems and glow worms sparkled from its walls, reminding Eve of a constellation. She latched onto Malak's arm and peeled it away to find Princess Snow. She didn't call for Hansel – not when there was a chance Malak could be dead. She focused on her breathing, pushing away the dark thoughts, and felt for a pulse.

Snow's eyes opened.

Eve sucked in a breath and the Princess sprung forth, her palm cracking against Eve's jaw. The Seeker stumbled, her surprise barely registering as the Princess lunged again.

Eve was knocked back and one of her blades went skittering across the rock as Snow's slender arms collided with her stomach. She backpedalled, then whirled, raising her remaining blade. The edge nicked the Princess's neck, but Eve stilled.

The Princess growled. *Actually growled.*

'Don't touch him,' Snow spat.

Eve choked back a laugh. This was not the dainty princess who lay asleep inside a crystal coffin. She was almost animalistic. Dirt was thick under her nails, blood smeared on her blue dress. She flashed her teeth, ready for battle.

Eve pulled back the knife an inch, though it went against every instinct. 'I'm not here to hurt you, Princess. I'm here to help.'

The Princess wove around her, and Eve followed her movements. She knew what the Princess was doing, blocking the only entrance to the cave to give herself an edge.

Like a cat hunting a small mouse, Snow moved with unnerving grace. Eve wiped the blood from her mouth; for such a delicate thing, the Princess had a solid hit on her.

'I'm a friend of Malak,' Eve said. 'Swear on the Fairy Godmother.' She crossed her fingers against her chest.

The Princess's eyes flicked towards Eve's knife. 'I've been fed lies before.'

Eve was about to respond when Snow attacked. One moment she'd been prowling and edging her into the corner, the next she had Eve's discarded knife in her hand.

'What the—' Eve started.

Snow spun, aiming for Eve's throat. She was fast, Eve gave her that, but she wasn't the Seeker. Snow's blade missed as Eve pivoted, using her own blade to counter.

Eve darted, barely dodging Snow's next attack. Her hand crashed into the cave wall and the glow worms darkened.

Snow hurled the blade at Eve's head. Eve ducked quickly and, with a roundhouse sweep, brought Snow's feet out from under her. Her head smacked the ground.

'Sorry,' Eve said, holding back her cringe. She stepped over Snow to collect her knives. 'If I were here to kill you, I'd have done so already.'

Snow lifted herself off the ground.

Voices echoed from the cave entrance. Pip and Hansel shoved at one another as they entered, freezing at the sight of the awakened Princess.

'You're awake?' Hansel said.

Snow beamed and ran for him. Hansel brought her in for a hug with his burly arms, and Eve pretended it didn't sting.

'Barely,' Snow replied, glaring at Eve from his shoulder.

Hansel turned around. 'Wasn't the goal to cure her curse, not beat her up?'

Eve didn't know whether to be offended or to laugh. When neither emotion won, she sheathed her blades, her voice hard. 'She attacked *me.*'

'It was a minor miscommunication,' Snow said, still holding onto Hansel.

Hansel registered Malak on the ground and slackened. Snow clung to him even as he released his hold and took a hesitant step forward, pain rippling across his face.

Eve wanted to reach out to him, to tell him it would be okay. She wanted to hold him, to hide him from the sight of Malak hurt.

But she didn't move. Not even when her mind screamed at her to do so.

Pip checked Malak for a pulse. A tut escaped his lips. 'He's alive.'

The tightness in Eve's chest eased at his words.

Pip pulled out his bag, rifling through its contents before producing some herbs.

'What happened?' Hansel asked.

Snow *still* hadn't let go. She nuzzled his neck, sighing out a breath that made Eve's fingers twitch towards her knives.

'I don't know,' she replied. 'I just woke up in here.'

Eve looked at Hansel, realisation dawning as she pieced the puzzle together.

'We're missing two.' she said, and all sets of eyes fell on her.

Hansel finally pulled away from Snow but kept his hands on her shoulders. 'Where are the dwarves?'

'What dwarves?'

'The two dwarves in the grotto,' he said, his voice rising. 'There were two dwarves, Beetle and Bon—' his voice cracked on the last word.

Snow's eyes watered. 'I don't know, I must have been asleep.'

Hansel raked his hand through his hair before lowering his voice. He embraced her again, murmuring something in her ear. A knife sliced through Eve at the sound. His voice was different with her. Gentle.

Snow grasped Hansel's shirt, opening her eyes like a puppy begging for food. 'I found him like this. There are no dwarves, I swear.'

Hansel stroked her cheek.

Eve couldn't take it. She turned on her heel and waved away Hansel's questions to storm out of the cave mouth.

When she'd climbed over the lip, Florian reached down and helped her up. 'What did you find?'

Eve dusted off her pants, not hiding the bite in her tone. 'Little miss princess is awake.'

Prince Florian's face glowed, then paled, and then dropped.

'What?' she asked, not really caring. She had to do something with her hands, something to ease the emotional swell of finding Malak and Snow. The dwarves were missing, and she wasn't in the mood for Florian's dulcet voice.

'I'd hoped it was going to be me,' he said, quietly.

Eve took a breath, managing to rein in her frustration. 'Yeah, well, it wasn't.'

Red bloomed up his neck and cheeks, his mouth a thin line. His eyes watered, and the sight jarred Eve. She was pissed off at Hansel, not Florian.

She swore under her breath. 'I'm sorry. That was mean. It's not your fault you weren't her true lo—'

Eve paused.

'What is it?' he asked, as Eve made her way back to the cave. He followed, panting as he tried to keep up. 'Eveline?'

'Who is it, then?' she said to herself.

'Who is what?' he asked.

But Eve wasn't listening. She was going over each possibility in her head. Each word of the prophesy. 'Who woke her up? Who's her true love?'

Florian shook his head, confused. 'I don't understand. What was in the cavern?'

'Not what,' Eve replied, 'Who.'

Malak.

She considered this new twist of events as she reached for a nook in the stone and hauled herself upwards. Had Malak been the key all along? Was their journey a useless voyage, or had her gift been wrong? It had led her to the Prince after all, but why? Why didn't it just point to Malak when they'd arrived here in the first place?

She clambered over the lip of the cave. Pip was lighting his pipe at the far edge of the entrance. The Princess sat beside Malak, gripping his hand, and shot a glance of disgust towards Eve. Hansel stood a little way off, watching them all, but his eyes immediately fell on Eve as she entered.

'Are you and the troll in love?' Eve asked.

Snow blushed, but she scoffed. 'If friendship is love, then yes.'

Friendship.

Could that have been enough to break the curse?

Hansel flicked his eyes to his friend. 'Malak loves Snow, that's why he made an oath.'

Eve stared down at Malak.

It hadn't been true love's kiss at all, but an *act* of true love. And if sacrificing oneself didn't constitute that, then she didn't know if anything else could.

Eve had scoped out the entire grotto, only to find blood and death. Thankfully, she'd found no dwarf bodies, which meant there was a chance they were alive. It was the best she could hope for after all the destruction.

It had taken all of them to haul Malak's unconscious body out of the cave. They moved him to the only remaining green patch – by the crystal coffin – and lit a fire in the hearth.

Florian scratched at his skin, and Snow laughed at a joke Hansel made. Eve rolled her eyes at the ease between them, at the high-pitched fake laughter that made her skin crawl.

Pip smacked his lips on the rabbit meat they'd caught. The silvery rabbit hide sat off to the side. Eve had thought it too beautiful to dispose of.

Snow went to check on Malak, so Hansel came and sat beside Eve.

'So' he said, a smile on his lips. 'Are you going to tell me why I'm getting the silent treatment, or do I get to guess?'

She scowled, staring at the fire, its hues of orange and gold wrapping into the red of the coals. She was acutely aware of his every movement, his every breath, but all she could hear was the echo of Snow's laugh.

'Eve?' he asked with a teasing tone.

It wasn't the soft caress he'd used with the Princess, but neither was it harsh. No, it was more of a surety with her. A quiet confidence in the way they spoke, with a dash of caution.

When he touched her arm, she finally met his gaze. He looked concerned.

'What is it?' Eve asked. She knew she was being ridiculous. He'd shown her his feelings. It didn't need to be spoken aloud. He'd shown it in a firm grip on her shoulder when she'd come down the snowy cliff. It was in the feather touch of his fingers before they faced the giant's wrath. It had been in the warmth of his palms when he'd caressed her face at the bottom of the mountains. It was in the explosion of stars as he'd kissed her.

It'd been unspoken, and at each scenario, she'd pulled away. Scared of the unknown. Scared of him and what it could mean.

Why, then, was she so worked up when he'd held the Princess and spoken to her in that way? It was an ugly monster that had reared its head. Porchid was the one known for outbursts, not her, so when her eyes pricked as she looked at those warm eyes of his, she blinked them away.

'What happens now?' she croaked, ignoring his questions. She didn't know why; she just knew either she cut it off or followed it through. Maybes were gone, and her oath had reached a fork.

One path led to the Queen, and the other led to revenge. Vengeance for her father had consumed her for so long. It was an illness, festering within her like an open wound.

Did she forge a new path? Did she follow him and forget about revenge? Would he follow her too? Or had he already chosen his path? She wasn't ready for disappointment, or the heartbreak it entailed.

'That's up to you,' Hansel said.

He walked off and sat on that same tree where he'd once told her his story. A deep ache infused her body. Not one of the flesh, but one of the soul.

For even though she wanted to follow, she did not.

Hansel leaned against the burnt tree, uncaring of the ash branding his clothes. He heard Snow before he saw her, the grass crunching under feet.

Snow lifted her skirts and sat down. She placed her arms on the edge of her knees and looked towards the sky. She didn't have to say anything, it was just a comfort having her close.

When Hansel wasn't on duty at the castle, he'd spent all of his free time with Malak and Snow. Some memories in the Silver City were tainted, but many were bright: Snow laughing as they snuck into the library; Malak and the Princess dancing in the gardens; the three of them guessing the shape of the clouds.

They had been his sanctuary. His sanity. His peace.

Snow huffed out a breath and ran her fingers through her tangled hair. She had a way about her, a fire that couldn't be doused. Her emotions ran hot, and he'd always admired that.

He hadn't known how she'd survived. How she'd retained her strength or patience or kindness. Where Hansel suffered in one way, she'd been dealt the Queen's jealousy. Where he'd been caressed, she'd been poked and prodded, brought to the mirror every few weeks.

Both their physical wounds were minimal, but it was the ones inside that cut the deepest. Hansel reached his arm around Snow in an embrace.

He turned towards the campfire where Eve was. She rolled over in her sleep. Where Snow was a storm, Eve was the calm.

Both were dear to him. One a sister and one a … A what? What was Eve to him? His friend? His companion? His love?

Snow shuffled under his weight and broke the silence. 'I don't like her.'

Hansel huffed out a laugh. Eve was hard to like, but he found it appealing. Porchid, at least, shared his sentiments. 'She has her moments.'

Snow rolled her eyes. 'Why is it that you always fall for the most hopeless of women?'

He shrugged. 'I guess something about them gives me hope.'

'You can't fix them all, you know.'

He knew that. He didn't want to fix them, though. Not really. He loved Eve. Loved all the broken pieces of her. To an extent, he'd perhaps even loved Myrenna too.

The two of them didn't speak for a while, sitting in stillness before Snow pulled away. 'It was an apple pie.' Hansel raised his brow and she sighed. 'Myrenna got me with an apple pie.'

Snow had never called her 'the Queen'; it had always been 'Myrenna' since the day her father had brought her home and declared they'd be wed. The Queen had won over her father with her baked goods in a competition judged by the royal family. Only the most talented of bakers were invited to attend, and the story went that once the King had tasted the Queen's apple pie, he'd fallen head over heels.

'You ate her apple pie?' he asked.

'I couldn't resist.'

He remembered that day. The smell of the delicious pastry drifting from the kitchen below. He remembered advising her not to go, placing a note in her palm.

A warning and a plea.

She is coming for you.

'You didn't heed my warning,' Hansel said with the shake of his head. 'And here I thought you smarter than that.'

She huffed. 'One bite was all it took, and I was gone.'

He picked at the grass in front of him. He wanted to be mad, but when she sat safely beside him, he couldn't bring himself to be. Relief was still the one emotion running rampant through his veins.

'She hired me to kill you, you know. I don't know if it was some sick joke, but she sent me to find you. I'm to bring back your heart.'

Her face softened and she touched his arm. 'She still uses you in a way that always hurts *you* more than others.'

His face was grim. Snow knew how it felt. The Queen had a way of worming her way in and lodging herself so deep it was almost impossible to pull her out.

'I missed you,' Snow said.

Snow was alive, and that was enough for now. Hansel smiled. 'I missed you too.'

Porchid was angry at Eve.

She was angry at Hansel. She was angry at the Princess.

Humans were stupid. She was sick of being the only logical being in a realm full of morons.

The only thing she wasn't mad at was the furry mattress under her. She snuggled down and looked at Eve's bed. Porchid understood her caution, but she had never understood the Seeker's ability to hold on to her emotions without release.

The Princess, it seemed, had that part down pat. How she'd ever survived containing herself around the Queen was a miracle.

This was going to be a rocky ride. Porchid would have to brace her shiny little wings for the tornado that was coming. She had sensed it from the moment she'd entered this place. This was not the end for them. They were about to feel whatever was coming, handle whatever fate had in store. No. This was not the end.

It was only the beginning.

Epilogue

The shackles at their feet chafed as the guard dragged them across the hard floor. Its marble shone in squares of black and white. Bonyx's reflection showed a bruised and bloodied face. His grey hair was plastered across his cheeks and forehead, and a bead of sweat dripped down his back.

Beetle was beside him, head towards the ground, his skin mottled and grey.

Before them lay a grand throne, and a large gold mirror pinned upon the wall. If Bonyx looked close enough, he could see movement behind the glass.

Beetle groaned. His arms were lifeless at his side, his eyes half lidded.

The skirt of Myrenna's black dress shimmered in the light, feathers shaping around her neck as it draped over her shoulders in a crystalline sheen. Her hair was wound upon her head, with a small tiara that sat daintily on her brow. She lounged on the throne, sharpened talons clicking on the metal.

Bonyx's age had become a burden. His weak bones called out to him; limbs that were once nimble were no longer as agile. And whilst his soul was strong, he was not sure of little Beetle.

The guards pushed them onto the tiles, his knees creaking in protest. He winced at the sharp sting of pain.

The Queen smirked. 'Tell me, dwarf, have you ever baked an apple pie?' She waved her hand over a bowl of fruit, as if deciding which to pick, and pierced the flesh of a small red grape with her nail.

Bonyx remained silent.

'Well?' she asked.

With effort, he shook his head.

'Pity,' she mused. 'You see, dwarf, to bake the perfect apple pie, you must have the right ingredients.'

She sucked the grape off her sharp, manicured nail. 'First, there's the moulding of the pastry, you have to mix it *just* right.'

His eyes darted to Beetle, but the dwarf only sobbed.

'Then there's the matter of the filling,' she said. 'You need the right amount of sauce with the right number of apples, cut in just the right size.' She let the statement linger before she continued. 'The trick is not to overfill it, otherwise the pie will drip, and you'll find yourself covered. Then there's the top layer, where you wrap it up nicely to place in the oven. It's all about getting the right shape to fit. Too big, and the ratio isn't right. Too small, and it's not a pie, is it?'

She rose and slowly walked down the dais, popping another grape in her mouth. Her movements were slow. Deliberate. 'Baking the perfect apple pie takes patience, precision, and perfection. Something our dear little Princess never bothered to learn.'

Beetle trembled, never looking up from the floor. Bonyx tried to shield him but failed, his chains too heavy. His heart sped up as the smell of lavender and blood emanated off the Queen.

'Baking is an art. Just as running a country is an art. And when you and she all die, I will be the one left standing.'

Her hand latched onto the back of Beetle's scalp and she yanked him off the floor. Tears ran in hot streaks down his cheeks. Bonyx sucked in his breath, his hand lifting towards his cousin.

'Just as an apple pie needs its baker, so does a princess need a kingdom.'

Myrenna caressed the side of Beetle's face. 'Do you know what secret ingredient they have in common, dwarf?'

Bonyx's pulse quickened. Dread filled him with what she might do, and yet he had no way to control the situation.

Myrenna's face twitched, her beauty gone in an instant. And with it, both anger and cruelty were unmasked. It made her a monster.

'No?' Myrenna asked. 'It's quite simple.' She lowered her voice. 'Both. Require. Heart.'

Myrenna lifted her arm and sliced into Beetle's back.

Bonyx tried to move, only to find he was met by an invisible barrier. He beat against it as Beetle stared back at him with wide eyes. Blood dripped from his mouth. A shudder. Then silence.

The Queen slid her hand out, covered in blood. And in her palm lay Beetle's beating heart.

Blood pooled towards Bonyx's knees. He choked, a silent scream escaping his lips.

Myrenna dropped Beetle's body, grabbed Bonyx's hand, and slid his cousin's still-warm heart into his palm. She lowered her face to his. 'Without the right heart, dwarf, the apple pie is a failure from the moment you begin.'

Bile ran up Bonyx's throat.

Myrenna licked her lips, a threat behind her eyes. 'You hid the heart I need, and I want it back.'

End of book one.

The Father and the Sisters Grimm

A SHORT STORY

Once, long ago, there lived a little girl and her merchant father.

The father lived for his daughter's laughter and doted on her. The little girl wore a crown of lilacs, and had the most beautiful voice. Her father would clap as if he stood in the grandest theatre with the finest company. They would dance until sundown and laugh until blue.

He would tell her stories by firelight, ones filled with dragons and swords and heroes.

Although they were poor – the house but a ramshackle cottage in a glen – the little girl never wanted for anything.

For he was her king, and she his princess.

One stormy night, the little girl fell ill.

The rose of her cheeks flushed upon her clammy skin, but no healer could aid her. After three days and three nights, with nobody to help, the merchant gathered what little coin he owned, and ventured into the shadow forest to seek out the three sisters Grimm.

Crones, they were, with nails of bone. Their cauldron was a carved mass of obsidian. Their eyes shone black; their teeth yellowed and decayed.

When the father pleaded for his daughter, the crones replied in voices of silk.

> *'For one bargain made,*
> *thrice you shall pay,*
> *for three we are and three we keep,*
> *three to brew what you seek.'*

When the father agreed, not heeding the warnings of the villagers, the sisters Grimm cackled in glee and brewed him a great potion.

> *'Three prices we shall claim,*
> *one by brightest moon and one by plain,*
> *last shall be by stormy night,*
> *when blackest sky shows rainbow light.*
> *We shall come, to collect the toll,*
> *and if not fulfilled, your mortal soul.'*

The father had agreed to a bargain, but he did not yet know its price.

When the little girl woke from her dreamless sleep, the father cried, relieved that the sisters Grimm's concoction had worked.

For many days life returned to normal. The father and daughter danced. He told stories of trolls and rings and magical things. He adorned her head with a crown of lilacs freshly grown from the newly turned soil.

But one night, when the wind whispered and the father awoke, he knew his time had come.

The father ventured deep into the forest and met the sisters Grimm.

'The first price owed by brightest moon is water
as sweet as a tart,

from a magic well entombed in stone only
found by a selfless heart.

But beware, young human, for its beauty is
deceiving, and if thirst consumes you,

you will not be leaving.'

The father knew of a mystical cave less than a day's journey, and the following night, by brightest moon, he set out to pay his debt.

The cave's mouth glowed iridescent as the merchant tied his horse and entered its depths. The darkness swallowed him whole. Left became right and up became down. When his water skin went dry, a thirst consumed him.

When he indeed stumbled into the fountain, it was something to behold. The carved rock was as ancient as the land itself, and the waters a crystal blue.

In his desperation, the merchant went forth and filled his pouch.

His mouth became parched – as dry as swallowed sand – and the water whispered to him.

'Drink me.'

As if his body was not his own, he indeed cupped his hands into the cool, soft surface. The witches' warning echoed in his ear as he brought the water close to his lips—

'Beware, young human, for its beauty is
deceiving, and if thirst consumes you, you
will not be leaving.'

As if pulled by strings, the merchant flinched back. With little ease, he dragged himself out of that cave and back towards his little kingdom in the little glen.

When he returned, the sisters cackled in unearthly delight.

'Indeed, you have survived a very great task,

but thrice was the price we asked.

One has been paid by brightest moon, but the
other will be by plain:

we seek a flower of greatest beauty, but it lies
among those slain.

Three cycles you have to find blood's bliss,

but beware of its petals for its death's sweet kiss.'

One night, under a blanket of stars, the girl asked her father to tell a story. And so, he told her of the sisters Grimm and a father's plea to save his only child.

He weaved it into a grand tale of adventure, one to please even the most critical of children, and when she fell into an almost slumber, the daughter made a wish.

Two cycles passed, and the father and his daughter travelled far and wide selling goods.

They crossed plains and mountains in search of the flower called blood's bliss. They passed villages and fields of long-ago battles shrouded in mists.

The night before his debt was due, the merchant's daughter woke with a terror in her heart, for her father was not laying in his cot. She crept from the wagon into the spring-filled air and found him kneeling.

With the tug of her heart, the daughter took her father's hand. She led him through the valley, and there, upon the knoll of a hill, lay a lone, ruby-red flower.

With the blood's bliss found, only one more task remained.

The cauldron boiled, broiled, and bubbled as the merchant handed over the flower, the sisters Grimm hungry for their prize. Their papery skin crinkled as they greedily fingered the petals and crushed it into a fine powder. By cauldron light, shadows danced, and they sang of the merchant and his pretty daughter.

On the child's birthday, the father made her a crown of roses.

They laughed and sang, fingers turning pink from icing. The food was bountiful with glazed pork, buttered potatoes, and rich cakes. Her beauty grew, and suitors came. Her father was promised grand sums for the future of her hand. But no matter the prize, she was not an item to be sold, bought, or bribed.

Her gift had become known, and even though they remained poor, they were rich in their hearts.

One night, the merchant returned to the glen to find the sisters Grimm waiting. There was still one prize left, a debt yet to be paid. Confident, the merchant dismounted his horse and met them unarmed.

'For one bargain made, thrice you shall pay,' they crooned, 'for three we are and three we steal, the time has come to finish the deal.'

The witches cackled, their wickedness stinking of rotting flesh.

'Twice you've paid, and yet thrice is due,
the last is that which means most to you.
For youth and beauty unbeguiled,
we seek the payment of your only child.'

The merchant refused the sisters Grimm and pleaded for another way. Yet they remained steadfast in their bargain and foretold that in three nights and three days they would come to collect.

For three nights and three days the merchant doted on and loved his daughter more than any other days before. He again told the story of the sisters Grimm, not only as an explanation but as a warning. For if he could save her from their wicked ways, then his soul was worth the sacrifice.

When the sky rumbled, the father hid his daughter away.

He met the crones then, and when their black teeth shone, he quoted the end of the bargain.

'Last shall be by stormy night,
when the blackest sky shows rainbow light.

For we shall come to collect the toll,
and if not fulfilled, your mortal soul.'

When the witches discovered his daughter was gone, their wrath filled the little kingdom. Lightning came down and set the ramshackle home aflame.

The sisters Grimm had never forgotten the bargain, nor had they forgotten the child.

Their potion grew black with the merchant's bones, their teeth thick with remnants of his flesh.

When the sisters Grimm sipped the potion, their skin became supple, their hair long.

They would not have youth and beauty as unrivalled as the girl, but it would do.

And as they had done for a millennia, they waited for her to seek them out and make a bargain the little girl couldn't live without.

The End

Acknowledgements

Writing is hard. It's a dream, and a big one at that. There's an age old saying, 'It takes a village to raise a child' but it also takes a village to write and publish a book.

It starts off with only you and that little man called self-doubt plonked right there on your shoulder. It starts with a daunting blank page and a simple idea. It starts with a burst of imagination and the realisation of how incredibly formidable the task ahead is.

But it also starts with a vision and a desire so strong that you cannot help but write it.

I started my novel writing journey by signing up to National Novel Writing Month (NaNoWriMo) in November of 2017 with the hopes of completing 50,000 words in 30 days. Impossible right? What a crazy idea.

Self-doubt was on my shoulder then but I came out with 30,000 words of a YA Science Fiction novel that month. This is still incomplete I might add. But did I feel unaccomplished? Or worthless? Or a failure?

Surprisingly, no. Somehow, that year ignited something in me I hadn't felt in a long time. An itch had been scratched. A dreamer, dreamed. It was a blur of colour, with characters so vivid I had no choice but to set them free.

So, by the time NaNoWriMo of 2018 came around, I pulled up my socks and I told self-doubt to find someone else's shoulder. I set my fingers to keyboard and by the end of the month I had written the first 77,000 words of The Gilded Mirror. An impossibility had suddenly become a *possibility.*

So, my first thank you is to NanoWriMo for existing. For helping me challenge myself and create the burgeoning beginnings of Eveline's story.

My next thank you is to my parents, who read to me every night and introduced me to fairytales. For sitting with me through spelling bees and rereading the same series over and over again. For both having grand book collections and letting me wander the bookstore whilst I searched for my next adventure.

Thank you to my friends and family, who didn't balk when I told them I wanted to be a writer. Who encouraged me and engaged with the story. Who sat with me over wine and let me babble about these imaginary people and insane ideas. For pushing me that little bit harder to get it done, and to shove self-doubt aside.

Thank you to my colleagues and staff at the time for being there on my writing journey and watching me slowly melt into a puddle of stress. Your encouragement each day was everything.

Thank you to my Beta readers, Mikayla, Jenna, Candi, Bri and Rae. We all fumbled along this writing journey together and I'm grateful you stuck around for future books.

Thank you to my editor Daniel Carr from The Write Stuff. You did such a fantastic job with 'A Glass Darkly' that I had to have you onboard for the re-edits of this series.

Thank you to my partner, Jared, who let me disappear into my mind and remained patient despite me tapping away on my phone or doing weird google searches. We were in the early stages of dating when I originally wrote this book but you're still patient with me.

For those who picked up the original book, thank you. Whilst this version of the book has been rewritten and re-edited, the core of the story remains the same. Thank you for waiting years for me to give this book the attention and love it truly needed — and for sticking around.

Thank you to the new readers and those who have shouted their love for this series. I'm excited to be on this self-publishing journey with you. Bookstagram and BookTok have changed the landscape of books and I'm so proud to be a part of this community.

Which means I also want to thank the writer's I've connected with on social media. You've championed me, taught me, laughed with me and made me feel a little less alone. You know who you are.

Writing, pitching and republishing as an indie author has been a journey. An exciting and surprising one, but a journey all the same.

I have always believed that when something magical comes along you must grab it. The crux of imagination or a dream or an idea. Whatever your age, grasp it firmly between your fingers and let it coat your skin like fairy dust.

Because if we all did that, we may just very well fly.

About the Author

K E Barden is an independent author based in Brisbane. Her first book, The Gilded Mirror was written entirely on a mobile phone and the dent in her pinkie finger proves it. When she isn't writing, you can usually find her spoiling her high maintenance cat, building fairy castles, or comparing her real boyfriend with her book boyfriends.

Her books are a combination of fiction, romance and fantasy with the express intent of stealing you away from reality and creating characters that will become your entire personality.

You can find Kim on social media @ KEBardenAuthor

Authors Note

Thank you for making it this far. I hope you enjoyed The Gilded Mirror.

Reviews are the lifeblood of indie authors. Without them, there's a very high chance our books fade into obscurity. If you enjoyed The Gilded Mirror (or loathed it) please take the time to leave a review on GoodReads, Amazon, Social Media, or anywhere you want to share.

Thank you, *Kim xx*